SALTY

Also by Mark Haskell Smith
Moist
Delicious

SALTY

Mark Haskell Smith

Black Cat
New York

a paperback original imprint of Grove/Atlantic, Inc.

Published simultaneously in Canada
Printed in the United States of America

FIRST EDITION

Library of Congress Cataloging-in-Publication Data
Smith, Mark Haskell.
p.   cm.
ISBN 10: 0-8021-7034-X
ISBN 13: 978-0-8021-7034-7
1. Rock Musicians—Fiction.   2. Americans—Thailand—Fiction.
3. Thailand—Fiction.   4. Kidnapping—Thailand—fiction.   I. Title.
PS3619.M592S25 2007
813'.6–dc22

Black Cat
a paperback original imprint of Grove/Atlantic, Inc.
841 Broadway
New York, NY 10003

Distributed by Publishers Group West

www.groveatlantic.com

07 08 09 10 11   10 9 8 7 6 5 4 3 2 1

For Mary Evans and Brian Lipson,
early adopters, first responders

One

PHUKET

The Andaman Sea stretches out for 218,100 square miles along the southern peninsula of Thailand, extending south until it tickles the shores of Indonesia, flowing west where it mixes with the dark water of the Indian Ocean. It is one of the most beautiful expanses of salt water in the world, teeming with pristine coral reefs and home to thousands of exotic sea creatures. Not that he gave a fuck.

Turk Henry stood on the beach and looked out at the ocean. It was amazingly clear, so clear it wasn't even blue or green or any of the colors you usually associate with ocean. It was like glass. You could see right through it, right down to the bottom. Clumps of seaweed, rocks, and sand; the occasional shadow and flash of fish darting beneath the waves. It wasn't like the water he'd seen growing up near the Jersey Shore, that was for sure.

Turk craned his neck, peering through his massive sunglasses—the kind that make you look like you're recovering from eye surgery—and looked for the boy. Turk liked the boy. The boy brought beer. Hand him a couple baht and he'd go sprinting off to the end of the beach where his parents and grandparents sat around giant coolers filled with beer, soda, green coconuts, whatever you wanted. He'd come racing back and hand you a beer. Ice cold beer; the three greatest words in the English language.

His wife had told him they were eight degrees north of the equator. She liked facts. Eight degrees north of the equator, for the layman, translated into unbelievably fucking hot. A zillion degrees Fahrenheit and humid like the inside of a dishwashing machine. Turk had never felt anything like it. The only thing that had even come close was when he and the rest of the band were stuck in an elevator with ten or twelve groupies. A couple of the girls decided to get frisky, and suffice to say an orgy broke loose. With all the fucking and sucking, the groaning and heavy breathing, the elevator got hot and humid in a hurry. A couple of the girls even fainted. Passed out from the sex. When the elevator doors were finally opened by the fire department, there were six or seven naked groupies lying in a pile on the elevator floor. That's how you become a legend.

But it was even hotter here, and Turk wasn't dressed for it. He'd rolled up the legs on his black linen slacks, the kind with the drawstring that hang loose and baggy and made him look thin, and dunked his feet in the water. The sea wasn't cooling or refreshing, it was warm. Almost like a bath. His wife had told him that the average water temperature in the Andaman Sea is seventy-eight degrees Fahrenheit. That felt about right.

Turk unbuttoned his black silk shirt, letting his large pale gut leap out into the sunlight, his skin so white that it bounced the light up, casting reverse double-chin shadows across his face and making him look vaguely vampirish. Despite the hiking of the pants and the unveiling of the paunch, he wasn't any cooler; sweat rolled off his body like he was melting. Fuck, he *was* melting. Where was that boy?

He turned around and looked for his wife. It was her idea to come to Thailand. She had nagged, pleaded, and cajoled until he finally broke down and agreed to sit on a plane for twenty-three hours—he watched five movies—as they flew from Los Angeles to Osaka to Phuket. It was her fault he was here, burning and roasting and sweating like a pig in an oven. Normally she was easy to spot—she was the only one here who actually wore a top. The rest of them, the Europeans and Australians, all lay out in the sun with their tits hanging out. They'd read books or play cards, sometimes get up and jump in the water to cool off; a couple of women were even throwing a Frisbee around, all of them topless. Not that it bothered Turk. He liked tits.

Sheila had told him that it was a five-star resort, superluxe, first class all the way. It was nice, he had to admit. It was isolated, away from the run-down little tourist town, smack in the middle of some kind of jungle with a private cove. The main part of the hotel was a modernist structure on top of a hill. It didn't fit with the local architecture, looking more like a billionaire playboy's fortress of evil than a Thai temple, but then Turk wouldn't know Thai architecture if it fell on him and besides, he thought the concrete and glass building looked pretty cool. The main lobby was a big open room with a soaring atrium. This was connected to a restaurant, a swimming pool, a fitness center with a personal trainer on standby, and most important, a bar that overlooked the beach and the tranquil little cove. The resort's rooms were actually freestanding cabanas dotting the beach and hillside surrounding the main building. You didn't get a room, you got a little house with a thatched roof, amid coconut palms and beautiful flowering orchids and other plants that Turk had never seen before.

He had to agree, it was very nice and if you were going to vacation in a third world country there was no better way to go. But it wasn't like he had never been in a fancy hotel before. Metal Assassin only stayed at the best hotels. It was in their contract.

If Sheila had told him that it was wall-to-wall breasts—like a nudist colony where only the women were nude—she wouldn't've had to nag him so much. There is nothing more relaxing for the stressed-out heavy metal musician than to kick back, drink a few cold ones, and watch a parade of nature's greatest triumph on display. If only Sheila were here to join in. Turk would be the first to tell you, his wife had a great rack. She'd put these other women to shame.

Turk remembered that she was off on some safari or something. She'd wanted him to go with her; she'd wanted him to ride an elephant. But he couldn't think of anything less appealing than straddling the massive gray hump of some monstrous beast as it lurched through the forest belching and farting like a sick Harley-Davidson. That was Sheila, though. She was always off doing something. She liked go to yoga retreats in Mexico or bungee jumping with her friends in some dusty canyon in Ojai; she'd spend an afternoon in an authentic Navajo sweat lodge or attend something called an "inspirational tea." Sheila made fun of Turk for not having an "adventurous spirit." But Turk liked to take it easy. Didn't people always say "take it easy"? Wasn't that something you were supposed to do?

He didn't mind that Sheila had her adventures; it was fine with him. That was the great thing about their marriage— they tried hard not to be codependent; they respected each other's space. Turk and Sheila were a mutual support squad, helping each other cope, keeping each other on their respective wagons. It may not have been the most passionate coupling in the history of the world, but it was certainly the most stable. Turk was happy to see Sheila go on her fulfilling adventures. He just preferred to putter around the house, listen to music, practice his bass, and maybe watch a movie in their home theater. Sometimes he swam in the pool. It was a quiet life, but it made him happy. Going snorkeling or jumping out of an airplane just didn't interest him. He often thought Sheila should've married an extreme-sport athlete, or maybe that guy who owned the airline company who was always jumping out of a hot air balloon on a motorcycle. She needed someone who enjoyed taking risks. That wasn't Turk. He enjoyed playing it safe. So while Sheila rode through a jungle on the back of an elephant, Turk did the safe and sensible thing and sat on the beach drinking beer.

His feet sufficiently soaked, Turk walked back to his umbrella and slouched into a chaise, grabbed a towel, and mopped the sweat off his head. He heard a voice speaking English with a light German accent.

"Excuse me, sir, but aren't you in Metal Assassin? You play the bass guitar, is that right?"

Turk looked up and saw a wispy young woman wearing nothing but a bikini bottom, her blond hair stuck in pigtails, her blue eyes gleaming at him from behind some Persols, and her perky little breasts pointing at him, looking almost accusatory, like he'd just done something wrong.

"Yeah. That's me."

"I love your music."

She smiled at him; beamed really. Turk was used to women throwing themselves at him. He knew it wasn't because he was super good-looking; it was because he was a rock star. Not that he was ugly. He had a chunky body—as round and expansive as the sound he conjured out of four strings and a massive Marshall back line; the kind of body a real bass player should have. It wasn't that he was out of shape; he worked out, and his arms and legs looked young and powerful, his articulated muscles standing in sharp contrast to his protruding beer gut. He had a large and colorful dragon tattooed up his right leg and his left bicep was inked with the Metal Assassin logo, the words written in flaming Iron Cross Gothic.

His face was fleshy, but handsome, with mischievous blue eyes and large curly muttonchops on the sides. His head was topped by a full mane of long stringy rock star hair that he had to dye to hide the serious streaks of gray sprouting from the temples. All in all he looked the part. He just kept his shirt on.

Turk smiled back at the girl. He'd had his teeth straightened and whitened just this year, for his forty-fifth birthday, and they looked so clean and gleamy that they appeared fake.

"Thanks."

"Really. You guys are my favorite band. I have all your discs."

Most of them did. Turk studied her nipples; they stood out like bright pink bits of Play-Doh that had been pinched into shape. He looked up at her face.

"Which one's your favorite?"

She bit her lip, appearing slightly stumped. Then she giggled.

"I don't have a favorite. I like them all."

Turk smiled and nodded. Sweat flipped off his head, scattering like he was some kind of wet dog.

"Cool."

The young German, or perhaps she was Swiss, on vacation from Zurich or somewhere, bit her lower lip, summoning up the courage to ask the big question.

"So? Tell me. Is it true?"

"What?"

"You are no more? Steve is really going solo?"

Turk nodded sadly, putting on that grief-stricken faraway look that the fans seemed to expect on hearing the news that Metal Assassin had finally called it quits.

"Yeah. He wants to do his own thing."

And not share the royalties. Selfish fucker.

"So, what are you going to do?"

Turk saw the boy trudging through the sand and waved to him. He then turned and looked at her. Normally, before he was married, before the years of therapy where he learned to recognize when he was in a *catalytic environment* and stop himself from *fantasizing* and *ritualizing* his sexual compulsions, he would've invited her back to his room for a quick shower and a longer blow job. But he'd learned to break that cycle. His therapist had drawn all kinds of little charts mapping out how his sexual addiction worked. The charts always ended with *anxiety, despair, shame, guilt,* and *self-loathing.*

It wasn't easy for him; he was a rock star, after all, his entire life spent in a *catalytic environment,* but Turk had learned to control his destructive urges. He'd been surprised at how good it felt to have some power over his desires. His therapist had suggested that the behaviors and compulsions came from his having low self-esteem, and indeed, controlling those behaviors made him feel good about himself. In other words, Turk had discovered that denying himself a good piece of ass actually made him feel like a worthwhile human being. Go figure.

On top of that he'd taken a vow to be true to his wife and he was going to do it, even though it'd been the longest year of his life.

"Are you starting a new band?"

The Swiss-German girl seemed genuinely concerned, so he gave her an honest answer.

"I don't know. For the time being I'm just going to drink a beer."

The boy arrived, grabbed the baht from Turk's outstretched hand, and then went sprinting off down the beach.

Two

Sheila was on her way to ride an elephant. It was something she'd always wanted to do. She didn't know what attracted her to the massive animals, but there was just something about them that she found adorable. She collected small statues of elephants, photos of elephants, and paintings of elephants. She hosted a fund-raiser to ban the sale of African ivory. She marched in a protest against a scrimshaw exhibition at the Museum of Folk Art. Last year she helped organize a "Rock the Habitat" concert. Elephants were her raison d'être. When she wasn't tending to the needs of her infantile rock star husband and his countless petty demands, she was doing something to make the world a better, safer place for the elephant. She even had a tattoo of pastel-colored elephants marching trunk to tail around her ankle.

Now she was stuffed in a battered Land Rover with four other tourists, careening down a dirt road in the forest, on her way to spend some quality time with the largest land mammals in the world. According to the brochure she would get to touch them, feed them some bananas, and ride on top of one as a group of them meandered through the tropical rain forest.

Her husband had made fun of her. Why did she want to ride some big smelly animal when she could stay in bed with him? Sheila had bit her tongue. She'd been tempted to say that being in bed with him was like riding a big smelly animal, but she didn't. If he didn't want to come along, well, it was fine with her. Better even. She was tired of listening to him complain; the big rock star bitching because it was too hot, the humidity was ruining his studded leather belt, why couldn't he have ice in his drink? Why was the food so spicy? Why was the toilet paper so flimsy? Sheila shook her head. Here they were on the trip of a lifetime and he was complaining about toilet paper. Why'd he have to complain about that? Why couldn't he just wipe his ass and enjoy the sights?

Sheila tugged on the ends of the red bandanna that was holding her hair up. It was growing steadily heavier from absorbing sweat, and she wanted to keep her hair from falling down. It was hot; she could agree with Turk about that. But instead of moaning on the beach like some half-dead walrus, she was out and about, seeing the sights, shopping—you'd be surprised at the number of small carved elephants she'd acquired already—and going on a jungle safari.

She looked out the window of the Range Rover as it rolled its way through the tropical forest. Catching her reflection in the glass, she unbuttoned one of the buttons of her special jungle-tested safari shirt; just because you're in the tropics doesn't mean you can't show a little cleavage. Christ, back at the resort nobody wore a top; it made her halter dresses, tube tops, and khakis look practically Islamic. Sheila didn't know why she balked at going topless. She had a great figure, and she knew it. But she didn't have anything to prove. She was beautiful, with green eyes, a wild spray of sandy blond hair, and smooth pale skin that came standard with her Nordic ancestry. She was graced with fine, delicate features, except for the large fleshy lips that seemed to turn outward for no better reason than to show off their lusciousness, like some kind of wildly succulent orchid.

Sheila had been a model since she was fifteen. She'd been topless in *Vogue, Glamour,* and *Women's Wear Daily,* and in countless ad campaigns. Maybe that was it. She was used to getting paid to show her breasts, not just give the view away.

She'd enjoyed being a supermodel. She'd made gobs of money, traveled the world, dated movie stars and movie directors—done all the things the super-beautiful get to do. She'd been to raves on Ibiza, had cocktails on Martha's Vineyard, sunned in St. Bart's, hiked in Greece, Carnivaled in Rio. She was a regular at Davé in Paris, where he always had her favorite vegan noodles ready for her. When she wasn't working she lived a vampire life, sleeping all day and spending all night in the VIP rooms of whatever club was currently the hotspot. She traveled in private jets, private cars, with private chefs. It was life in a luxurious bubble world, and when the bubble occasionally popped, she could take the edge off harsh reality with a hit of X or a line of blow.

Sheila had been a card-carrying, hard-partying member of the in crowd. But after a while, the drugs, the drinks, and the passage of time took their toll. The makeup artists and photographers had to work a little harder to hide the lines and the dark circles under her eyes. In an industry powered by taut glowing skin and youthful sex appeal, Sheila wasn't so young anymore.

The drop in her bookings coincided with a kind of life-style crisis. The in crowd had become insular, incestuous, boring in its fabulosity. Night after night it was the same people, the same places, the same drugs. It was a static life, like being stuck in place, frozen in time. Nothing ever changed and nothing ever happened. Only the constant reassurances of their mutual fabulousness gave Sheila and her friends any comfort.

At her thirty-second birthday party, Sheila realized she needed to change. This insight crystallized for her when she found herself stoned on the same mushrooms, having sex with the same Brazilian DJ, in the same hotel and in the same position as she had the year before. Sheila realized that if it was always going to be the same, she might as well be married to some rich guy, grab a little slice of security before gravity took hold of her body and her breasts and butt headed south like a bad junk bond.

While it used to be fun to drink champagne and do coke all night, to club and carouse until dawn, now she found herself exhausted, her body paralyzed with a profound weariness. At first she thought she might have chronic fatigue syndrome or perhaps a newer, trendier virus that had yet to be named, but after a detoxifying vacation at an ayurvedic clinic in Mexico she realized that she was just tired.

She met Turk at the rehab center. She was there for cocaine; he was there for some kind of sex addiction. They bonded right away; somehow they had an innate understanding of each other's addictions, and ended up dating for a year—as Turk struggled with his addiction—before the doctors finally declared he was cured, and he proposed. They were married a year ago.

Being married to a rock star, being Mrs. Metal Assassin, hadn't turned out to be as much fun as she'd hoped.

. . .

A sunburnt American woman sitting next to Sheila tapped her shoulder.

"Do you mind? I'm trying to get a picture."

Sheila leaned back, out of the way, as the woman stretched herself over her and tried to focus her camera on the dense jungle whipping by. The woman's shirt was soaked through and Sheila felt her skin crawling slightly as her shirt absorbed the woman's sweat. It felt clammy, foreign, and unclean.

Sheila was relieved to hear the digital click and whir of the computer chip as the woman finally took a picture. She could only imagine the image. A blur of deep green.

"Just one more."

The woman persisted, leaning a little more on Sheila, pressing her dampness into her. Again the excruciatingly deliberate focusing of the camera, the waiting for the exact moment; and then, finally, she pushed the button.

"Thanks so much."

"No problem."

Sheila looked down and saw that the woman had left a large, moist splotch on her. She shuddered.

There were six of them crammed into the car: two couples—one British, from London; the other, the sweaty ones, from Seattle—herself, and the disinterested Thai driver who handled the car with the nonchalance and fearlessness of someone playing a video game. Sheila realized that the car was meant to accommodate three couples, but she was glad

Turk wasn't with her; she could hear him complaining about the uncomfortable jump seats already.

The couple from Seattle began to brag about their shopping expertise. Southeast Asia, according to them, was a bargain hunter's paradise. Anything could be had for a price —from rare antiques to souvenir tchotchkes—and any price could be haggled down. It was, according to them, your duty as a representative of the industrial world to pay as little as possible to the citizens of this developing nation. The Seattle-ites looked at the locals as if they were cunning used car salesmen, rip-off artists gouging the wealthy Westerners with their inflated claims that the meticulously hand-carved Buddha statue was actually worth the suggested price.

"Never pay what they ask. Never."

They were especially proud of the fact that they had negotiated some local craftsman down to half the asking price for a beautiful cabinet that they planned to ship back to the States. According to them, you were really doing the locals a favor by securing the lowest possible price. As if getting less money secretly made the Thais happier. Sheila wondered about that. How is it that people with lots of money get poor people to lower their prices so they're poorer? How is it that a rich man who makes his money selling "branding strategies" and "marketing concepts" can hardball someone who actually makes something real? What kind of world do we live in?

The woman from Seattle turned to Sheila.

"Just today, we had lunch at this little restaurant."

Her husband chimed in.

"A little place. Way off the beaten path."

"You could order fresh seafood. Really fresh. And they charged you by how much it weighed. But the best part is, you got a bowl of rice and this great coconut curry sauce with the meal."

"And a mango salad."

She turned and corrected her husband.

"Green papaya. With the peanuts. You know?"

Sheila nodded. She was familiar with the green papaya salad called *som tum;* in fact it was everywhere, served at every meal. It was like chips and salsa in Mexico, ubiquitous.

The woman smiled at Sheila, rubbing her hands together in glee.

"You know what I did?"

Sheila shook her head.

"What?"

The woman leaned in, looking like she was about to divulge some lucrative insider-trading tip.

"I ordered one shrimp."

Sheila blinked.

"One?"

The husband came to his wife's defense.

"They were real big. Prawns. Really. Bigger than shrimp."

The wife smiled.

"I had one shrimp. *Prawn.* The curry, rice, and salad came with it. You know how much it cost me?"

Sheila shrugged.

"Remember, they charged you by weight. How much does a shrimp weigh?"

"Not much."

The woman nodded.

"I had lunch for less than a dollar."

The husband beamed at his wife.

"I did the math. All that food for seventy-nine cents."

The wife nodded, sharing her husband's excitement. "We love Thailand."

Sheila smiled at them, tuning them out, as the Seattle couple continued their story. They also drew a hard line when it came to tipping. It seemed that giving gratuities to waiters, porters, cabdrivers, or various other helpful people actually perverted the local economy. It made the locals reliant on tourists and could destroy their self-sustainability. The husband, a man who was comfortable talking about anything with great confidence, began to lecture about this at length.

Sheila never haggled or bargained with the locals. She always overtipped. It was, she felt, the least she could do.

. . .

Sheila rolled down the window—the air conditioner in the Land Rover was hardly working—and tried to let the breeze dry off her shirt. She looked out into the forest as they flew down the road. Although it was morning and the hot sun was blazing above the canopy, there were sections of the forest that were pitch black, places sunlight had never visited, primordially dark, like something out of a science fiction story, gateways to another dimension. It gave her the creeps.

Eventually they pulled into a clearing, the dirt crunching under the tires as the Land Rover skidded to a stop, and the tourists began climbing out. Sheila immediately began stretching her legs as the couple from Seattle bickered about who packed the trail mix and the couple from London took turns applying heavy doses of sunscreen to each other's faces. She walked toward some kind of structure made from small tree trunks and topped with palm fronds, like a primitive carport. There were two picnic tables placed under the roof. The driver was already there, sitting in the shade, gazing out at the trees, whose lower branches had been mysteriously stripped of leaves and bark.

Sheila stood and flexed her legs, grabbing her foot and pulling it up behind her until it touched her ass, stretching the quadriceps. The driver gave her a look that made her want to button her shirt up, and lit a cigarette.

"You like elephant?"

Sheila nodded.

"Yes."

"You ride elephant before?"

"No. This is my first time."

The driver laughed and shook his head. He turned and blew a plume of tobacco smoke into the thick humid air.

"Always first time."

...

She felt it first—the thump, the vibration under her feet. It felt like the floor in their house when Turk was in his studio playing the bass. She turned as she heard the sounds of heavy chains rattling and chiming to see four large elephants being led toward the clearing. A group of mahouts, scrawny Thai men wearing vibrant blue cotton shirts with matching pants cut off at the calves—looking like some bizarre surgical team —were leading the elephants along. Sheila saw the beautiful animals—when you were up close to them, they really were bigger and more amazing than you could ever imagine—and immediately felt conflicted. Large metal shackles kept the elephants hooked together as they shuffled forward like a prison chain gang. The driver sensed her distress, or maybe he was just used to animal lovers from the West pitching a fit when they saw the elephants chained together like that.

"No problems, miss. They take the chains off."

"Why do they have them on?"

The driver looked at her like she was an idiot.

"So they don't run away."

It never occurred to her that an elephant might do something like that. Where would an elephant run?

The mahouts began whistling and shouting, tapping the elephant's legs with sticks, bringing the coffle to a halt. Sheila was relieved to see them take the chains off as several of the mahouts, using the ears for leverage, pulled themselves up to the top of the animals. They straddled the elephants' heads, their legs dangling just behind the giant flapping ears, and expertly guided them into a line, steering by rubbing their legs against the elephants' necks and pulling on their massive ears with sticks.

Sheila had been so awed by the size of the animals and so distracted by the chains around their ankles that she hadn't noticed what was tied to the elephants' backs. They looked like seats from an old school bus, cushioned by some blankets and stabilized by a couple of planks, roped tightly around the animals. She turned to the driver.

"We ride up there?"

He grinned.

"Don't fall. Long way down."

There was more whistling and shouts from the mahouts as Sheila and the other tourists were led up a wooden walkway and past a kiosk selling film, drinking water, booklets about the animals, and dozens of pachyderm-themed T-shirts that the couple from Seattle deemed a "ripoff." A well-worn rope stretched out to keep the paying customers from stepping off the edge and dropping ten or twelve feet into piles of elephant dung below. It was here, raised off the ground, that they boarded the bench on the elephant's back. There was no climbing up the trunk, no holding on to the ears; it was all about comfort and safety. Like a ride at Disneyland.

...

Sheila had been on the elephant only a minute or two when she realized that, as far as transportation goes, this was easily the most uncomfortable ride she'd ever taken. Perched on a hard bench a good fifteen feet off the ground, she was thrown from one side to the other, left, right, forward, and back, as the animal strolled down the jungle trail. She had to hold on tight and shift her weight as counterbalance to the peculiar force whipping her around. At one point, as her bench pitched violently forward, she thought she might fall, and let out a startled squeak. The mahout turned to check on her. She waved him off.

"I'm okay. I'm fine. Just getting used to it."

The mahout smiled to reveal teeth stained a vibrant red. He used the back of his hand to wipe crimson drops of spittle off the side of his mouth. Sheila was taken aback. It looked like he'd been smacked in the mouth and was bleeding, but then she saw him dip his hand in his pocket and pull out a betel nut. He grinned as he popped it into his mouth. He chewed vigorously for a few minutes and then let a long stream of bright red saliva fly off into the forest like some kind of wayward arterial spurt.

A sweet breeze, heavy with the scent of rain, came off the ocean and rattled the palms. It felt good, cooling her skin as the sun continued to beat down. Despite the constant lurching, or maybe because of it, she began to feel sleepy. Like she was being rocked to sleep by the heat and the slow-motion rhythm of the elephant's gait. Every now and then she'd hear one of the other elephants trumpet or honk and she'd look behind at the other couples. They seemed to be enjoying the gut-churning ride as much as she was.

They meandered like this for about an hour—the mahout spewing cherry-colored drool into the woods, Sheila clinging to the seat with white knuckles, and the elephant stopping to grab morning glory vines with her trunk, rip them out of the ground, and stuff them into her mouth with a big wet crunch.

Sheila thought she might be dreaming, might've dozed off for a second, but all of a sudden she was awake and there were men shouting. Men pointing serious-looking guns, like the rebels and insurgents you see on the news. They were shouting in Thai at the mahouts.

They wanted her to get off the elephant.

Three

I want to rape you."

At first Turk wasn't sure what she'd said. He was taken aback, startled by her aggressiveness. The door to his cabin wasn't even closed when she grabbed him, pressed him against the wall, and whispered those words in her breathy Swiss-German accent.

"What?"

"I want to rape you. Right now."

She pressed her lips against his and reached down for his crotch. It was then that he understood that English was not her first language.

"'Fuck.'"

She stopped and looked up at him, batting her blue eyes like she'd done something wrong.

"I'm sorry?"

"You want to fuck me. That's the word you should use. 'Rape' is not the word for what you want to do."

"Yes. Okay. Thank you. I want to fuck you. Right now."

Turk pushed her away, gently.

"Honestly, I'd love to. But I can't. I'm married."

She didn't look like she believed him.

"But you are famous for screwing with girls."

Turk shrugged. It was true. He was famous for screwing girls.

"That was before."

He walked over to the mini-fridge and pulled out a can of beer. He offered it to her, but she shook her head.

"You don't like me?"

Turk looked at her—the lean young body, the Swiss Miss pigtails, the pale and perky breasts, the big blue eyes—and popped open the beer. Of course he liked her; what's not to like? He knew the drill. She wasn't going to go away until she got something from him. A story, a stain, an experience, some kind of souvenir.

"I don't want to cheat on my wife."

"I won't tell."

Turk flashed on the years of counseling, session after session where he slowly came to realize that his addiction sprang from a deep feeling of inadequacy that had haunted him from childhood. Having sex with her, giving in to his promiscuous nature, would only open up those feelings again. He had worked hard, he had struggled, but he eventually overcame the urge to fuck every moving thing in his vicinity. He wasn't going to backslide now. He looked at her and shook his head.

"That's not it. I promised myself I wouldn't. And I'm not going to."

He wasn't going to go into all the gory details of his newfound sexual sobriety. She put her lips in a pout and walked toward him, unwrapping her sarong to reveal a thong bikini bottom. She stroked her bare nipples for a moment and then turned her attention to his crotch.

"Can I see it?"

"What?"

"I read in a magazine that you have a very big cock."

Turk shook his head.

"I'm not going to show you my cock."

He knew that once it was out, she would need to touch it, and once she touched it his willpower would crumble. She must've sensed that, too, or maybe it's just common knowledge. Once that thing sees the light of day . . . well, we all know that the rest is inevitable.

"Please?"

"Sorry."

She gave him her sexiest look.

"I will be very, very nice to it."

"No."

"Just a look? I won't touch it. I promise."

Turk shook his head, he was about to say something to make her feel better, but then he saw her expression change.

"Schiesse!"

And with that she turned and stomped out of the cabin.

Turk heaved a sigh of relief and flopped down on the sofa. He'd been tense. They didn't understand, did they? They didn't know how hard it was to say no. When something was so ripe and ready, so juicy and sweet, it took superhuman rock star strength to say no. For Turk it was hell. Being monogamous was the hardest thing he'd ever tried to do in his life. It'd have been easier to do a triathlon, or climb Mount Everest while figuring out his income taxes. For him, monogamy was a slow and brutal torture, a battle to the death between good and evil for control of his soul. The only good thing about it was that now he could look at himself in the mirror and not think that he was a bad person, a pig, a drunk, a waste, a loser, a fucking asshole. Now he felt good about himself. He might still drink too much, he might not be the brightest bulb in the chandelier, but at least he didn't cheat on his wife. It was something.

. . .

Turk turned and caught his reflection in the mirror. He raised the beer in a little salute to himself and his all-around monogamous goodness. He was proud, and rightly so. He'd been tempted by a very sexy half-naked Swiss-German teenager who wanted to rape him, and survived. Turk considered jacking off as a kind of reward for his display of willpower—while the image of her standing naked and pleading was still fresh in his mind—but the beer and the heat got to him and he slowly faded into a nap.

Four

The hood smelled like dried shrimp. Briny, fishy, and hot. It was loose at the bottom—otherwise she might've suffocated—but it was tight at the top and she could feel the equatorial sun beating on her forehead through the coarse, rank fabric. As Sheila struggled to breathe through the thick cloth, she felt her arms and legs attacked by a ravenous swarm of bloodsucking insects. Her hands were bound behind her and she was powerless to stop the mosquitoes' feeding frenzy. She had tried flapping her arms and kicking her legs to shake the hungry bugs off her flesh, but every time she did she received a sharp poke in the ribs from the barrel of a gun. It was safer, she realized, to let the bugs eat.

It was only when they started moving that she felt the insects stop. They were in a small boat; she could hear the sound of outboard motors and water slapping against the hull. For a while she'd heard the outraged shouts and complaints of the couple from Seattle. They made belligerent demands and grew increasingly irate, threatening everything from lawsuits to a full-scale invasion by the United States Marines to the nuclear annihilation of all of Southeast Asia. Then she'd heard the distinct sound of a blunt object cracking skull. The kidnappers, skinny brown people without access to expensive legal counsel or nuclear launch codes, apparently didn't appreciate being harangued by the overfed, white, and privileged.

Sheila didn't know how long they'd been on the water. Despite her fear, the heat and lack of air had caused her to swoon. She didn't know if she'd been asleep or just kind of out of it, but she'd lost track of time. They could've been traveling for twenty minutes or two days, she couldn't tell. She felt the boats slowing, the men chattering to each other in Thai, and then someone removed the hood from her head. Her first reaction was to gasp and suck in air like she'd been holding her breath underwater for an hour. Then she looked around.

She was riding in a long thin boat—like a strange canoe with a V-8 engine hooked to the back. Made from wood that looked like teak, the boat was barely wide enough for one person, yet long enough to accommodate herself, the two couples, and a half-dozen kidnappers sitting single file. She saw that one of the kidnappers, a young man who looked to be about twenty-two, was smiling at her with a disturbingly random-looking row of teeth in his mouth, a few large incisors littering a pocked, dark gumline. Even though Sheila's father had been a dentist and she found rotting gums and unruly teeth repulsive, she smiled back. She didn't want them to put the hood back over her head.

The kidnapper was wearing Army-issue fatigues and was cradling some kind of scary-looking machine gun casually in his lap. When he crossed his legs, Sheila saw that he was wearing Nike brand flip-flops.

. . .

Sheila wondered where her sunglasses were. They were Chanel and expensive. She didn't want to lose them. She'd expected to be blinded by the light, but they were in some kind of swamp, the boat gliding under a canopy of mangled trees, the roots rising up from the water in a riot of skeletal fingers, branches twisting out like tortured ligaments, the dappled gloom sporadically punctuated by shafts of searing tropical sun. The water smelled brackish, like dead shrimp, like the hood that had been over her head. But the swamp was alive; snakes slithered on branches, fish jumped in the water, hundreds of birds honked and hooted all around them, and, as the boat slowed even more, a dense cloud of bloodsucking insects descended like a fog.

Five

BANGKOK

His assistant, a handsome young Thai with a name so long and convoluted that the Americans at the embassy just called him "Roy," had brought in a durian for Ben to try. It was large as a pineapple, brown, and covered in hard spikes like some kind of alien football. Just looking at it you wouldn't want to eat it. Smelling it you definitely didn't want to eat it. In fact, you didn't want it in your office. Now he understood why it wasn't allowed on public buses and why shops kept it piled on the street; even the locals didn't want the stinky fruit brought inside. Ben tried to think of what it smelled like. The only memory that came close was the time his Siamese cat—named "Nomo" after his favorite baseball player—got run over by a car and he'd sadly bagged her body in a plastic bag and dropped it in the trash can. Five long hot summer days later and the smell coming out of the can was unbelievable: a fetid, overripe, and rotting carcass, it made you gag to go near, as if the boils of hell had been lanced and were oozing into the atmosphere. That's what the smell of durian reminded him of, only sweeter.

The embassy building on Wireless Road in Bangkok is built like a cross between a corporate headquarters—USA, Inc.—and a kind of fortified bunker. The windows are sealed shut for your protection. All the air comes through secure, massive, air-conditioning units. Great for keeping a large building ice cold in the boiling tropics, terrible if you're trying to sneak a cigarette or get a funky stench out of your office.

Ben told Roy to take the reeking fruit outside; he'd taste it later. He wanted the smell to go away before he barfed. He was a special agent for the Bureau of Immigration and Customs Enforcement. An ICE agent—he always liked the sound of that—stationed in Bangkok who right this second would've preferred a canister of sarin gas to be released than to smell the aroma reeking off that ripe durian.

But at least it was something to do.

Ben had joined Immigration and Customs Enforcement for some excitement. A little action. Some patriotic terrorist hunting. But the job consisted of sitting on his ass behind a desk scrutinizing visa applications—just in case a dangerous individual might try to enter the United States—and looking at flight manifests for any Arab-sounding names. If he found one, he'd check it against the terrorist watch list. In other words, Ben spent his day, increasingly bleary-eyed from the computer screen, sifting through hundreds of names on lists.

On the rare occasion something did come up, he'd spring into action and ride with the Thai police to the airport to intercept a suspected terrorist. This inevitably meant keeping some innocent Saudi businessman in a holding room for hours on end while his documents were checked and rechecked against various databases in Washington, D.C. Of course, Ben didn't speak Thai or Arabic, and the Thais didn't speak English or Arabic, and the suspected terrorist only spoke Arabic and some random language like Urdu or Farsi, so much of the day was spent trying to communicate basic things like "I'm hungry" and "I need a toilet."

But it got him out of the office. When he first took the posting, Ben had thought he'd be tracking down Muslim separatists in Malaysia and Indonesia. He'd be the eyes and ears of Homeland Security in Southeast Asia. *Keeping tabs on the hot spots.* It didn't work out that way. The regional security officer, the legal attaché, and members of the Diplomatic Security Service—Ben was sure they were CIA—all had dibs on the exciting stuff. Even though he was told when he signed up that ICE agents had "broad powers" to do all kinds of crime-busting terrorist tracking, the reality was that he was given broad powers to sit behind a desk and look at lists of names.

Still, it was better than his previous job. He'd been bored out of his mind as a "service consultant" at the Land Rover dealership in Pasadena. Day in, day out, listening to rich people whine about how important they were and how they needed their car. Ben wondered why they didn't buy a reliable car, a Mercedes-Benz or a Toyota. Even Ben's Honda Accord never had a problem like those glamorous SUVs.

Sometimes the cars had real problems—like a leaky transmission or a malfunctioning door—and sometimes the problems were due to the car owners' overactive imaginations. Ben never heard the phantom rattles that drove the well-heeled Land Rover owners to threaten litigation. He never

saw the mysterious "gaps" in the rear door that allowed car-
bon monoxide to leak in and reverse the Botox treatments
that the ladies had paid a fortune for. It never bothered him
that the air conditioner took five minutes to turn the car from
an oven to a walk-in freezer. Five minutes was too long?

But he couldn't say that. He had to cock his head like
an obedient Labrador and nod. He had to make them all feel
listened to and special, to soothe and coddle the rich and
spoiled. It was horrible. He hated it. Ben Harding was not a
coddler.

He was a fairly good-looking kid with sandy blond hair
and all-American features: the milky pink skin of the suburban Caucasian, blue eyes that would've been attractive if they
weren't a little too close together, big ears, and a cartoonishly
squared-off jaw. Ben looked like a football player, only he
wasn't particularly athletic, never played any sports; he was
just big and chunky.

He'd joined the Army right out of high school, hoping
to use the G.I. Bill to pay for college when his enlistment was
up. He'd wanted to be a helicopter pilot; he liked their cool
helmets, and they had awesome insignias on their flight suits.
But he didn't score high enough on the test for that, so instead he trained to be a helicopter mechanic. It wasn't that
glamorous or exciting, but it was okay. He liked to tinker and
he learned a lot.

When his time in the Army was up he didn't feel like going
back to school. Who wants to sit in classrooms all day listening to some old fart drone on and on? So he took a job working at a car dealership. He had learned a lot about engines,
electrical systems, and hydraulics; it seemed like a good fit.

But the coddling, the ass-kissing, killed him. He wasn't even at the dealership for a year before he sent in his application to the Bureau of Immigration and Customs Enforcement and, because he was ex-military and single, was hired, and sent to Bangkok.

Ben was happy to go somewhere exotic, but he didn't have the slightest idea why they picked him to go to Thailand. He didn't speak Thai. Couldn't begin to tell you what the signs on the buildings and streets said. He knew nothing of the customs, food, history, or political situation. He knew there was a king, but was surprised to learn it was also a democracy. Once a guy from the Defense Attaché Office told him they always sent single guys to Bangkok. Too many wives complained when their husbands were stationed there. It was all that sex.

Sex and Buddhism, Buddhism and sex. It was everywhere you looked. *Wats*—Buddhist temples—their strange winged roofs and odd spires jutting skyward, dotted the landscape, monks walked around in red and orange togas, and it seemed like every house, every business, even the United States Embassy had some kind of altar heaped with flowers, fruit, and cookies as offerings for the Buddha. Ben figured that the insane traffic of the city was directly related to Buddhism. As if a fervent belief in reincarnation was all that was required to get a driver's license. You don't make it across the street? That's okay, you'll come back in another life.

The other striking characteristic of the city was all the massage for sale. Foot massage, Thai massage, hot oil massage, scalp massage, fifteen-minute massage. This was a place where people wanted to touch you. Sometimes they wanted to do more than that.

Ben had been to Patpong, the notorious red light district; he'd seen the sex shows. But watching a woman shoot Ping-Pong balls out of her vagina kind of freaked him out. Not that it wasn't an impressive feat. If he hadn't seen it with his own eyes he might not have believed it possible. Yet there she was, doing splits on the bar, picking up a ball with her labia. Slowly rising off the bar with the ball in her grip, she'd hula-hoop her hips around and shoot the ball across the room with deadly accuracy. Ben was mesmerized by this trick. Imagine the muscle control, the hours of practice needed to do that. Even though he felt embarrassed by what he was seeing, he couldn't take his eyes off her.

But that evening took a terrible turn when one of the Ping-Pong balls splash-landed in his glass of beer. His friends and coworkers immediately insisted he drink it. That was the last thing Ben wanted to do. His mind spun with various germ warfare scenarios he'd studied during his training. Horrible photographs of smallpox and anthrax attacks, viral infections, leprosy, Ebola, and influenza; not to mention HIV. But his friends didn't care. They chanted for him to chug it. Ben broke into a cold sweat as he imagined all the thousands and thousands of penises that had penetrated that Ping-Pong ball launch pad. No way did he want to drink his beer; he'd rather drink elephant piss. But his friends were obsessed, and continued to chant and cheer him on to victory. What was Ben going to do? Punk out? Become a laughingstock? The reputation of Immigration and Customs Enforcement was riding on his shoulders. The last thing he wanted was for the State Department and the FBI to think ICE agents were pussies. So he did the heroic thing—he removed the Ping-Pong ball and chugged the beer down in a couple of massive gulps. Then he excused himself, went to the bathroom, and puked all over the floor.

He never went back to Patpong again. He realized that he was just too square to be carousing in sex clubs. The clubs were humid, sticky, and moist. Humans were copulating in various ways in every corner of the place, the smell of spent semen mingling with cigarettes, beer, sweat, and the faintly sweet and floral smoke of burning opium. The air was laden with germs, free-floating microorganisms just waiting for a host to come along and inhale them.

Ben had felt vaguely queasy ever since the Ping-Pong ball flew out of the Thai prostitute's pussy and splashed into his beer, as if he'd become infected by some mysterious pestilence or parasites had taken up residence in his body. If he got too hot, he thought it was the first sign of disease. If he felt a chill, that was evidence of something going horribly wrong. He had become a tropical hypochondriac, supersensitive to smells, tastes, any sensation at all different from what he knew. For Ben, Bangkok had become a festering bacteria breeder, a plague incubator, a virus-producing apparatus bent on destroying him. It all just creeped him out. Which was why he wanted the smelly durian out of his office.

Ben reached for the antiseptic hand cleaner that he kept in his pocket at all times and began to rub his hands together in a frenetic effort to rid them of deadly germs.

Normally he hated being stuck as the duty officer at the embassy, but the regional security officer was at a conference in Tokyo and the legal attaché was on maternity leave, so he had no choice. But when the phone rang and the Thai police commander on the other end told him about the kidnapped tourists, Ben realized this was an opportunity. If he handled this right, he could make a name for himself, a reputation within the Homeland Security community. Maybe he'd get a promotion. Maybe he'd get transferred to a country where you could drink the water.

Six

PHUKET

Sheila had never seen a dead body before. But there he was, the whiny cheapskate from Seattle, his head bashed in by the butt of an AK-47, his body dumped on the ground like the proverbial sack of shit. Hundreds of black flies were already swarming around the blood-spattered gash on his head, laying their eggs in his nostrils and eyelids.

A lean and muscular Thai man, his hair cropped into a thick flattop, his eyes hidden behind a stylish pair of Ray-Bans, identified himself as Captain Somporn.

"Please cooperate. We don't want to kill anyone else."

He was deadly serious, scary even, and yet there was something about him that disarmed Sheila. Maybe it was because he was handsome.

Sheila looked over at the dead man's wife. The woman sat on the ground in shock, staring at her feet, rocking slowly back and forth. Sheila noticed that the woman had shit herself, soiling her expensive safari shorts. She thought about going over and comforting her, but then she remembered the grotesque sweat stain the woman had left on her shirt and her husband's indignant howls of outrage that an American should ever be subjected to anything but gratitude and servitude by the inhabitants of the "third world." He'd even had the audacity to say, "Don't you know who I am?" to the kidnappers. Totally uncool. No wonder they bashed his head in.

"We are holding you for ransom. Please inform us of the proper contacts."

Captain Somporn stood in front of them, going through their wallets and purses one by one. Asking what hotel or resort they were staying at, dutifully writing down the information in a little notebook with a pink "Hello Kitty" picture on the cover, developing mini-dossiers on each hostage. Sheila was surprised that he had a vaguely British accent, like he'd been schooled in London or, perhaps, Hong Kong.

When Somporn got to Sheila—and this is where she noticed that he had a mischievous twinkle in his eye behind those stylish shades, as if he were an actor pretending to be a kidnapper—he stopped and lifted the sleeve of her shirt to reveal her Metal Assassin tattoo.

"You like Metal Assassin?"

Sheila nodded.

"I was very disappointed to hear they broke up."

Hoping for favorable treatment, Sheila said, "My husband was in the band."

She realized instantly that she'd made a mistake. She could almost see the dollar signs ka-ching in Somporn's eyes.

"Which one? Is it Steve?"

She shook her head.

"Bruno?"

Somporn winked at her and added, conspiratorially, "He's my favorite."

"It's Turk. Turk Henry."

Somporn stepped back, impressed, and studied her intently.

"You are the famous model he married? Yes?"

"I'm not that famous."

Somporn smiled.

"You're too modest. I had your calendar. The one with the dirt bikes."

Sheila was surprised. That was a pictorial she'd done in Holland where she posed nude and seminude with various Husqvarnas and Bultacos at famous motocross tracks around Europe. The photographer was a young German, a demanding sadist and a protégé of Helmut Newton's, who insisted on her crouching, doggy style, in the dirt with mud smeared provocatively on various parts of her body and a helmet covering her head. Despite feeling demeaned and exploited, she had to admit that the photographs were interesting, and it hadn't hurt her career at all. In fact, she realized, the calendar would be a collectible now, worth hundreds of dollars auctioned over the Internet.

"'Maiden of the Motocross.'"

Somporn laughed.

"Yes, that's the one. I used to have it on my wall."

He leaned in close to her. She could smell the strong scent of fresh tobacco on his breath.

"You and I have much in common."

Sheila realized that she was scared; her legs were shaking. She steadied herself, trying not to cry.

"Cool."

Somporn's eyes studied her breasts.

"Call me 'Captain.'"

Sheila nodded.

Captain Somporn had his men—and there were at least a dozen of them, toting machine guns and pistols—herd the hostages into a small wooden hut. There, Sheila and the woman from Seattle, her shorts giving off a rancid fecal reek, were handcuffed together and made to sit on the floor across the room from the British couple. Then they were left alone. She could hear the comings and goings of various people in the camp, soft murmurs of Thai being spoken, the sound of a car starting. Closer to her was the constant drone of flies trying to get into the soiled American's shorts and a parade of mosquitoes feeding on them both.

The Seattleite continued to rock gently back and forth, occasionally uttering some gibberish prayers or something. Sheila tried to whisper words to console her, but mostly she kept her face turned away to avoid the stench.

Sheila realized that the British couple hadn't uttered a word since the kidnapping ordeal had begun. She looked across the room at them and forced a smile.

"They just want money."

The man, a double-glazing salesman named Charlie Todd, nodded. His wife, Sandrine—her mother had taken several ferry rides to Calais in her youth—younger than her husband and with one of those plain yet attractive faces, started to whimper.

"Why did this happen to us? This is our vacation."

Her husband gently shushed her, trying to keep her calm.

"Don't worry dear, Rupert will come through. He always does."

It was true that their son, Rupert, was extremely reliable. In fact reliability was their company's claim to fame. It said so right on the side of their van:

Todd & Son Double-Glazing Specialists. Reliable and Tidy. Call for a Free Estimate.

Working out of a converted carriage house in the Crouch End section of north London, Charlie had built his business through honest estimates and elbow grease, until he'd finally saved enough money to take his wife on a real vacation. Sandrine had wanted to go somewhere exotic. She had always chided her husband that he had "no sense of adventure." But the fact that they now sat on the floor of a small hut in the middle of a mangrove swamp suggested perhaps they'd got a little *more* adventure than she'd hoped for when they'd booked the trip.

Charlie watched as a mosquito landed on Sandrine's shoulder. He blew puffs of air on her, hard as he could, to interrupt the insect's feeding. Sandrine turned and looked at him.

"What are you doing?"

"Mosquito. Don't want you to catch malaria."

Sandrine didn't care.

"Stop it. It's annoying."

"Less annoying than malaria, I'd imagine."

Full, the mosquito buzzed off. Charlie looked at the crude open window cut into the bamboo walls.

"You know, a nice bit of polycarbonate would go well there. Keep the bugs out. Keep the place cool."

Sheila looked over at him.

"I'm sorry?"

"A window. Double-glazed polycarbonate. Argon-filled's the best, you know. Best for insulation."

Sandrine elbowed her husband.

"Charlie, please."

Seven

Turk woke up with the sour taste of stale beer in his mouth. Over the huff and throb of the air conditioner he could hear the clanging and mewling of a group of Thai dancers and their accompanying musicians as they began their cocktail hour concert on the beach. It was dark in the room, and Turk fumbled around for the light. Once he could see where he was going, he went to the bathroom.

Even with the air conditioner cooling the room, he was sweating. Thailand, he realized, was a country that opened your pores. Wake up sweating as the morning sun begins roasting the landscape, sweat all day in the steam room humidity, eat some spicy food that makes you sweat even more, and sweat all night long as you attempt to sleep. It's a wonder the people didn't just shrivel up from all that sweating.

Reminding himself to stay hydrated, he grabbed a cold Singha beer from the minibar and stepped into the shower. He shampooed his stringy hair, letting the cool water—there was no way you'd want to take a hot shower—run down his pear-shaped body. He toweled himself off and sprayed deodorant under his arms. It was annoying how the deodorant never actually dried; his underarms smelled nice enough but they were constantly clammy.

Turk slid into some black cotton pants with an elastic waistband and pulled on a T-shirt. He checked himself in the mirror. His hair was a wet, frizzy mess and he definitely needed a shave, but he was hungry and wasn't about to miss the buffet. He tugged his pants up, dropping the end of the T-shirt over his belly. The T-shirt had an American flag in the background and written over the flag was the message: *These colors don't run—fucking deal with it.* Turk liked that. It was simple. Clear. Patriotic.

Turk stepped outside into the buggy night. Moonlight hit the ocean and bounced back, casting a silvery-blue glow across the beach. He walked along the sand, sending hundreds of tiny crabs skittering back into the waves, following the sound of the music toward the glow of several dozen tiki torches.

Twenty or so couples were grazing at the buffet—a giant U-shaped setup staffed by a dozen Thai chefs in crisp white uniforms—piling their plates as high as they could and sitting at little tables scattered around the beach. Turk looked for Sheila; she should've been back from her safari by now, but he didn't see her. He'd promised her they'd eat dinner together but he was hungry, so he went to check out the food.

Turk stopped and watched as a young Thai woman carved a watermelon to look like an intricate peony. Various lotus blossoms and other flowers cut from mangoes, papayas, chili peppers, and radishes were arrayed in front of her. She smiled up at Turk, inviting him to put one of the carvings on his plate. Turk smiled and told her they were too beautiful to eat. Unlike you, he thought. He started to say something else, but immediately caught himself and hurried off. He reminded himself of what the shrink had told him over and over again, beating it into his head. Be vigilant. Stay on guard. The addiction can come back when you least expect it. It's not just backstage after a show or at a party when you have to be on guard—the *catalytic environment* again—but times like these. Looking at women carving fruit to look like flowers.

Turk began to survey the buffet like a general inspecting the troops. There were live blue and black crabs moving in slow motion in a large plastic bucket, huge prawns laid out on a bed of ice waiting to be grilled, platters filled with fiery Thai salads—Turk didn't quite understand why you'd want to eat a salad made of red-hot chili pepper duck with mangoes. There was a rice and curry station with vats of meat bubbling in various chili-choked stews. Turk was still trying to understand the food. It looked great—it was beautiful—and tasted good, but why was it so fucking hot? One bite and your lips and tongue would burn and begin to swell. The stuff slid down your gullet easy enough, but once it got to your stomach it felt like a gas burner had been switched on. The worst—and the mere thought of this made Turk cringe—was the next morning. Digestion didn't appear to affect the chilis at all; they were just as biting and potent coming out as they were going in. No amount of beer could dilute the raw, burning sensation he felt after sitting on the toilet in Thailand.

A chef threw some strange-looking vegetation into a white-hot wok. The wok exploded in a fireball of oil and vegetables as the chef deftly flipped and tossed the contents up in the air. Turk walked over for a closer look.

"What's that?"

"Morning glory vine."

"You eat that?"

The chef nodded as he continued to juggle the fireball. "Very good."

Turk was impressed. It reminded him of the pyrotechnic show Metal Assassin had used on its last two tours. When all the other bands had turned to lasers and holographic projections and high-tech crap like that, Metal Assassin had decided to go old school: smoke and flames and explosions.

Rock 'n' fuckin' roll, man.

Even though vegetables weren't his strong suit, Turk ordered a plate of morning glory vines. He wanted to watch them blow up again. When the chef flipped them out of the wok and they fireballed, Turk couldn't help himself—he let out a shriek and pumped his arms into the air, his first and pinkie fingers extended in a devil horn salute to the wok master.

Turk took his vegetables and, what the hell, a half-dozen grilled jumbo prawns back to a table to settle in to wait for his wife. A cold Singha materialized at his side. Turk accepted it without hesitation, popped a prawn in his mouth, and washed it down with the beer. Out of the corner of his eye Turk noticed the young Swiss-German girl making a show of ignoring him. He wasn't surprised: hell hath no fury and all that. So he ignored her ignoring him and turned his attention to the show.

Three slender Thai women, dressed in traditional silk robes, sporting golden crowns and long metallic fingernails, swayed to the strange plucking and clanging of the music as they waved their hands in the air. Their movements were sensual and dreamlike, their bodies undulating in erotic slow motion. This was no hula; it was something else. Watching them gave Turk a boner.

There were assorted gongs and drums being thumped and whacked by the musicians, creating a slow, mysterious beat. Too slow for Turk—he would've pumped it up a couple of notches—but it didn't suck. Three other players sat off to the side, one tapping out a strange melody on a xylophone type thing called a *ranad-ek* while another one sawed away on a two-string Thai fiddle and the third bleated out bird-calls on a bamboo flute. The whole thing had a mellow jazzy vibe punctuated by irritating shrieks and tweets.

Turk might've ignored the music completely if Sheila had been with him. They would've talked about her day and had a laugh. But since he was still alone, his plate now emptied of prawns and morning glory, he ordered another beer and leaned back in his chair.

The song fizzled out and died. Turk applauded. He was always conscious about supporting his fellow musicians; not many were as fortunate as him. He watched as the fiddle player pulled a strange-looking instrument from behind him and began to play what Turk could only call a riff. The instrument, a *jakhae,* looked like a kind of square guitar flopped on its back. It was not the coolest ax Turk had ever seen, but the sound that came out of it was fantastic. It reminded Turk of the time their lead guitarist, Bruno Caravali, had played a solo on a sitar. Bruno sat a few inches in front of a double Marshall stack with the amps cranked up all the way; it was so loud in the studio that the air crackled with a static charge that made your hair stand on end. Bruno, who had no idea how to play a sitar but was somewhat of a guitar virtuoso, started wailing on the sitar strings. The sheer volume of the amps caused all the other strings on the sitar to vibrate and resonate violently, as if its rivets were about to pop. The sound that came out was incredible, an otherworldly buzzing. Like a dragonfly perched on the string, only a million times louder. That sound became the signature intro for the Metal Assassin hit "Drop in the Bucket."

The guy playing the *jakhae* wasn't amplified, but somehow the sound was similar. The music touched Turk; it drifted in the sea air and came to him, gently filling an empty spot inside his chest. Sheila would say it was his heart chakra. That it was proof he was yearning to play music again; that he missed his bandmates. But that was Sheila. She was from California. If it couldn't be feng shuied, ayurveda-ized, aromatherapy-ized, Qi Jonged, or acupunctured, then it couldn't be helped at all. She believed all that stuff. Turk didn't disbelieve it. Just like he didn't disbelieve that maybe some concerned and wise old man with a big gray beard might be looking down on him from heaven, making sure he was okay.

But Sheila would've been right about one thing: He did miss the band. Breaking up hadn't been his idea; that was Steve's ego trip. Turk would've been happy to rock with Metal Assassin until they pried the bass guitar out of his cold, dead fingers. But what could he do? It wasn't like it hadn't happened before. Rock bands are always breaking up, and Turk had been in bands since he was in high school.

There was that first band, Gangplank, which played a kind of punk rock disco. Three guitars that were never in tune, a bass, and a drummer with the largest drum kit Turk had ever seen. To this day he hadn't been in another band where the drummer had a gong.

While they weren't exactly accomplished musicians—they created an excruciating noise—playing in Gangplank was fun. After school they'd go to the drummer's house and rehearse in the basement. They'd get amped up on root beer and Cheetos, making a wonderful racket until the drummer's dad came in and kicked them out. Turk could still remember walking home through the tidy little streets of working-class suburban Teaneck, his ears ringing, his bass slung over his shoulder in a gig bag, and a smile on his face.

I'm in a band.

But Gangplank never got out of the basement. They never played a gig. Just when they'd arranged to play at a party—a college party with kegs of beer—the lead singer got grounded because he was failing chemistry.

Turk played with a couple other bands—he couldn't even remember their names—experimenting with punk rock, fusion, and Top 40; everything but country. He played in bars, art galleries, house parties, and rented halls; he played at weddings, bar mitzvahs, bachelor parties . . . anywhere he could plug in his amp.

Eventually he hooked up with some musicians from New York City. They were forming a group called Play Loud. Turk had always played as loud as he could, and in the other members of Play Loud he found like-minded individuals. They performed a kind of art school heavy metal, with the entire band outfitted in costumes that made them look like extras from a *Mad Max* movie who'd accidentally found themselves at a Dadaist happening.

The lead singer, Jimbo, and his girlfriend designed the outfits: the lead guitarist outfitted in striped tights and leotards with feathers, Turk saddled with a chain mail T-shirt, a leather jockstrap, and a kind of Viking helmet/hockey mask on his head. They looked ridiculous, but were immensely entertaining, and the band soon gained a small amount of notoriety and started to make a little bit of money.

Turk dropped out of high school a month shy of graduating and got his GED. He didn't need a diploma to rock. But Jimbo had delusions of grandeur and quit the band after a year to go to Hollywood and become a movie star. Play Loud never lived up to its potential, but the experience gave Turk some credibility as a bass player and put him on the map as a talent to watch. Soon after Jimbo's decamping, Turk found himself auditioning for Steve, Bruno, and the band that was to become the worldwide megaselling sensation, Metal Assassin.

Now, after twenty-seven years of rocking the world—years that had gone by in what seemed like a flash—Turk sat on a beach in Phuket wondering where the fuck his wife was.

He was interrupted by the hotel manager, a tall and attractive Frenchwoman named Carole Duchamp.

"Monsieur Henry? I must talk with you. It concerns your wife."

Eight

LOS ANGELES

Jon Heidegger had just pulled his new Mercedes coupe into his personal parking spot—his name carefully stenciled in silver paint on the brick wall—when his cell phone rang. The caller ID displayed an impossibly long string of numbers, and normally he wouldn't have answered, but not that many people had his personal cell phone number, so you never know.

"Heidegger."

There was no immediate response. He could hear some kind of delay, a ghost of an echo, the static hiss of time and space as his voice went into outer space, bounced off a satellite, and was beamed down to another part of the world.

"Hello?"

Jon pulled down his visor and checked his teeth in the mirror. He'd paid a lot of money for the good veneers, the best ones, and he still couldn't believe they were his teeth. They said it would make him feel more confident, and they weren't kidding. It was like he'd stolen the beaming smile off that movie star who's so famous for grinning and talking about Scientology.

He heard a wash of white noise and then, faintly, sounding like he was trapped in an echo chamber, Turk.

"One million. Cash. Important. Hurry."

Jon noticed that one of his eyebrow hairs had gone crazy and was curling up in a weird spiral and jutting out over his designer horn-rims. That was the bitch about getting old. Your hair suddenly turned on you, sprouting out of your ears and nose, going all bushy and crazy on your eyebrows, dropping off your head and yet growing robustly on your neck and back. Like his gardener trying to control the ivy taking over his Hollywood Hills home, his hair needed twice-monthly waxing and tweezing to keep him from looking like fucking Sasquatch. He grabbed the offending eyebrow hair and yanked it out.

Jon flipped the visor back into position.

"Now what do you need that kind of money for? Hookers can't cost that much. It's Thailand, for Chrissakes."

He heard a garbled rant coming from the other side of the world.

"Turk . . . dude . . . this connection sucks. Give me your number and I'll call you back in five minutes."

Jon scribbled down the number. It was long—how many numbers does it take to call Thailand?—drifting over three lines on the little memo pad he kept in his car.

. . .

Jon Heidegger was over six-two, tall and lanky. That meant he couldn't just step out of his nimble little Mercedes, he had to extricate himself from the driver's seat in three careful movements. First his legs pivoted out and he carefully placed the soles of his Prada shoes on the pavement so as not to scuff them, his red socks—he always wore red socks—peeking out from under his black pants; then he did a twisting maneuver that put him in an ass-forward position—he didn't like to remain like this for very long, due to his belief that his ass looked too big; and finally he ducked his head, stepped back, and emerged from the vehicle. Then he took a moment to straighten his shirt, jacket, and pants. He spent a lot of money on clothes; no reason to let them get rumpled. Sometimes he wished he'd gotten a big car like an Escalade or something, a massive hunk of steel that you climbed up into—no folding, twisting, or bending required—but as he closed the car door and walked away, the German-engineered electronics detected this fact and the Mercedes locked and alarmed itself automatically. He loved that.

Heidegger strolled into his office—a funky industrial building reclaimed by an extremely expensive modernist architect and stocked with a collection of rare Danish modern furniture and pricey artwork by contemporary Japanese painters—and turned to his personal assistant.

"Miss Monahan. Get Karl on the phone. It's urgent."

His assistant, Marybeth—she loved it when Jon went old school and used her last name—nodded and started dialing. She didn't need to look the number up—she dialed it several times a day. Karl was the investment banker. He handled the money and, well, rock stars and their money was always a complicated subject. But where some people might be judgmental, even critical, of the rampant waste and extravagance of millionaire rockers, she didn't care. As far as Marybeth was concerned, they'd earned it, and blowing it on mansions, private jets, custom cars, and all kinds of assorted weird shit was just part of the lifestyle.

She loved rock music more than anything else in the world, and working for JH Management allowed her to rub elbows with all the greats. *Franz Tulip?* She helped him shop at Barneys when he was in town. *Hellvetica?* She'd been to a party at their house in Malibu. *Aimee LeClerq?* Marybeth had gone to the Kabbalah Center with her and now wore the protection string around her wrist like it was diamonds from Harry Winston. *Rocketside?* Signing them had been her idea. *Metal Assassin?* They were her favorites.

Marybeth Monahan was not shy about detailing her wild weekend in Paris with guitar god Bruno Caravali to anyone who would listen. Even if it only lasted a couple of minutes, letting Bruno lift her skirt, rip her fishnets, and take her from behind on top of the Eiffel Tower at midnight was the highlight of her life.

What girl didn't dream of something like that?

Marybeth punched a button on the phone system.

"I've got Karl."

While Heidegger handled their careers, Karl was the gatekeeper to their vaults, the man who made sure the incredible bounty of musical El Dorado wasn't completely wasted on paternity suits and trips to rehab. Karl wasn't about to turn over a million dollars of Turk's money—even though it was, technically, Turk's money—until he understood the true nature of the crisis.

"Couldn't keep it in his pants, could he?"

"I don't think that's it."

"Drugs?"

"He's been clean for six months."

"If he's in a jam, he should just call the American consulate. They'll get him a lawyer or whatever."

Heidegger heaved a sigh. Mostly he was glad that Karl was so hard-nosed, but sometimes it was just a pain.

"I'm supposed to call him and tell him the cash is on the way."

"Tell him I'll pull it together, but I want to know what it's for."

He hung up, pushed his glasses up his nose, and proceeded to dial the string of numbers Turk had given him. No manager likes to deliver bad news to his or her clients, but since the breakup of Metal Assassin it seemed like all the news Turk ever got was bad. Though Steve and Bruno both got record deals, no one was interested in a Turk Henry solo project. Despite his musicianship, Turk's reputation for excess—and in rock star terms that meant excessive excess—got a quick rejection from everyone Jon had talked to. Still, it wasn't like Turk was broke. He had at least a hundred million dollars in various bank accounts and investment schemes. If Turk had bothered to ask, Jon would've told him to call it a day and go raise horses on a ranch or buy a winery. But that wasn't what Turk wanted to hear. Turk wanted to keep rocking.

He waited about thirty seconds, then heard a voice on the other side of the world.

"*Sawadee.*"

"Hi. Turk Henry please."

A sequence of pips and beeps followed, and then Turk's voice came over the line.

"Did you get it?"

Turk sounded edgy, excited.

"Karl's working on it. But listen, he wants to know what it's for."

There was a pause on the line.

"I don't want this getting out."

"How many times have I covered for you? Your secret's safe with me."

"They said they'd kill her if it got out."

He could hear Turk breathing hard.

Heidegger sat up in his chair.

"Turk. Tell me what's going on."

"Sheila's been kidnapped."

He couldn't be sure, but it sounded like Turk was crying on the other end.

"Relax. We'll get her back."

"Promise?"

"I'll do my best. Now let me get the money sorted out with Karl."

"Thanks, Jon."

Heidegger hung up, and, despite his concern for Sheila, he couldn't help himself: he smiled. This was fantastic news. This was human interest. *E!, VH1, US Weekly, People, MTV*—everybody would be all over this story. Turk's plight would be splattered all over the media: his life after the tragic breakup of Metal Assassin, his struggles with a variety of addictions, his marriage to a supermodel—and now her kidnapping. Barring another invasion of a Middle Eastern country, Turk would be on center stage in the world media. The public would talk about him, worry about him. They would feel Turk's pain and, best of all, they would buy a new Turk Henry CD. This was Turk's career rising from the ashes like the proverbial phoenix. How could he keep it quiet?

As he began to draft a press release in his head, he sent an instant message telling Marybeth to roll calls to his publicist and to the A & R man at Planetary Records. They had work to do.

Nine

PHUKET

Captain Somporn watched as two of his men, Saksan and Kittisak, bundled the dead American's body into the back of a battered *tuk tuk,* a rickety three-wheeled golf cart. They tried, unsuccessfully, to prop him up like a sleeping tourist, but even with rigor mortis setting in the body would flop unnaturally in the backseat —a marionette with its strings cut—the head lolling and swinging like some kind of freak tetherball in the wind. There was no way to stop it, so Somporn told his men to go fast and hope no one noticed. Besides, the body was starting to smell and the flies it attracted were annoying.

Somporn was fond of his men. They had once been a crack narcotics interdiction unit—the fierce *Thahan Prahan* —patrolling the Thai-Cambodia border. Perfectly attuned to the jungle—the rustle of leaves, the snap of twigs, the scent of a distant cigarette—they had ambushed dozens of convoys in their day, carting off hundreds of pounds of raw opium, delivering it to their grateful superior officers. They were so daring and ingenious that they were eventually brought to the attention of their commanding officer, General Chuengrakkiat, who offered them a generous bonus if they would turn their attentions to protecting the convoys instead of annihilating them.

Although he was a captain—he had attained this rank through diligence, bravery, and the uncanny ability to look the other way without being told to—Somporn was, like his men, a poorly educated boy from working-class parents. In fact, Somporn's mother and father ran a fairly successful green papaya salad—*som tum*—and sticky rice business on one of the side streets in Bangkok. Somporn had always assumed he would spend his days working in the family trade, grating green papayas and making their homemade *nam pla*—it was his great-grandmother's secret recipe—when the draft interrupted his plans.

His parents weren't wealthy enough to bribe the Army officials and get him out of it, so it was no surprise when his name was called. Somporn sometimes wondered if his parents had just decided they'd like to have a little more room in their cramped apartment and that's why they let him go, maybe even wanted him to. Either way, it didn't matter now. The world of cluttered Bangkok streets and the smell of fresh green papaya were in the past. If pressed, he could still brew up a tasty *nam pla,* and his men often implored him to make the spicy fish sauce for them.

When Somporn looked at his soldiers now, he had to laugh. They had slowly transformed from steely-scrubbed, clean-cut representatives of the best of the Royal Thai Army to . . . well, they looked like a cross between one of those techno-hippie bands from Japan and a ragtag group of sea pirates. They were a lean and, frankly, frightening group of men. Wearing their hair long and stringy, with scruffy and sparse goatees and Fu Manchu–style mustaches, their preferred dress code was a ripped-up T-shirt featuring an English band like The Clash or a product logo like Motorola splashed on the front, mixed with a pair of baggy surfer shorts or khakis cut to the ankles. Only Apirath sported tattoos—he had decided he would use his part of the ransom to buy a Harley-Davidson motorcycle—but they all had multiple ear piercings and wore all kinds of necklaces and jangly bracelets. It was a decidedly effeminate look—balanced by the automatic weapons slung electric-guitar low from their shoulders—that was not improved by the fact that a couple of the men had begun wearing the sunglasses of the captured women day and night.

Somporn walked back along the beach to his cabin/command post—really nothing more than a small wood frame room with a thatched roof and a few crude furnishings—and sat down on the floor for a smoke. He lit a Russian cigarette and inhaled. He would've preferred a Marlboro or a Camel but now that Americans weren't smoking anymore you couldn't find those brands as easily. He wasn't a heavy smoker—he enjoyed the occasional cigarette—but a mangrove swamp wasn't the best place for a hideout unless you took pleasure in feeding mosquitoes, and the smoke kept the little bloodsuckers away. That was the choice: malaria or cancer; either way, he had to get out of this swamp soon or it was going to kill him.

Somporn squashed a big mosquito against his arm and allowed himself a smile. The plan, as pathetic and desperate as it was, had turned out a stunning success. Who knew they'd catch a millionaire rock star's supermodel wife when they'd gone hunting for tourists? It was like snatching an old lady's purse and finding it filled with diamonds.

The original plan had been to kidnap a few *farangs*—Westerners—cash in on their safe return, and use the money to purchase opium from a grower he knew near Chiang Mai. After taking the opium to Hong Kong and selling it to a heroin lab, he'd have enough to give everyone a bonus, buy a small boat, and get back into business. It was a solid enough plan.

But it was nothing like the glory days when Somporn and his men had terrorized the South China Sea. They'd been real pirates then, using the element of surprise and sheer audaciousness to take down some major scores. Attacking at night, their small inflatables almost invisible in the black water, they'd drift up on a big oil tanker—sometimes a natural gas tanker—use hooks and ropes to climb aboard, disable the communicators, and take the crew hostage. Since Somporn and his men had been elite commandos in the Thai Army, they were well trained and highly efficient, able to overwhelm a boat's crew in a matter of minutes.

They would sail for a small, uninhabited island and dump the crew there with a couple of gallons of water and a few cans of food. Then it was a quick change of flag—Somporn always liked to use the Venezuelan flag for some reason—a couple of gallons of paint to change the name of the vessel, and they could sail right into Shanghai harbor and sell the gas or oil to a dealer he knew. It was an extremely lucrative business.

Less lucrative were the Pai Gow tables in the casino at the Hotel Lisboa on Macau. That's where Somporn always went after a heist.

He had a ritual. He would take his cut of the score and wire several thousand dollars to his local *Wat* in Bangkok for good luck and blessings from the Buddha. Then he'd stash a large chunk of cash in a safe deposit box at his Hong Kong bank. This money he was saving for the day when he could afford to buy a real pirate boat. He'd then have several new suits made for him at a custom tailor he liked in Shenzen, so that when he checked in to the hotel, he looked sharp, respectable, and anonymous, like a successful businessman on vacation.

Even though the island of Macau is connected to the Chinese mainland by a bridge, the European architecture and the fact that some people still spoke Portuguese made him feel like he was far away from Southeast Asia. Captain Somporn always stayed at the Hotel Lisboa. It was his hideout: opulent, extravagant, and the last place the authorities would look for a rugged Thai pirate. He'd spend a month, maybe two, sitting at the Pai Gow tables sipping single malt Scotch and listening to the gentle clicking sounds of the tiles as they were shuffled, stacked, and sorted into eight piles of four. He loved that the game was filled with ritual, like a religious ceremony, the tiles waiting in neat rows as the dealer shook the dice to determine the order in which they'd be dealt. He loved that the dealer had to be as lucky as the player; no one really seemed to have an advantage, and most of the hands ended up a tie, a "push hand," where nobody won and nobody lost. It was, for him, the time when he felt the most at peace.

When he was out of money, he'd make a phone call to Bangkok and alert his crew that they were back in business.

This went on for a number of years, and eventually the safe deposit box in the bank in Hong Kong contained enough money for him to invest in a very fast, Russian-made, armored assault boat—specifically, an OSA Class Type 205 Fast Patrol Boat. It wasn't that expensive. He'd bought it off a disgruntled

Russian Navy crew that had deserted and were trying to get to New Zealand, where they were planning on buying some land and starting a winery.

Somporn adored that boat. Even though he couldn't read any of the instrument panels—they were all in Cyrillic—and even though the dual diesel engines used barrels of fuel, for some reason that ship made him feel like a real pirate. Maybe it was the large and relatively well-appointed stateroom, with an actual air conditioner and private bathroom; maybe it was the radar that helped them track other ships; or maybe it was just the nifty little rocket launcher and the four .30mm guns mounted on the bow and sides that gave him that extra frisson of danger. The boat didn't have any missiles—the Russians had already sold those to some Chechens—but it didn't matter, it looked intimidating and most ships were happy to surrender without putting up a fight.

Outfitted with a fast warship, Somporn and his crew went to work terrorizing the Strait of Malacca between Indonesia, Malaysia, and Singapore for two fun and profitable years before a Thai fighter pilot managed to get their coordinates and lock on a couple of missiles.

Most of the crew managed to escape the explosions and elude the helicopters that hunted the water for survivors. Somporn, however, was unlucky—it seemed the thousands of dollars sent to the *Wat* had been for nothing—and was scooped out of the water by the Thai Navy. Perhaps he should've sent more money to the monks; perhaps it was just his karma. He used the rest of his savings to bribe the officers and crew of the Navy boat to let him go. Once the cash transfer had been confirmed, they were happy to help him, setting him adrift in a rubber raft fifty miles off the Thai coast in shark-infested waters.

Defeated, dehydrated, hungry, and broke, he finally washed ashore and began the slow process of reassembling his crew. That's why he was here, feeding mosquitoes in this mangrove swamp; but this was just the beginning. Soon he would return to his pirate life, the high seas, easy money, and the Pai Gow tables of Macau.

. . .

Somporn swatted another mosquito. He hadn't noticed this one feeding on him, and it had filled itself with his blood. The bug exploded in a burst of crimson. Somporn stood and went over to his bed. He rummaged through his duffel bag until he found a bottle of Calvin Klein's Obsession cologne for men. It smelled nice, sophisticated, and he wasn't stingy as he splashed it on his face. He turned and checked himself in the mirror, running his hand through his hair, making sure there wasn't anything stuck in his teeth. Somporn started to leave and then stopped himself. He took the bottle of Obsession and shook a few drops down his pants, onto his pubic hair. He'd never met a supermodel before.

. . .

Captain Somporn didn't knock. It wasn't about being polite; it was about control. He carried a battery-powered lantern—the light swarming with a variety of exotic insects—into the hut. The smell was the first thing that hit him. Sharp, astringent, and nasty: shit mixed with fear. He'd smelled it before, once when a Cambodian drug lord took his patrol captive and several of his platoon mates were executed in front of him. It happened so fast and was so terrifying that the men lost control of their bowels. Somporn didn't like to be reminded of it.

He saw the four miserable hostages leaning against the walls of the hut, their faces pale and exhausted, their skin clammy and bug-bit.

"Are you hungry?"

The British couple nodded, the woman from Seattle whimpered and pissed herself, and Sheila glared at him.

"You've got to let her clean herself."

Somporn smiled.

"Perhaps if her husband had shown a little more respect."

"If not for her, then for me. Please. It's disgusting."

Somporn's expression changed; he stared at Sheila for a moment, then bent down and unlocked the handcuff holding her.

"Come with me."

He quickly—because he didn't like the smell any more than Sheila did—cuffed the Seattle woman's hands together, and led Sheila out of the hut.

. . .

Once outside, Sheila took a few deep breaths to try and clear her nostrils. She looked around the camp and saw several of the kidnappers sitting around a fire, drinking beer and eating bowls of noodles. A few women sat on the ground listening to a transistor radio and peeling mangoes. For the first time since she'd been kidnapped, her stomach growled.

"Captain? Why don't you help that woman? What you're doing is cruel."

Somporn looked at her, sympathetically.

"It's not that I'm cruel. It's a psychological technique."

"Letting her sit in her own shit?"

"I want you and the others to understand that if they act out, like that woman's husband, they will be killed and their spouse will be made to suffer. Then they will understand that what's happening to them isn't so very bad."

"Where'd you learn that? Kidnapper school?"

Somporn led her into his cabin.

"I'm not a kidnapper. I'm a pirate."

Sheila looked confused.

"A pirate?"

Somporn nodded as he set the lantern down and lit a second, gas-powered lantern that was surprisingly bright. Its hiss and clear white glow reminded Sheila of camping trips with her family.

"Right now I'm a pirate without a ship. But that is about to change."

Somporn pulled a bottle of whiskey and two small Chinese teacups out of a cupboard along the wall.

"Would you like a drink? It's Jack Daniel's. World-famous."

"Sure."

Somporn poured some into each cup and handed her one.

"I'm sure you'd like to wash up. I have a shower. Over there."

Somporn pointed to the corner of the cabin, where a small showerhead hung from the end of a plastic tube. Bamboo slats were cut into the floor for a drain. It was crude, but it was a shower.

Sheila couldn't believe it. There was nothing more in the world she wanted right now than to cleanse her body of the Seattle woman's excrement. If the smell was nauseating— it clung to her like a putrid aura—the actual sensation was even worse. But the thing that really freaked her out, the bacterial thought that echoed in her head, was the cold and thick and slimy truth that she had spent the day sitting in another person's shit. She wasn't sure she would ever get over that.

Captain Somporn was offering salvation: soap and water, a chance to get clean. Still Sheila hesitated.

"I don't know."

"The water is not warm, but it is clean. And there's some soap."

Sheila sipped her whiskey. She could feel it going down, trace its journey past her throat and into her stomach. It warmed her, and she began to relax. She studied Somporn. She watched as he sipped his whiskey. She saw how he was sitting, relaxed and in control.

Sheila had been a beautiful woman long enough to understand what was going on.

"You want to watch me shower?"

"I can't have my hostage escaping."

"I need some clean clothes. I can't put these back on."

"I have clothes you can wear."

Sheila looked at Somporn. The Captain, she realized, was like a lot of men she'd met in her life. Like the actor she had lived with, the one with the famous dimples; or the movie director, the cerebral one with the glasses and shaved head; even that ridiculous television producer, obviously gay but wanting a beautiful female model to front for him at parties.

All of them so insecure, so scared of women and their bodies that they had to hide behind fame, status, and money. Incapable of intimacy, they had needed to dominate her. They needed the feeling of power, of control. As if being equals would emasculate them, cause their dicks to shrivel up and retreat like turtleheads. They had desired her because it enhanced their status among other males. She had been as important to them as a Maserati, a vacation home, or a Rolex watch.

Sheila often wondered why men were such babies. What was their problem? What were they afraid of? What would they lose if they opened up and shared themselves with a woman? How would they feel if they let themselves be taken, conquered, and dominated?

Maybe they would like it.

She began unbuttoning her shirt. Somporn sat cross-legged on the floor and lit a cigarette. He watched as she took her shirt off. She was nonchalant. Not coy, not embarrassed. He assumed she was used to getting undressed in front of others; isn't that what models did? But nothing could have prepared him for what happened next. As Sheila removed her bra, Captain Somporn's jaw dropped. Although her breasts were large and voluptuous—perfect, yet with a Japanese raku–like imperfection that made them more than perfect—it wasn't the size or shape that caused his astonishment. It was the color of her skin under the tan line; he had never seen skin so white before. Where the rest of her body was brown and golden, her breasts were white and shimmering, almost translucent, like fresh squid. Her nipples were a shade of pink that Somporn had seen only on coral reefs. She slipped off her pants and revealed an equally pallid ass.

"How is it your skin is so white?"

Sheila stood under the showerhead and removed a clamp on the hose. Cool water began trickling over her body, and Somporn noticed that her nipples jerked erect the moment the water hit them.

"That's the color of my skin."

"But in the pictures you are so brown?"

Sheila squirted some soap into her hand and began lathering her body.

"I used a bronzer."

Somporn rose from his chair and picked up the lamp. He began walking toward her.

"What are you doing?"

"I've never seen such white skin before."

Sheila stopped washing and instinctively covered herself for a moment, then realized there was nothing she could do about it and dropped her hands to her side. She watched Somporn's eyes as they studied her breasts. They were wide in amazement, yet focused in discovering ever nuance and detail. Even her dermatologist didn't look at her this intently.

"This is your natural skin?"

She nodded.

"Why did you color yourself brown?"

Sheila shrugged.

"It's called a healthy tan."

Somporn shook his head in dismay.

"But your white skin . . . it's so beautiful."

Somporn reached a hand out to touch her breast. Sheila stepped back against the wall.

"Please, Captain. I'm trying to wash."

Somporn caught himself.

"I apologize."

He walked back to his spot on the floor and sat down. He refilled his whiskey and lit another cigarette. Sheila watched him. She could sense that he was suddenly troubled by something.

"Where are you from?"

"The United States."

"But there are black people, brown people, in your country. Not everybody is white like you."

Sheila nodded.

"My mother was from Denmark. My father is Norwegian."

Somporn considered that for a moment as the water in the shower slowed to a trickle and stopped. Sheila grabbed a towel—a nice one, pilfered from a four-star hotel—and began to dry herself. Somporn was watching her, entranced, and yet she could tell that his thoughts were elsewhere. Finally he spoke.

"Scandinavia."

He said it like it was a magical word.

Ten

Turk's head was spinning. His nerves were jangly, his hands quivering in a kind of speedy tweaker palsy, and he had a splitting headache. Maybe it was all that iced tea he'd guzzled. Turk got cottonmouth when he was nervous, and he must've sucked down a gallon of the stuff. He should've stuck to beer, but somehow that didn't seem like the right thing to do as he talked on the phone with Heidegger and then with the guy from the U.S. Embassy in Bangkok. If people saw him drinking beer they might not think he was taking this kidnapping seriously.

He was taking it seriously, very, but he didn't know what to do, he was out of his league. He didn't have the skill set or the temperament for dealing with a crisis like this. He was a rock star, for fuck's sake. He had people who handled things for him. Your flight gets delayed, you call the tour manager or Marybeth. They call someone or something, whatever it is they do, and you're on another flight. If there's a problem with that flight, they charter you a fucking plane. It's all taken care of. You just have to sit in the executive lounge at the airport, watch ESPN, and drink cranberry juice. If the gigantic Mack truck pulling your gear gets stuck in a snowstorm while you're on tour, nobody calls you and says that your equipment won't make the gig; somehow equipment arrives and is set up, ready for you to rock. You don't even hear about it until days later, when it's become a funny anecdote about how the stranded crew were kept entertained by a couple of truck stop whores; they even made an amateur porn video about it. That's why you keep an army of managers, tour managers, booking agents, lawyers, trainers, nutritionists, travel agents, and roadies on the payroll. The real world starts to burst your bubble or bum your party head and, snap, someone's there to deal with it. It's all taken care of; it's handled. That's how rock stars roll.

Turk lay down on the bed in his hotel room. He kicked his flip-flops off and adjusted the pillows. He tried to relax, taking a deep breath of air in through his nostrils and letting it whistle out through his lips; he tried to let his thoughts go. He wasn't sure what that meant, exactly, but that's what the yoga teacher Sheila had hired to help him "open up" had said to do.

He knew he should calm down; a U.S. official was on his way. He was going to liaise with the Thai authorities. By "liaise" Turk assumed he was going to talk to them or tell them what to do. Having the American government take over should've put his mind at ease. But it didn't. At the end of the day, Turk just didn't trust "the man."

He remembered the time he and the other members of Metal Assassin got in trouble in Tampa Bay. They'd had a bit of a sex party with a group of willing young women, only to find out that the oldest was fifteen. The police were called. Charges were filed. It looked like they were in the soup for sure. They even considered going on the lam and relocating to Düsseldorf or Hamburg. There was a big audience for metal in Germany. But their manager and lawyer and record company were on the ball. Turk never got the full story of what happened or how they did it but suddenly the charges got dropped. They vanished. Disappeared. Expunged from court records. The press never got wind of it. No one was the wiser. Even the parents of the fourteen-year-old that Turk and Bruno had banged in the limo—Turk taking the front end, Bruno the back—were all smiles, asking for autographs, getting their pictures taken with the band. They seemed to understand that no one in Metal Assassin, not Turk, Steve, Bruno, or Chaps the drummer, knew the girls were underage. Later, in therapy for his sex addiction, Turk wondered if it would've mattered to him if he'd known.

But who was going to handle Sheila's abduction? The guy from the embassy? The Army? The President? Jon Heidegger? Somebody had to do something. Turk could feel the stress building inside him. There was a tightness in his chest that worried him. He was supposed to live a nonstress kind of life. Being stressed was part of the problem that led to his addictions. The shrinks had warned him that stress triggered something in his brain that could make him fall back into his old cycle. Turk didn't want to fall off the wagon. He'd spent too much time and money and energy trying to get right.

Why did Sheila have to go ride an elephant?

Why did they have to kidnap Sheila? If someone else he knew was kidnapped and he was stressed out about it, he could have sex with her. Now he was on his own. Turk thought about calling his sponsor, then decided he'd do it in the morning.

He sat up, climbed off the bed, and went over to the minibar for a Singha. The Thai beers were pretty good—cold and slightly bitter; the brew gurgled down his gullet and soothed his sizzled nerves.

Feeling somewhat better, he went into the bathroom and rooted through Sheila's toiletries until he found a bottle of prescription sleeping pills. He couldn't remember if you were supposed to take one or two, and the label on the bottle was all smudged. He didn't want to just feel groggy, he needed to *sleep,* so he popped two, washing the pills down with the rest of the beer. The subsequent burp tasted faintly of pharmaceuticals.

Turk lay back down and made himself comfortable. He wanted to get a good night's sleep. He had to be sharp for his meeting with the authorities in the morning.

He waited for the drugs to knock him out.

Eleven

en Harding, ICE agent, had never been to Phuket. He'd never been to the other "hot" tourist destinations either, like Krabi, Ko Phi Phi, or Phang Nga Bay, with its bizarre limestone spires jutting up out of the water. Even if he'd wanted to go, the tsunami fixed that. No way was he going near the ocean, not after the pictures he'd seen. It wasn't the idea that you could be asleep in your bed when the ocean suddenly decides to rise up and destroy everything that freaked him out. That would, at least he hoped, be a quick way to go; swept out to sea, drowned under millions of gallons of water. It was the aftermath of the tsunami that caused his skin to crawl. The stink of corpses left on the beach, the dead animals hanging from trees. The sewage systems—already primitive at best—overwhelmed and spewing fecal matter everywhere. From Ben's point of view, the tsunami was bacteria's best friend. If he thought about it long enough, imagined being trapped in that germ-intense environment, he'd break out in a cool sweat and feel tingles of imaginary fever—cholera , smallpox, yellow fever—beginning to spread through his body.

For most of his tour of duty he'd been in Bangkok, and while the capital city had its share of fetid and scary places, it was for the most part modern, with hot running water, antiseptic soap, Western toilets—all the things you needed to keep from getting sick. Armed with a bottle of antibacterial hand gel, he could go out into the city with confidence and slowly acclimate to the strangeness, the clamor, humanity, and humidity of life in Southeast Asia. Now he was going out into uncharted waters. Even though it was only a one-hour flight, he'd be leaving the quasi-sanitary comforts of the big city.

To prepare for the trip south, Ben had started taking a course of antibiotics as a prophylactic. Be prepared.

...

It didn't surprise him that tourists had been kidnapped. The south of Thailand butts up right next to Malaysia, and, as everyone knows, Malaysia is a Muslim country. And a Muslim country is a place teeming with potential terrorists. It would be easy for one of these "terror cells" to go up to Phuket and assault tourists from the developed world. Like the disco bombing in Bali, where hundreds of Australians were killed, Ben was just surprised it hadn't happened sooner.

Ben was surprised by the mix of people on the plane: Thais, Saudis, Norwegians, Swedes, Brits, Australians, French, German, Chileans. He was the lone American. Mostly they were families or couples going on their honeymoon. People ready to lie around on the beach, snorkel, and get sunburned.

Ben didn't understand it.

People paying good money to fly on germ-infested airplanes and land in germ-infested countries where they'd sit around and eat food that was guaranteed to teach them the ABCs of hepatitis. A honeymoon, an anniversary trip, a vacation spent soaking in a pandemic soup.

The sex tourists were the worst. Didn't they know that HIV infection rates were soaring in Southeast Asia? Why did they arrive in droves and head, salivating, to the seediest brothels in the world? Why did they risk their lives? Was Thai pussy that good?

…

The airport in Phuket was small and tidy, like an airport in Duluth or Boise. The only strangeness was a large section of rows of identical orange chairs with a sign saying: RESERVED FOR MONK. Ben didn't see a monk anywhere.

He followed the rest of the passengers down corridors lined with ads for undersea adventure, coral reef exploration, Thai dining and dancing, parasailing, deep sea fishing, and other assorted resort activities. The good life. A perfect target for terror.

At baggage claim, a driver from the resort was standing by the door wearing a khaki uniform and white pith helmet. He held a little sign that read: MR. HARDING, USA. Ben shook his head in dismay. If the terror cell was watching the airport, his cover was blown.

Ben nodded to the driver.

"I'm Harding."

The driver bowed stiffly and handed him a manila envelope.

"This is for you, sir. Do you have any bags?"

"Just this."

The driver took Ben's small carry-on.

"The car is waiting."

...

It was hotter in Phuket than in Bangkok. But at least the traffic was mellow. It was rural, relaxed. The roads were clear and the streets seemed clean. Ben was glad that the driver had left the car running, the air-conditioning blasting at maximum, turning the interior of the little Toyota into an icebox. Ben sat in back and opened the manila envelope. It was the information he'd requested on the kidnapping victims. He immediately set aside the information on the British couple—they weren't his concern—and concentrated on the Americans. Although he'd heard of Metal Assassin—who hadn't?—he couldn't claim to be a fan. Ben didn't have many CDs; he just listened to whatever was on the radio. But he did remember a power ballad by Metal Assassin that he'd liked. Though he couldn't remember the title, he did recall the chorus. It had something to do with love breaking a chain or smashing a door. Maybe that was the name of the song, "Unbroken."

He was relieved that the musician from Metal Assassin, Turk Henry, hadn't been kidnapped. How could he keep that away from the media? They'd be on it like piranhas. And what do terrorists like more than killing Americans? Publicity. For all their talk about injustice and Islam, they were really just egomaniacs, media whores with bombs strapped around their waists. Sign them to a good PR firm and give them a couple hours on *Oprah* and they'd probably stop blowing people up.

But it wasn't Turk Henry who was abducted; it was his wife. Apparently she had been famous about ten years ago, but was now just a footnote on the back page of *Vogue*. Ben was certain that he could get Mr. Henry to cooperate—there was always the veiled threat of an IRS audit to keep people in line—and keep things on a need-to-know basis until he'd sorted this out.

...

Turk heard a banging on his door. Or maybe he was dreaming of someone at the door. No. That was really someone at the door. Turk croaked.

"Wait."

The banging didn't stop. Turk tried again, only louder.

"Fucking hold on a second."

That stopped the banging. Turk sat up, his head still swimming from the sleeping pills. He heard a muffled voice on the other side of the door.

"Mr. Henry. Mr. Henry. They are waiting for you in the manager's office."

Turk stood, steadied himself, and waddled over to the door. He pulled it open to reveal a young man holding a tray with a pot of coffee, a cup, and some kind of fruit juice in a little glass sealed with plastic wrap.

"Compliments of the hotel."

Turk stepped aside and the young man slipped in and deposited the tray on a little table.

"They are waiting for you."

"Who?"

"The American government man. USA."

Turk nodded. He didn't know what the fuck this guy was talking about, but whatever, coffee sounded good.

"Give me a half hour."

"Half hour. Okay."

And then he was gone. Turk closed the door and blinked. He opened the door again and looked out. There were the coconut palms, the beach, even a couple of topless Dutch women out for an early-morning tit bake. He wasn't dreaming. He poured himself a cup of coffee—he had trouble opening the sugar cube wrappers, but eventually wrestled the cubes free—and then sat on the bed and let the sweet lukewarm goodness slide down his gullet.

He stared off into space for a while, waiting for pharmaceutical Morpheus to release the grip on his head.

...

Sheila had returned late, well fed, clean, and slightly tipsy. The Captain had been kind enough to handcuff her away from the woman from Seattle. It was a good thing, too, as the woman had added to her repertoire of shit and piss with a spectacular bout of projectile vomiting. This was followed by a steady stream of diarrhea that flowed up her panties and out the waistband of her shorts like a volcano oozing noxious brown magma.

The British couple were suspicious, certain Sheila had fucked the Captain for the clean T-shirt—one celebrating Real Madrid's tour of Asia—camouflage pants, and flip-flops. Of course, she hadn't fucked him. But the thought had crossed her mind. Not for sex—basically, she was over sex—but for survival. Even though the Captain had seemed friendly, he had still kidnapped her. His men had murdered someone right in front of her. She knew that her luck could change at any moment, and she didn't want to die. Not yet anyway. Sex for survival? Why not? To Sheila it seemed like her survival always depended on sex. She realized she'd have to bring that up with her therapist. Although she'd have to find a new shrink, as the last one had tried to fuck her.

Sunlight was beginning to filter through the hut. Sheila looked over and saw Charlie, the double-glazing king of Crouch End, staring at her.

"What'd he make you do?"

"He just wanted to talk."

The wife looked at her.

"I'd like some clean clothes. Maybe he'll talk to me."

Charlie elbowed his wife.

"Hush now. There's no need for that."

Sheila heard some mumbles from the Seattle woman. She looked at her, feeling pity and revulsion. The woman was curled into a fetal position, lying in puddles of various viscosities. The insects had homed in on her. They swarmed around her, occasionally rising simultaneously like a dark blanket and then settling back down again. Sheila could see that the woman was sick; she quivered with fever, alternating between wild sweats and teeth-chattering chills.

That's what happens when you order one shrimp.

She thought about protesting to Captain Somporn, but then she remembered his warning: someone has to be treated badly. Sheila averted her eyes.

· · ·

Ben had never met a rock star before, but he'd read about them in some of the glossy weekly magazines that drifted around the embassy. He always made a point of scouring any publication for news, reviews, and gossip, anything that smacked of America. He liked to sit down at his desk with a Coca-Cola, freedom fries, and a hamburger from the Embassy commissary, read *People* magazine, feel the A/C cranking; and it was almost like home. The magazines kept him informed. He knew who was adopting a Cambodian baby, which celeb was getting her implants removed, which was having an affair with the other, who was bulimic and who was anorexic. Magazines taught him everything he knew about rock stars— their fast cars, drug problems, and tattoos. He knew they partied hard and lived a kind of outsider existence. Millionaires above the law. Of course, when he thought about it, most rich and famous people acted above the law. Were rock stars so different from CEOs?

Ben realized he would have to scare Turk, control him, and get him dependent so he would call Ben before he even thought about calling anyone else. If Ben could control Turk, he could control the investigation, and that would allow him to resolve it before Diplomatic Security and the legal attaché could swoop in and steal the credit.

Carole, the manager of the resort, had been nice enough to provide Ben with some fruit, coffee, and croissants. Ben didn't care for baked goods in Thailand. Not that these weren't okay—he was sure they were fine—but he was suspicious of anything with butter in the tropics. Butter wasn't natural in this kind of heat. There was probably a reason why the natives never ate it. Pasteurized? Doubtful. He was sure it would be swimming with bacteria, a fatty microbe spread.

Ben drank some coffee and ate the fruit. He was particularly fond of the mangosteen—a strange fruit that was purple on the outside but looked like a pale orange on the inside—and the rambutan, a scaly red globe covered with spiky hairs that you had to crack open to extract the translucent sweet-sour fruit. He preferred to eat fruits with skin. That was key to avoiding a parasitic infection.

Ben expected Turk to be a bedraggled, bleary-eyed scruffian with long greasy hair and a torn T-shirt, so he was not disappointed when Turk was finally ushered in to Carole's office, the faint scent of stale beer wafting in the air behind him.

The two men shook hands. Ben produced his badge and U.S. government identification. He handed Turk a business card. Turk looked at it.

"Immigration and Customs Enforcement?"

Ben nodded. "ICE has a broad mandate."

"ICE? You're an ICE agent?"

"Yes."

Turk couldn't help himself—he laughed. "You're serious?"

"I assure you, Mr. Henry, ICE is very serious."

"What about Mr. Freeze?"

Ben winced, as if he'd heard that joke a million times and didn't think it dignified a response.

"Coffee? Mr. Henry?"

Turk nodded.

"Thanks."

Ben poured him a cup and did what he'd been taught in counterterrorism classes: he observed the subject, looking for any telltale sign of duplicity, involvement, or untruthfulness.

"I need to ask you a couple of questions, just to establish a time line."

Turk nodded. This is exactly what they did when they interviewed people on those police procedural shows that were on every channel, every night. He'd seen hours of them, and somehow having this agent asking the same kinds of questions was comforting to him.

"Why weren't you with your wife?"

"*Why?*"

"She went on the excursion alone. Is that not correct?"

Turk had to think about it. "She went with a group."

"But you didn't go?"

Turk shook his head. "Riding an elephant isn't high on my to-do list."

Ben took a small notebook out of his pocket and scratched a few facts onto a page. Turk looked over and saw the word "Phuket" scrawled on the top.

"When did you hear about the ransom?"

"That night. That's how I knew she was kidnapped."

"How did the message reach you?"

"It came to the hotel. The French chick got it."

Turk watched as Ben made some more notes. It was just like on TV.

"They asked for a million dollars?"

Turk nodded. "U.S."

"That's a lot of money."

Turk shrugged; his relationship to money was not like most people's. "My banker is already sending it."

"You didn't wait to consult with your own government?"

"I'm consulting with you now."

Ben leaned forward and looked him in the eye. "Do you want my professional opinion?"

Turk nodded. "Yeah. For sure."

"Seems to me they knew that your wife was going to be taking that elephant ride. That means they have organization, on-the-ground intelligence, planning, execution. All the hall-marks of a terrorist cell."

Turk blinked. "Terrorists?"

Ben nodded. "They don't want you to know this, but southern Thailand is a hotbed of terrorist activity."

Turk thought about all the topless Europeans lying on the beach. Ben continued. "It's the proximity to Malaysia."

"So they're Malaysian?"

"We don't have confirmation on that."

"So they could be from Thailand."

"Mr. Henry. They could be from anywhere. What's to keep an Iraqi insurgent or a Moroccan terrorist from coming here and starting a sleeper cell?"

Turk shrugged. "Fuck if I know."

Ben nodded. "Exactly. We just don't know."

Turk rubbed his hands together nervously. He didn't know where this conversation was heading, but it wasn't going the way he'd thought it would. "So what happens next?"

"What do you mean?"

"What are we going to do? You know? To rescue Sheila?"

Ben sat back in his chair. "Officially our hands are tied."

"What?"

Ben looked at Turk with a slightly sad and very sincere

expression, as if he were about to deliver bad news to a small child or a retard.

"The United States government doesn't negotiate with terrorists."

Turk's jaw dropped.

"That's always been our policy."

"But how do you know they're terrorists? An hour ago they were kidnappers."

Ben leaned forward conspiratorially. "I can't reveal my sources. You understand."

Turk shook his head. "No. I don't understand. Are you saying you know where they are? Can't you do some kind of rescue? Send in commandos?"

"You'd have to take that up with the Thai authorities, but I doubt they'll be much help."

Turk slouched in his chair and stared at the floor. This was not what he had been expecting. He wished his coffee would magically turn into beer. A beer would taste really good right now.

Turk continued to stare at the floor while Ben rattled on about national security, government policy, and stuff that Turk didn't even listen to. It was all just a bunch of fucking excuses. It was annoying. Like the time he bought a new, custom-shaped electric bass that wouldn't stay in tune. No one could fix it; no one seemed to know what was wrong with it. It was beautiful, but irritating. One day he'd had enough and, without even the benefit of an audience, he'd smashed it into the floor until it was reduced to splinters and strings. Ben was starting to look a lot like that electric bass.

"Fuck it. I'll make the deal myself."

Ben, who had been watching Turk for some kind of reaction, something that he might put in his report, spoke in a firm, official voice.

"We can't allow you to do that."

"What do you mean? You already said you couldn't help. You have your reasons, fine. So stay out of it. This is none of your fucking business."

"You are a U.S. citizen, Mr. Henry. It is a violation of the Patriot Act to aid any terrorist or terror organization. If you try to pay them the ransom for your wife, I'm afraid you'll be arrested. If convicted, you could receive ten to fifteen years in prison."

"But what about Sheila? She's a citizen."

Ben put his notebook away.

"I'll level with you, Mr. Henry. We're at war. Think what those terrorists could do if they got ahold of a million dollars."

"Maybe they'd stop being terrorists and open a restaurant or something. That's what I'd do."

Ben shook his head. "They'll purchase nuclear arms. They'll make a dirty bomb and blow up Cleveland. Hundreds of thousands could die. How would that make you feel?"

Turk shook his head. "Cleveland? Why would they attack Cleveland?"

"Or St. Louis, Kansas City, Des Moines. Anywhere in the heartland is vulnerable."

Turk couldn't help himself. He laughed in Ben's face. "You're fucking joking."

"Let me assure you, there is nothing funny about a dirty bomb detonating on American soil."

As often happened when confronted with information, rules, or regulations that went counter to his desires, Turk lost his temper.

"I find it hard to believe that Malaysian terrorists want to nuke Cleveland. Besides, have you seen the Cuyahoga? It's *already* toxic."

Ben put on his most sympathetic expression. It was the same expression he'd used when he worked in customer service at the Land Rover dealership. A fake look of pained, shared exasperation at the small everyday tragedies that turn a pampered life into a living hell.

"I'm sorry. I know how you feel. But in every war there are casualties, innocent people who find themselves in harm's way. I'm sad to say that your wife is just one of them."

Turk stood up. He wasn't going to sit around and listen to any more of this bullshit.

"She's not a casualty yet."

"Sit down, Mr. Henry."

Turk did as he was told.

"I'm going to do you a favor."

"Okay."

"I'm going to look into this, personally. But you have to promise me something."

Turk nodded.

"You have to promise me that you won't tell anyone about this. Just sit tight and let me handle the terrorists."

Turk was thinking about it when the door opened and a uniformed Thai policeman interrupted them.

"Agent Harding? Could we have a word?"

Ben turned to Turk.

"I'll be right back."

...

Captain Somporn had given it some thought and come to the conclusion that making multiple exchanges with the hostages exposed him and his men to arrest, imprisonment, and the inevitable execution that comes with abducting foreigners and jeopardizing the lucrative Thai tourist trade. It would be better, he realized, to do one extremely lucrative exchange and walk away from the kidnapping business forever. It was only sensible. Somporn relayed this plan to his men, who quickly agreed. Holding hostages was boring work, like being a waiter in a restaurant filled with pissed-off diners. They were tired of bringing them food, cleaning up the shit. Although several of the men, notably Kittisak, wanted to murder the remaining hostages and dump their bodies in the sea, Somporn talked him out of it. It was, he said, more trouble than it was worth.

He had his men serve the hostages breakfast, a nice hot bowl of rice porridge with dried shrimp and some wild spinach. They'd be angry, outraged, when they got back to their hotels. So he thought he ought to feed them, make them happy, and show them a little kindness before he kicked them loose. It would take the edge off their outrage, stifle their screams for justice, complicate and conflict their emotions.

...

Sheila sat on the ground eating her porridge. She was surprised how good it tasted; perhaps it helped to be really hungry. She found a spot where the sun filtered through the trees and allowed herself to be warmed by it. She looked over when she heard Captain Somporn shouting to one of his men. The man jumped up—Sheila noticed that he was wearing her Chanel sunglasses—and hurried over to her with a paper umbrella. He drove the sharp end of the pole into the ground, angling it so that it shaded her.

Sheila looked at Somporn.

"I like the sun."

Somporn wagged a finger at her.

"Your skin is too dark. I am saving you from skin cancer."

Sheila heard Mrs. Double-Glazing make a tut-tutting sound. As if this were proof of something.

They watched as the woman from Seattle was carried out of the hut by a couple of Somporn's men. They carried her toward the beach, dragging her shit-smeared ass across the sand and into the water. Sheila could tell that the men weren't happy to be dealing with her. While one held her head and shoulders above water, the other one carefully stripped off her clothes.

They kind of swished her around in the water—moving her body back and forth—then dragged her back and dumped her on the beach. She lay naked on the sand, her heavy white skin exposed to the sun, her breasts hanging low and heaving as she took in deep, terrified breaths. Undressed and rinsed off as she was, the festering insect bites were now clearly visible on her body, making it look like she'd slept on a bed of hot nails. The salt water stung her wounds, and she writhed around, trying to focus, struggling to figure out where she was. Occasionally she let out a groan.

Somporn looked at Sheila and pointed to the woman's naked body.

"Better without a tan."

...

Turk sat in the back of the police car. The ICE agent sat in front with the Thai police officer. Turk didn't know where they were going, but it had something to do with one of the people who had been abducted with Sheila. They were hoping Turk might be able to identify someone. Turk didn't want to go. But they'd insisted, making him feel like he was under arrest.

They pulled into the parking lot of some kind of big department store. It was all concrete, modern, with brightly colored flags flying from poles. Looking like it'd been dropped out of the sky from the New Jersey suburbs, it could've been a Wal-Mart or a Target. A large orange sign said something in the indecipherable curlicues of the Thai alphabet. Maybe it said "Wal-Mart" in Thai. When had Turk ever been in one of those? He wouldn't know a Wal-Mart if it landed on him.

The car pulled up next to an ambulance and another police car. A small crowd of curious Thais stood around looking at a dead body on the ground. Turk was shocked.

"Shouldn't they put a sheet over him or something?"

The Thai officer shrugged.

"Then there's nothing to see."

They got out of the car. Turk hesitated. He didn't want to get any closer. He looked at the man—the poor guy looked like he'd been worked over with a baseball bat—and then quickly turned away and tried to climb back into the car.

"Nope. Never seen him before."

Ben grabbed his arm.

"I know it's not pleasant. But it's important."

He dragged Turk within a couple of feet of the body.

"Take a good look."

Turk looked. He didn't know it, but it was the dead cheapskate from Seattle, his head bashed in, his skull deformed, blood caked across his face, the ever-present flies still swarming the wounds.

The first thing Turk thought was that it was a fake. It wasn't a dead guy. It was some kind of prop, a special effect concocted to freak him out. He looked around; there had to be a hidden camera somewhere. But Turk's state of denial didn't last long. One whiff of rotting carcass and he knew it wasn't anything you could fake. His stomach turned. He didn't barf or gag, but somewhere deep inside his guts queased up on him.

"Let's go."

Ben pulled out his notepad.

"Do you recognize him now?"

Turk nodded.

"Looks like Freddy Krueger."

Ben wrote that in his notebook.

"Where do you know Mr. Krueger from?"

Turk looked at Ben and shook his head. He didn't want to be an asshole, so he walked back to the car.

On the drive back to the hotel, Ben tried to impress upon Turk the importance of the U.S.'s adopting a no-nonsense policy in dealing with terrorists.

"Now you see what they're capable of."

Turk lifted his sunglasses and fixed Ben with his petulant —fuck-off—rock star glare.

"And that's supposed to make me what? Not want to get my wife back?"

Ben tried to be reasonable.

"You have to understand. We don't make deals with terrorists. It only encourages them."

"So how is getting Sheila back encouraging them? They're already totally encouraged; you said it yourself. Are there different levels of encouragement? Like are we on an orange encouragement alert? Or is it a red one?"

Ben could see that Turk was angry, but he didn't know what else to say.

"It's possible that when they realize we won't be paying them, they'll release her."

Turk glared at him.

"How is that possible?"

"It could happen."

"Has that ever, in the history of hostages, happened before?"

Ben nodded. Turk knew a line of bullshit when he heard it, and grew increasingly irate.

"If they are terrorists like you suggest, then it's also possible they'll chop her fucking head off and show it on TV. Isn't that a possibility?"

"I can't make any guarantees."

"Seems to me that paying a million bucks to keep my wife from getting her head chopped off is a bargain."

Ben could see that Turk just wasn't going to be reasonable about this, so he decided to take a hard line, an approach he hoped his supervisor might later commend him for.

"I'm sorry. But if you try to contact them or give them money in any way, you'll be arrested and prosecuted under provisions of the Patriot Act."

"You've got to be kidding."

"Like it or not, Mr. Henry, the United States is at war. We take the war against terrorism very, very seriously."

Turk looked at Ben for a long beat, and then used an extended middle finger to push his sunglasses back up his nose so they covered his eyes.

...

When they got back to the hotel Turk stormed off to his room without saying a word to the ICE asshole, the Thai policeman, or the hotel manager. As far as he was concerned they could all go fuck themselves, or each other, or their mothers. He didn't care.

Turk entered his cabin and went right to the minibar. He cracked open a Singha and took a nice long drink. The cold beer burbled down his throat like the clear mountain brook they always showed in those stupid ads. Sure, it was refreshing, clear, and cooling, but those ads annoyed Turk. You couldn't drink water from some mountain stream. It'd have raccoon shit in it, or acid rain, or toxic runoff. Mountain streams were teeming with parasites, mercury, DDT, all kinds of stuff that would kill you. But beer refreshed and relaxed. Beer was better than stream water any day. Turk burped. Then he picked up the phone and called his manager.

Heidegger's assistant, Marybeth, picked up the phone and immediately bombarded Turk with questions. Was he okay? How was he doing? Did he think Sheila would be all right? Was there anything she could do for him? Anything? Her voice was warm and honey-coated, filled with empathy and concern. Turk tried to remember if he'd ever fucked her. It seemed to him he had. He must've. Right?

But he didn't have time to chat, and told her to connect him to Jon right away. Turk heard a beep, a blast of new wave rock, and then Heidegger's voice came on the line.

"How's it going? Did you talk to the authorities?"

"They're fucking useless."

"What do you mean?"

"Some asshole from the government told me they'd arrest me if I tried to pay."

"What?"

"He said she's been abducted by terrorists. It's against the law to pay ransoms to terrorists."

"Terrorists?"

"That's what he said."

"That's unbelievable. Can they really do that?"

"What the fuck do I know about it? He seemed to think they could. But then he told me to sit tight and he'd try and deal with it on the QT."

The line was silent for a moment. Finally Heidegger spoke.

"What does that mean?"

"I don't know."

"Listen, Turk. I don't like this. You tell that government anus that if they arrest you for trying to save your beloved wife they'll have every media outlet in the known fucking universe doing a story on how they're a bunch of soulless bureaucrat cocksuckers. Keeping things on the QT is the last fucking thing we're gonna do. You get your money and save your wife. The embassy twat can go fuck himself."

Turk loved when his manager got angry. That was the great thing about having "people" and "handlers." It was Heidegger's job to be a raging asshole, whiny baby, righteous advocate, avenging angel, and whatever else his clients needed him to be. He could say the things Turk wanted to say without actually having to say them and come off sounding like a big fat jerk.

"Did you get the money?"

"Yeah. Everything's cool. Let me give you the address so you can pick it up."

Turk looked around the cabin.

"Wait. I need a pen."

"No you don't. It's the Bank of Phuket on Phuket Road in Phuket Town. Just keep sayin' Phuket and you'll find it."

"Thanks, Jon."

"After you get her back we need to talk. I think I got you a record deal."

Turk brightened.

"Really?"

"Save the day. Then we'll talk."

"Okay. I'll call you later."

"Oh, and Turk. Listen. Take a big suitcase. It's a lotta fuckin' money."

...

The transcript of Turk's conversation with Jon Heidegger appeared as an e-mail on Ben's Blackberry. He'd had the foresight to request that the intelligence station back in

Bangkok tap Turk's hotel room phone line. Any calls the rock star made would be recorded and sent to him. Ben had to squint a little to read it, the type being so small, but he got the gist of it. Turk Henry was going to be a problem.

Twelve

heila slipped out of her clothes, carefully folding them and putting them on the floor, and walked over to the makeshift shower. Captain Somporn had provided her with a new loofah, some expensive moisturizing soap, and a jar of all-natural coconut oil. It was like he'd turned this little corner of his hut into some kind of spa.

"Is there anything else you need?"

Sheila turned to look at him. He was sitting on the floor, his legs crossed in front of him, a cold bottle of beer in one hand, a smoldering cigarette in the other, watching her, like a patron in a cabaret waiting for the show to begin.

"No. This is fine."

"The coconut oil is for your skin. It's very good. Very healthy."

Sheila smiled and then stood under the hose and unhooked the clamp. Warmish water trickled out, and she began to soap her body, building up a thick, rich lather.

The Captain's attentions reminded her of the ad campaign she'd done for a French soap company. They had wanted her skin to be glowing, healthy, and blemish-free and had sent her to a series of experts who prescribed exotic scrubs, herbal wraps, mud baths, and moisturizing sessions. They'd even hired a nutritionist to prepare her meals and make sure she drank four liters of water every day. For two months all Sheila did was get treated like a prize pig before the state fair.

The French soap company had spared no expense; it had hired a famous Dutch photographer, and the best, most creative makeup artist, a tomboyish British woman with a yogarific aura, had been employed to dust her skin with subtle orange-gold hues. They'd gone so far as to bring in Carlos Lemoyne, the world-famous eyelash specialist. He'd arrived with a whole team, shoved the makeup artist and photographer aside, and got to work. He spent three hours hand-painting each of her eyelashes so they became miniature works of art. Sheila loved them, because they made her green eyes pop out of the photo. Even though her breasts were fully exposed, people noticed her eyes; they couldn't help it, they looked that good.

That campaign should've made her an icon, the rare supermodel who's forever attached to a hugely successful product, like Cheryl Tiegs and Olympus cameras or Tyra Banks and Victoria's Secret. Sheila would've been set for life, but her daily habit of hoovering several grams of Peruvian marching powder had finally caught up with her. Her left nostril had sprung a leak, bright red blood gushing from it like a broken water main.

It had taken about an hour, but she'd finally got it to slow to a trickle. The photographer and makeup artist had worked valiantly to control and conceal the constant ooze but they only got off a handful of shots before it became impossible to continue. As the makeup artist ran off to get more cotton gauze, and the photographer stomped off in a hail of unintelligible curses to smoke a joint, Sheila calmly chopped herself a couple of lines of blow and snorted them up her good nostril. What with all the drama going on, she needed a bump.

When Carlos saw that, he had become so enraged that he physically attacked her, knocking her to the studio floor and attempting to remove her eyelashes with a sharp pair of tweezers.

Sheila had been left with a deviated septum and a destroyed reputation.

Still, the photographs were strikingly beautiful. They became the central image of the ad campaign. Sheila's face and body were plastered on billboards, in magazines, and on the products themselves.

No one had paid that much attention to her body since then, not even her husband, and although she was a little confused and frightened by Captain Somporn, there was no mistaking the intensity of his gaze.

Sheila poured some shampoo into the palm of her hand and began to wash her hair. She turned her back to the shower, letting the water rinse the soap out of her hair, giving the Captain a full frontal view of her body.

She looked over at him, hoping to see a sign, some clue of what he was thinking. A lick of the lips, a twitch of the eye, a boner maybe. But the Captain was stoic, unreadable. He would calmly take a drag on his cigarette and watch.

When she was finished washing and drying herself off, he asked a question.

"What do they eat in Sweden?"

Sheila had never been to Sweden but she had been to IKEA, the Swedish furniture megastore.

"Meatballs, mostly. Salmon. And lingonberries."

Somporn finished his beer and reached for another one in the cooler near the wall.

"Lingonberries?"

"They love 'em in Sweden."

Somporn opened a Singha for her and held it up. Sheila didn't bother to cover her breasts with the towel as she bent over and gratefully took the beer. She noticed that Somporn inhaled sharply as her breasts dangled close to his face, but he made no move to touch them.

"What do they look like?"

"Lingonberries?"

Somporn nodded. Sheila tried to remember the lumpy red smear of sauce that came with the meatballs in the IKEA cafeteria.

"Little. Round. Red. They make a sauce with them."

Sheila sat down on the edge of Somporn's small bed. She let the towel drop and picked up the jar of coconut oil. She slowly began to cover her body with the sweet-smelling emollient.

"Have you tasted them?"

Sheila nodded.

"They're sweet and sour. Kind of like the fruit here."

"Like a mangosteen?"

Sheila didn't respond; she was watching as her body began to glisten from the oil. It felt good on her skin. Better than any mud bath or herbal wrap she'd ever experienced.

It suddenly occurred to her that she and Somporn were lounging around like lovers, relaxed and warm in the afterglow of sex. This was normally the time Sheila enjoyed the most, the sex being either fun or not so fun; it was during the aftermath that she actually felt close to someone.

Somporn lit another cigarette.

"Those things aren't good for you."

The Captain nodded and waved his hand in agreement.

"The smoke keeps the mosquitoes away. I would hate for them to bite you and ruin your beautiful skin."

Sheila calmly rubbed the coconut oil onto her breasts, neck, and shoulders. Then she looked at Somporn, their eyes meeting.

"Would you do my back?"

He nodded and took the jar. Sheila turned around and waited. Captain Somporn sat on the cot and began, very slowly and gently—she could feel his hands trembling—to rub the coconut oil into her skin. She tried to relax but, alarmingly, she found herself getting aroused.

With her back to him, facing a dark corner of the hut, she couldn't see anything, just their shadows projected on the wall by the lantern, like a Balinese puppet show. But Sheila felt the touch of Somporn's hand, the sweet oil nourishing her skin; smelled the earthy odor of the tobacco mixing with the strong scent of coconut and the malty tang of beer; heard the hiss of the lantern, and the wet sounds of the oil he was lathering onto her body.

Sheila realized, with diamondlike clarity, that this was what it felt like to be intimate with someone. It had nothing to do with sex.

· · ·

Uncharacteristically, Turk had asked the front desk for a wake-up call. Under normal circumstances he let his circadian rhythms wake him up when his body was rested and his dreams were done, but today he wanted to get up bright and early. He wanted to be at the bank when the doors opened.

The phone rang in his room. Loud and jangly and annoying as hell. Wake-up calls, Turk realized, totally suck.

He climbed out of bed and rumbled into the bathroom. He figured he'd better shave, clean up, and look presentable. No one was going to give a million dollars in cash to a guy looking like a bum.

Dressed in a clean white shirt and tight black jeans—his gut extending out over his belt like some kind of rogue ocean wave, a spare tire, a flab tsunami—Turk emptied his suitcase, dumping all his clothes on the sofa, and headed out the door.

Several bellmen offered to carry the suitcase but Turk shook his head; it was light and he was in a hurry.

There were no taxis at the hotel entrance, and a thoughtful doorman offered to telephone for one. Turk noticed a dirty *tuk tuk* parked in the drive and asked about that. The doorman tried to convince him to wait for a cab, the *tuk tuk* being loud and smelly, but Turk didn't care. He was a man on a mission.

Turk climbed into the backseat of the *tuk tuk* and told the driver to take him to the Bank of Phuket on Phuket Road in Phuket Town. The driver flipped a switch and the *tuk tuk* gave a violent shudder, backfired loudly, and roared to life in a cloud of noxious fumes. As the three-wheeled transport lurched into gear and sped out of the hotel's driveway, Turk got the distinct feeling that he was using a broken lawn mower as a getaway car.

The driver smiled at Turk as he performed a blind merge onto the main road. A tour bus honked and then blasted past. Turk couldn't help himself.

"Holy shit! What the fuck're you doin', man?"

The driver nodded his head and smiled.

"Bus. Big bus."

Turk had to agree.

"Yeah. Big bus. Dead bass player."

Turk noticed that the *tuk tuk* had been custom-painted. The seats were upholstered in bright fabric with geometric designs and a little crescent moon dangled from the rearview mirror. Arabic writing covered the inside of the roof and above the windshield someone had written in English: *All Praise Allah! The Highest Honor Is Death in His Service!*

Turk clung to the frame of the *tuk tuk* as it went screaming down a long hill, the engine revving faster than it had been designed to do, the suspension—if there was one—shaking and rattling like a Japanese Zero on a kamikaze mission.

Turk realized he was scared. What if the ICE agent was right? What if this part of Thailand really was crawling with terrorists?

The highest honor is death in his service. What the fuck?

Turk held on to the side of the *tuk tuk* with all his strength.

As they got into town, Turk felt a little better. The traffic served to naturally slow down the *tuk tuk* as it careened along the roads, dodging the squat metal trash cans—at least Turk thought they were trash cans—set in front of houses, and jockeying with motorcycles, scooters, cars, and other three-wheel jalopies for some invisible advantage in a phantom race.

When the driver finally skidded to a stop in front of the Bank of Phuket, Turk felt a sense of relief. He shakily climbed out and paid the driver, giving him a ridiculously inflated tip—as if in gratitude for not getting him killed—and carried his suitcase toward the bank.

He was pleased to see that it actually looked like a modern bank. Like one you'd find in your neighborhood in Wichita or Albany.

Turk walked through the door and stopped. The air-conditioning was on and the cold, clean air felt so good he just stood there, taking a moment to feel the sweat evaporate from his skin. There was definitely something to be said for air-conditioning.

The bank manager, a guy with a name overstuffed with vowels and so long that Turk couldn't remember or repeat it even though it was written down on a business card in his hand, jumped up to meet him. He enthusiastically *waied* several times —bowed quickly with his hands clasped in front of him—then shook Turk's hand "Western style," with a grip so hard that it actually caused Turk's knuckles to pop and crackle.

After offering him a cup of tea—Turk declined—the manager checked his passport, had him sign a couple of documents, and then led him past several guards with submachine guns slung over their shoulders into the vault.

Turk watched as the manager fussed with a set of keys, opening a door about the size of a bathroom cabinet, pulling out a big metal drawer on wheels, flipping the lid open, and then unlocking a second box. It was like one of those Russian dolls: a locked metal box within a locked metal box within a locked metal locker within a locked metal vault within a locked concrete bank.

All the security made Turk feel a little weird about dragging the money out of the bank in an unlocked suitcase. It wasn't even leather.

The manager, Mr. Incredibly Long Name, took Turk's suitcase and placed it on a table. Then he began handing bundles of U.S. currency to Turk.

"Mr. Henry. You count, please."

Turk held a couple of the bound bricks of greenbacks in his hand and looked at the manager.

"I trust you."

The manager shook a finger at Turk.

"No. No. Please assure yourself that everything is in order."

Turk realized that he'd never counted to a million before. He wasn't even sure what a million was. A hundred hundred thousands? A thousand ten thousands? When was the last time Turk had been confronted with a math problem? He didn't even remember taking math in high school, and he hadn't bothered to go to college. The last math problem he ever solved had involved trying to figure out how many joints he could roll from a dime bag of weed he got off Zoë Levine's little brother at the video arcade. Turk tried to think of mathematic facts. A kilometer is 1.6 of a mile. Is that right? Or is a mile 2.2 kilometers? Or is a kilogram 2.2 pounds? A liter of soda is bigger than a normal bottle. The big plastic ones at the store were all liters. Weren't they?

Turk stood there, trying to make sense of it all as the manager kept handing him money. When he realized that his arms were full, he dumped the load into the suitcase, working quickly to stack them tightly into some kind of order. As he did this he pretended to count.

It took about fifteen minutes. When the suitcase was full, Turk turned to the manager.

"That looks good."

The manager smiled at Turk.

"Very funny, Mr. Henry."

Turk laughed. He didn't know why.

"Twenty-five thousand more."

Turk shrugged, embarrassed.

"You got me."

Turk unzipped some of the side pockets on the suitcase and stuffed the cash in. The manager handed him a form and indicated where Turk should sign.

"This money is your responsibility now."

Turk nodded.

"Thank you, Mr . . . um, sir."

The manager bent in another deep *wai.* Turk attempted to return the gesture, bowing forward from his hips and almost pulling a hamstring. He stood and opted to shake hands vigorously with the bank manager. Turk zipped the suitcase closed and hoisted it off the table. He let out a surprised grunt: a million bucks in cash was heavy lifting. He plopped the suitcase down on the floor, pulled out the telescoping handle, and wheeled it out of the bank.

. . .

Turk popped his sunglasses on as he walked out of the bank. Several *tuk tuk* drivers waved to him, offering their services. Turk shook his head—this time he was taking a taxi. He wheeled his suitcase—it followed him like a dog on a leash— to the corner and scanned the road for a cab. He realized he should've had the bank manager call him one, but he hadn't thought of it and now that he was outside, he didn't want to go back in. Turk saw something called a "Resortel" a couple of blocks down the street and figured he could find a taxi there. He'd started to walk down the road when a familiar voice came up behind him.

"Need a lift?"

Turk turned and saw Ben Harding, the man from ICE, standing there.

"I'm fine, thanks."

Turk tried to continue on, but felt the suitcase suddenly stop rolling.

"I can't let you do it."

Ben had grabbed the end of the suitcase. Turk played innocent. It had sometimes worked with police officers; he'd avoided arrest for possession of marijuana several times in his career.

"I'm sorry?"

Ben heaved a sigh. He took off his sunglasses and gave Turk his serious, protect-and-serve stare.

"Remember nine-eleven? The attack on the World Trade Center?"

How could Turk forget? Metal Assassin's entire North American tour had been canceled.

"Of course."

"How do you think that happened?"

"Some pissed-off guys flew planes into buildings."

Ben nodded. "Guys who went to flight school."

Turk squinted his eyes, trying to see what Ben was talking about. "Can't say they graduated."

"What did you say?"

"Can't say they graduated. You know, from flight school."

Turk could see that Ben was getting angry, and he tried to explain. "Because they crashed. Which is, in my opinion, what flight school should teach you how *not* to do."

Ben shook his head, slowly, conveying his disappointment. "You're making a joke."

"No. I'm just saying—"

"You're mocking America."

"I'm not."

"Sounds to me like you are."

Turk looked at Ben. It was ridiculous, two grown men in a playground argument.

"What's your point? *You* brought up nine-eleven."

Ben pointed to the suitcase. "Somebody gave money to those terrorists."

"It wasn't me."

"Not that time. But I know what you're up to, and I'll give you a chance to do the right thing. Why don't you turn around, take that suitcase back into the bank, and go home."

Turk felt a surge of anger rise in his throat. Who the fuck was this guy to tell him what to do? Turk wanted to punch Ben in the face, maybe a couple of times, hit him hard, bust his lip, break his nose, knock him down. And then kick him in the ribs while he lay there. Maybe stomp on his face, too. And piss on him. *Yeah. Motherfucker.*

Turk composed himself; he wasn't going to get in a fight now.

"I'm not going home until I get Sheila back."

With that, Turk jerked the suitcase out of Ben's hands and turned to walk away.

"Turk Henry. You're under arrest for violating the Patriot Act."

Turk turned to face him. "All I've done is withdraw some money from the bank."

"With the intent of giving aid and financial support to terrorists. That's conspiracy."

"You can't prove that. Maybe I'm just going down the road to a whorehouse."

Several locals stopped to watch the two *farangs*. A young woman with a cartful of fresh fruit offered them some.

"Don't make me do anything you'll regret. I'm well trained in the martial arts."

Turk couldn't believe his ears. First Sheila is kidnapped, and now a man from ICE is threatening to kung fu him. Turk said the first thing that popped into his head.

"Do you know who I am?"

Ben nodded. "Of course."

"Then you know beating up a celebrity is not something you want to do."

"You're not above the law."

"I'm not breaking any law. It's my money, and if I want to take it out of the bank and buy enough beer to fill the Andaman Sea, I can."

Ben narrowed his eyes. "You have a history of drug problems."

Turk looked at Ben with disgust. "You can't be serious."

Ben adjusted his stance, standing in a way that said he'd seen a few Bruce Lee movies.

"Listen, Mr. Henry, and listen good. I could arrest you right now and ship you off to a secret detention center in Romania. You wouldn't have the right to an attorney; you wouldn't get to make a phone call. You'd be thrown into a dank fucking pit and visited by nongovernmental contractors who could do whatever they wanted to you. No one would know where you were or what happened to you."

Turk swallowed. He remembered something his shrink had told him. A technique he'd used when Steve had started ranting and screaming.

"I hear what you're saying."

"Good. Now get your ass in the car."

...

Turk didn't say anything in the car; with the threat of extraordinary rendition hanging over him, he wasn't sure if he should. It was probably better to just keep quiet until he was out of this asshole's sight.

As they pulled into the long circular drive leading to the front door of the resort, Ben finally spoke.

"I told you I would look into this. All you had to do was lay low."

Turk pouted.

"Sorry."

"Consider yourself under house arrest. You can't leave the resort without my permission."

"How long's that going to be?"

"I have to talk to my station chief."

Ben pulled up in front of the hotel, got out, then helped Turk from the car.

"What about my suitcase?"

"Consider it impounded until I consult with Washington."

With that, Ben climbed back in the car and slammed the door shut.

"Can I get a fucking receipt for that?"

But Ben didn't hear him. He was already driving away.

...

Somporn stood over the American woman's corpse and shook his head. It hadn't gone exactly as he'd planned. She wasn't supposed to die on him. But that's what happened. Sometime during the night, she'd succumbed to her fever. Somporn realized that he should've paid a little more attention to her; she had looked pretty sick. But then, Americans were notorious whiners, complainers, big overfed babies always demanding special treatment, so he'd ignored her condition. Besides, he'd been busy with Sheila.

Somporn didn't want his men to think he'd gotten sloppy, carelessly letting one of the hostages die, but he had to admit that his attention had been elsewhere, his mind not as on the ball as usual. But no matter how hard he tried to act the part of ferocious pirate captain, he couldn't help himself. Watching Sheila shower had become a compulsion. It was all he thought about.

Not that he was doing anything to her. He was just looking at her, marveling at her incredible white skin. She'd let him touch her last night, smoothing coconut oil on her back. Somporn felt a shiver of delight zip up his spine as he remembered how soft and clean she was. He couldn't explain why he was so attracted to her milky skin; he just was. It touched something deep in him, her beauty almost moving him to tears. Not that he thought the dark brown skin of his fellow Thais wasn't beautiful; it was, but it didn't move some powerful and mysterious thing in him. Who knew why anyone preferred one thing over another? Some people loved chocolate. Somporn preferred the sharp-sour flavor of ripe mangoes. The Buddha would say that he was predisposed to alabaster white skin because of something that had happened in a past life. The attraction was imprinted on his mind stream; it was part of his karma that would follow him from life to life to life until he finally broke the cycle of suffering and rebirth and attained nirvana.

There were, Somporn realized, worse fetishes to have. There were people who liked to be wrapped up like mummies, women who liked to wear dog collars and eat out of bowls on the floor, men who enjoyed being hog-tied and pissed on by beautiful librarians. He had once met a man who was turned on by watching Japanese women pick their noses. The man had collected hundreds of videos and DVDs of schoolgirls in *Sailor Moon* outfits, businesswomen, even geishas, all stuffing fingers up their nostrils and pulling out a variety of boogers and stringy mucus.

The dead woman from Seattle was not a pretty sight. Her body had become a festering bug buffet. Somporn's first instinct was to take her out past the reef and drop her body into the ocean. The tides, sharks, sea turtles, and gulls would take care of the rest. But that wasn't the best strategic move. Better would be to make an example out of her, get the rock star really freaked out, maybe up the ransom to two million.

Somporn decided on a two-pronged approach. He'd release the British couple in town and dump the body in a bay near one of the fancy resorts. It would be a message to the American rock star: There was only one hostage left, and he should expect to pay top dollar for her safe return. Captain Somporn wanted Turk to know he was serious.

...

Turk walked through the hotel lobby in a daze. Something was wrong. He could feel it. How did the ICE agent asshole know he was picking up the money? Was his room bugged? His phone tapped? Did someone rat him out?

Turk went to the hotel bar and plopped into a cushy chair. A waitress scurried over to take his order.

"Gimme a beer. Please."

"Thai beer?"

Turk nodded and she went off to get his drink. He stared off, out the giant open doorway, at the ocean. Turk realized that he was in over his head. He needed some advice, a reality check. Turk normally trusted his instincts, his intuition, and right now his instincts told him that the agent was full of shit. Terrorists don't kidnap tourists on an elephant ride. There's nothing terrorizing about that. Terrorists blew up trains in Madrid or buildings in Nairobi. They got their money from exporting Afghan opium and Kashmiri hash. Sheila's kidnapping seemed like your typical criminal enterprise. Snatch a rich guy's wife and make him fork over some dough. It's a crime, pure and simple, not the clash of civilizations.

Turk didn't think they'd send him to a secret prison somewhere. He was a rock star. But he wasn't sure he wanted to press his luck either. Who knew what these bureaucratic zealots were thinking?

Turk needed to talk to Heidegger. He needed advice, pronto. But it was a risk. If he met Heidegger in the resort, the ICE agent would overhear everything. Turk needed neutral ground. He needed to get out of the resort. Turk didn't want to violate the Patriot Act, but it wasn't like he had a choice. Sheila was out there.

He thought about what his mom used to say: "You want scrambled eggs, you gotta break 'em first."

The waitress came back with the beer. Turk thanked her, picked up the Singha, and headed toward the manager's office.

Turk entered without knocking. The Frenchwoman looked up at him and offered a sympathetic, concerned smile.

"Ah! Mr. Henry. How are you?"

"I need to use your phone. And I want to be moved to another room."

The manager nodded. "Of course." She stood up and offered her desk to Turk.

"Thanks."

Turk sat down and dialed. The manger gave Turk an apologetic look as she knotted her long brown hair into a ponytail.

"Do you require privacy?"

"What's the best hotel in Bangkok?"

The manager thought about it for a second.

"I would stay at the Oriental."

Turk waited until he heard Heidegger answer on the other end, then spoke into the phone.

"Bangkok. Oriental. Tomorrow night."

Turk hung up the phone and looked at Carole.

"You didn't hear that."

"Of course."

There was an awkward pause.

"Will you be leaving us?"

Turk shook his head.

"I'm keeping a room here until I get my wife back."

...

Jon Heidegger looked at his cell phone like he'd just gotten a transmission from Mars. What the fuck was that about? It was obviously Turk's voice, but why the code, the cloak and dagger? *Bangkok*. All right. That was the city in Thailand. *Oriental*. Yeah. It was in the Orient. So? But *tomorrow night?* Was he nuts? Heidegger couldn't just drop everything and go see what Turk wanted halfway around the world. He'd sent him the money. What was the problem?

Even though it was ten o'clock at night, Heidegger decided he needed to do a little research. He called Karl at home and learned that the money had been sent and that Turk had received it and signed for it earlier that day. Then he got out his laptop and Googled the words "Bangkok" and "Oriental." The Bangkok Oriental hotel popped up as the first answer.

It occurred to him that perhaps Turk wasn't very good at the cloak-and-dagger stuff. He wouldn't be able to get to Bangkok tomorrow; that was for sure, not with the launch of Rocketside's new CD. But that didn't mean he wouldn't be represented. Jon Heidegger prided himself on being a good manager, the kind who takes care of his clients even if they've gone crazy and talked in spy code. He flipped open his cell phone and dialed Marybeth.

...

Ben should have taken the money back to the bank and had it secured in the vault. That would have been the official protocol. But he was tired and didn't feel like going to the bank. Besides, he was curious.

He dragged Turk's suitcase into his hotel room. He bolted the door behind him, plopped the suitcase on his bed, and unzipped it. He gasped when he saw the money; his legs got wobbly and he had to sit down. There was so much of it. A pile of greenbacks; a huge block of Benjamins. Ben had never seen anything like it. As he gawked at the cash, his awe and amazement only served to harden his resentment of Turk.

That fucking rock star. How did he get to be so rich? What had he done to earn it? He played electric bass—only four strings—and wore tight pants. He pranced around a stage waving his long hair. He married a model. It was a useless life, and for it he was rewarded with riches beyond imagine. Where was the justice in that? What kind of world were we living in where bass players became millionaires? It was wrong. Just plain wrong.

Ben Harding had paid his dues. Hadn't he? Wasn't he the guy who busted his ass keeping helicopters in the air in Afghanistan and Iraq? Wasn't he the guy who joined Immigration and Customs Enforcement to protect freedom and spread democracy? Wasn't he on the front lines in the war on terror? He was a red-blooded, freedom-lovin' American man, a first responder. At the last election, he'd voted for the candidate who promised to bring America back to greatness. He did everything the way it was supposed to be done and he paid his taxes on time. So how come some pudgy middle-aged rock star got to be a millionaire while Ben scraped by on his meager paycheck? It just wasn't fair. It wasn't just. Ben got paid about the same as your average elementary school principal in Asslick, Kansas. Better than the teachers, sure, but not really what a man who's protecting freedom deserves.

It irritated him even more to think that this wasn't even all of Turk's money. It was like pocket change. The rock star had millions more. He could just phone his banker and have another million sent over by tomorrow afternoon.

Ben stood up and zipped the suitcase shut. He didn't want to look at it. He squirted some sanitizing hand gel on his palm and rubbed his hands together. He grabbed a bottle of cold water from the minibar—some French brand, not the local stuff—and drank it as he paced back and forth. He didn't want to think about the money, but he couldn't think about anything else, so he forced himself to not think about anything even as he thought about everything.

Eventually he lay down on the bed next to the suitcase and stared at the ceiling. He couldn't believe it. A million bucks lying on the bed right next to him. One million dollars. A one followed by six zeros. Seven figures. He could buy a house in the mountains. Live in the woods away from all the people and pollution, the germs and the noise. He wouldn't have to work again. Not unless he wanted to. With a million dollars he could live in Hawaii. He could play golf every day.

As Ben daydreamed about all the things he could do with a million dollars—maybe he should've been a rock star—his hand reached out to the suitcase next to him and gently caressed it. It was a well-made piece of luggage. Manufactured with some kind of high-tech ballistic nylon, it was lightweight yet durable, practical yet fashionable. The kind he'd buy if he had a million dollars.

Ben considered the traveling he might do with that kind of money. Maybe he'd go to Alaska. He'd heard it was clean up there. Fresh air, pure water. For sure he wouldn't go anywhere in Southeast Asia. The hot and humid viral breeding grounds of Thailand, Vietnam, and Malaysia were too much for him. Way too many people; way too much weird stuff. Where else in the world could SARS, the avian flu, and God knows what next come from? With a million dollars Ben could avoid all that. He could get the hell out of Thailand and its festering melting pot of virulent disease. A million dollars could save his life.

Ben lay next to the suitcase. The money had an almost irresistible pull, like a beautiful woman wasted on tequila; it set his pulse racing, it turned his palms clammy and his mouth dry.

It was wrong, he knew that, but the tension was more than he could bear; he had to reach out and touch it. He couldn't help himself. Like a teenage lover he fumbled with the zipper of the suitcase, his hands trembling, eager to get in and yet scared of what he'd find. He slowly tugged the zipper down until he could just slip his hand in. His fingers were damp and unsteady as he reached in and stroked the cool soft bricks of paper. They were so smooth; his fingertips could just make out the ink raised on the face of the bills, the firm band holding them together.

It wasn't premeditated. He hadn't planned on it, not at all. It just kind of happened. Ben realized that he would never have this opportunity again. He would never have a million dollars to call his own, ever. His life just wasn't going that way. And yet sometimes, when you least expect it, something enters your world and your life takes a turn. Everything changes. Like falling in love.

Ben decided to keep the money.

. . .

At first Sheila was confused. Why was she sitting on the floor? Why were the handcuffs so tight? Where had the Captain gone? As she thought about this change of circumstance, this twist in the story, she slowly began to feel a strange and alarming sensation. It was the sting of rejection.

Had she been dumped?

She had been the pet pupil, the star hostage. Now she was back where she started, sitting on her ass with her hands and feet bound, sweating like a pig. It was as if all those peep show performances she gave the Captain had been for nothing. Her face flushed crimson; she was suddenly embarrassed that she'd exposed herself. What if Turk found out? What if the other hostages were recounting her escapades to the authorities right now? It was horrible, humiliating. She cursed herself under her breath as she squirmed to get comfortable on the bamboo floor.

It wasn't that the ropes around her ankles chafed or that the handcuffs were too tight. The Captain had locked her up personally—and not without a touch of tenderness—and told her he was taking the British couple into town and releasing them. It was being locked up in the first place. Sheila had assumed that they were past that. Weren't relationships supposed to be based on trust? She was sure she'd read something like that in one of those best-selling marriage books her sister had given her before she married Turk.

Sheila didn't know that the woman from Seattle—the shit-smeared cheapskate—had died; all she knew was that someone had paid the British couple's ransom and they were being delivered back to their hotel. So what was wrong with her husband? He had plenty of money—she had signed a pre-nup limiting the amount she could claim in the event of a divorce—and should've paid her ransom immediately. Even if it had been five million dollars, ten million. He had the cash. So what was the holdup?

It occurred to her—the thought came bursting into her consciousness like some kind of toxic aneurysm exploding in her brain—that Turk didn't want to rescue her. He didn't want her back. For all she knew he'd already returned to Los Angeles and was auditioning new wives—younger, blonder, dumber—in their custom Jacuzzi.

Sheila shifted on the hard wood floor. She was agitated, angry. Her physical discomfort wasn't helping either. Her skin was hot and prickly, her clothes sticking to her and making her skin itch, and her ass had fallen asleep. Her stomach growled loudly, and she realized she was getting hungry. She'd eaten some kind of rice soup for breakfast but no coffee, no tea, not even bottled water. Why was the Captain suddenly treating her like a regular hostage? Had she done something wrong? Why couldn't she take a shower?

Sheila glared at the floor—there was nothing else to do—and thought about the men in her life. Men, she realized, were the root of all evil. This thought, combined with a sudden and calamitous drop in blood sugar, plunged her into a depression.

But as the hours passed and her stomach stopped growling, she began to see things a little more clearly. Maybe, just maybe, it was her fault. Why was she relying on these ridiculous men? She needed the Captain to feed her and not kill her; she needed Turk to save her. It was absurd and, at the same time, fitting. The story of her life. Why did she always rely on men and not herself? Why was she waiting for some man to take care of her, to rescue her? Why not take matters into her own hands and escape?

The thought of escape excited her—although she realized she couldn't take her captors lightly. They had killed the guy from Seattle. They had guns. From what she could tell, they seemed serious and would kill her if they caught her. And then there was Captain Somporn. He was a wild card. She could tell he wanted something; she knew that much. She could see the desire in his eyes. He didn't want to fuck her, but he wanted something. Something sexual. Something that embarrassed him.

Turk was another story. Pampered, spoiled, unable to do his laundry or mow the lawn. How would he ever figure out how to save her? The most menial tasks stupefied him. Sure, he could play the bass really well and even sing a little, but ask him to use a can opener or read a map and he was useless. Lovable in his way, and sweet to be sure, but deeply flawed and a mediocre lover. That's the thing that cracked her up, the irony of it. The famous lothario—a legendary cockmaster—with hundreds of notches on his belt was boring in the sack. Sheila had been excited when they first became intimate. She'd expected all kinds of Kama Sutra craziness: bondage, role-playing, crazy sex toys, mind-blowing orgasms, and nights of unquenchable desire. But Turk was actually very meat-and-potatoes in his sexual appetites. Not that she minded that much. Sheila supposed that if she'd asked Turk to do something different he'd have readily agreed, but she was a little embarrassed by some of her desires.

She and Captain Somporn had that in common.

...

Turk watched the broadcast in his cabin. Laid out on the bed, a bottle of beer balanced on his stomach, the volume turned up. Turk didn't know it, but it was a riveting performance.

Charlie and Sandrine Todd read their lines perfectly and acted with real emotion. Ben had gotten to them, getting them to change their harrowing hostage story to one about becoming accidentally lost in the jungle while on a hike. He'd convinced the British consulate to help him, citing "national security" and "ongoing antiterror operations" as reasons for the change of story. Ben was surprised at how cooperative everyone was being. His plan to keep the incident quiet was, apparently, running smoothly.

Charlie recounted their tale of survival in the wilds with pride. A mix of cunning, ingenuity, and naturalist skills he'd picked up watching BBC adventure shows. Charlie also admitted to praying for their safe return, adding that he'd asked God to help Fulham avoid relegation and stay in the Premier League.

Turk flipped through the channels, but the story was buried as a kind of afterthought on BBC Asia.

Turk looked at his watch. The fact that the kidnappers had released everyone but Sheila was making him nervous. He didn't like being kept in the dark. Steve and Bruno had always made the big band decisions without him; he hadn't liked it then and he didn't like it now. If the ICE agent wasn't

going to share information, Turk would find out himself—
or, more accurately, hire someone to find out for him. Turk
wasn't going to sit on his ass and wait for someone else to
make life-changing decisions for him ever again.

Although Ben had told him he was confined to the hotel,
Turk knew he had to make a move. He'd already reserved a
plane ticket to Bangkok. A cab would be picking him up near
the resort's trash facility in a few minutes. Turk didn't know
if someone was watching the hotel or what, but he hadn't
taken any chances. He'd arranged everything quietly, in person, not over the phone. He needed money, reinforcements,
someone to help him figure this shit out. He had to get to
Bangkok tonight.

...

Marybeth looked at her suitcase. She'd already packed her es-
sentials: the black leather miniskirt, the fishnet stockings, the
see-through paisley shirt with the ruffly sleeves, her studded dog
collar necklace, her makeup kit, a purple polka-dot bikini, a
Metal Assassin tour T-shirt with the sleeves cut off, and a fresh
box of Trojan "Twisted Pleasure" lubricated condoms.

But what else would she need? What did they wear in
Bangkok anyway? All she could visualize were small brown
women wearing sandals and those loose fitting sarilike things.
They had to be loose and light; it was really hot there, she
was sure of it. Hot and steamy. So the leather pants were out.
The last thing Marybeth wanted was a yeast infection.

Thirteen

BANGKOK

When King Rama I founded this magnificent city on the banks of the Chao Phraya River he named it *"Krung Thep Mahanakhon Amon Rattanakosin Mahinthara Ayuthaya Mahadilok Phop Noppharat Ratchathani Burirom Udomratchaniwet Mahasathan Amon Piman Awatan Sathit Sakkathattiya Witsanukam Prasit."*

Which roughly translates to:

"The city of angels, the great city, the residence of the Emerald Buddha, the impregnable city of God Indra, the grand capital of the world endowed with nine precious gems, the happy city, abounding in an enormous Royal Palace that resembles the heavenly abode where reigns the reincarnated god, a city given by Indra and built by Vishnukarn."

Turk didn't know it, but Thailand had never been invaded or occupied by any foreign nation. It was never ravaged by imperialism. It was not an outpost of colonial conquest. Overlooked and unmolested by marauding armies, Thailand was allowed to grow on its own, unique and exotic, like a wild orchid in the deep jungle, until it mutated into something extraordinary, almost alien to the rest of the world.

. . .

The wheels of the sedan beat out a syncopated *ka-chunka chunk* as they cruised along the elevated freeway at midnight. Turk sat in back, staring out the window. He felt strangely disconnected from himself and from the world as he knew it, like he was in that half-state between waking and dreaming.

Bangkok spread out below him, the orange glow of the freeway lights cutting a path through the blue haze above the city. Lights twinkled from houses and apartments that seemed stacked on top of each other in a random jumble that spread out as far as he could see. Small fires glowed from late-night street corner carts, and Turk could see the slender silhouettes of people gathered around them.

Larger buildings, not quite scraping the sky, popped up alongside the freeway, their modern architecture made surreal by the signage—a kind of indecipherable dream language. There were billboards plastered with smiling Thai faces and pictures of products. Turk tried to read them but the alphabet was foreign, not offering a clue as to where a word began or ended or even what the letters were. He searched the signs for something to hold on to—some punctuation, some kind of connection to the world he knew. When he saw the word "Panasonic" he felt a warm sense of relief. He hadn't left the planet. It just seemed like it.

In the distance he saw moonlight reflecting off a shiny black river as it snaked along one edge of the city.

"Is that where we're going? By the river?"

The driver nodded.

"Chao Phraya."

...

The driver had met him at the airport—standing stiffly at attention in his white suit with white gloves and hat, he looked more like a naval cadet than a chauffeur—and had taken his bag, leading him to what looked like a fancy Toyota Corolla. As Turk got into the car the driver saluted and said, "Welcome to Krung Thep."

Maybe that's what gave Turk a sense of unease. He had flown to Bangkok but arrived in Krung Thep. He was going to the Oriental Hotel but the driver called it Chao Phraya. Turk sighed and took a sip of the cold bottled water the driver had handed him. Normally Sheila—or the tour manager—would've handled all the arrangements. He would be whisked to wherever he was supposed to be without giving it a thought. Turk was proud that he'd managed to do it on his own; he'd actually arranged something. And not just anything—he'd pulled off a secret mission. Although the more the driver talked the more Turk had a nagging suspicion that he'd fucked everything up.

When he arrived at the Oriental Hotel, his uneasiness vanished. The hotel employees, concierge, and night manager greeted Turk like he was visiting royalty. They took his Visa card. They offered him a cold fruit juice. They asked if he'd like something to eat. This, Turk realized, was the way it was supposed to be.

Turk followed the bellman, passing under a massive and slightly bizarre-looking chandelier dangling from the ceiling, strolling past a tranquil, flower-covered fountain burbling in the middle of the lobby, and headed for the elevator.

In his room, Turk tipped the bellman and closed the door behind him. Ignoring the deluxe fruit basket filled with all kinds of tropical delights, Turk headed straight for the minibar. He really needed a drink.

Turk sipped his second Singha and opened the window. A blast of humid air and the fragrant fertile smell of the river blew in and smacked him in the face. Normally he might've wrinkled his nose at the smell, but he belched instead, and the yeasty beer mixed with the smell of the river to create a lively perfume. Moonlight bounced off the Chao Phraya in blue-black flickers, and across the river in the distance Turk could see some strange building jutting up into the night sky. A couple of barges drifted downriver, passing a boat that looked like a big loaf of whole-wheat bread puttering slowly against the current.

Turk thought about Sheila. He wondered what she was doing, if she was all right. He was worried. It was natural, right? A man should be worried about his wife, especially when she's in the hands of kidnappers—or worse, terrorists. Turk wondered if the ICE agent was right. *What if they are terrorists?*

He took another sip of his beer. It was selfish, he knew, but he didn't care who they were—kidnappers, terrorists, headhunting cannibals, or crazed fans—he was determined to get her back. Turk was going to get Sheila back, and he didn't give a flying fuck what the U.S. government thought about it.

Turk went to his dop kit and shook out an Ambien. He downed it with the rest of his beer and closed the window. He needed to get a good night's sleep. Tomorrow was going to be a big day.

...

The nights are extremely pleasant in Bangkok. The traffic dies down and the wind clears the smog out of the air. The temperatures average around seventy-seven degrees in the hot season, and blooming plants scent the air with their fragrant pollen. But when the sun comes up, the temperature rises dramatically, and nine million people start their cars, motorcycles, trucks, and scooters.

Marybeth had grown up in Los Angeles. She'd experienced gridlock. She'd been a victim of traffic snarls caused by various Sigalerts, Amber alerts, brushfires, earthquakes, and mudslides. She'd seen the 405 freeway backed up with six lanes of traffic for as far as the eye could see. She'd spent an hour trying to go two miles on a road so clogged with cars that it moved slower than magma.

But she'd never seen anything like Bangkok at rush hour.

It didn't help that she had to pee. Marybeth realized she should've gone at the airport, but there had been so much commotion, all those people waving at her with flyers offering cheap hotels, guided tours, places to eat, cars to rent, things to do; it was overwhelming. She had grabbed her suitcase and wheeled it out to the taxi stand without thinking. She just wanted to get out of there. Get in a car. Get to the hotel.

But now she was stuck in an ungodly mass of slow-moving metal. As if the entire country of Thailand had decided to park their cars on the road and let the engines idle for a few of hours.

Maybe this is the cause of global warming.

While the cars weren't moving, all manner of two-wheeled transportation was flying by in the narrow gaps between vehicles. Countless motorcycles and scooters raced past, shooting down the narrow lanes created between cars as if they were on the wide-open road. Marybeth saw one sagging Honda 250cc, a man driving it, a woman sitting behind him with a small child sandwiched in between them and a toddler perched on the handlebars. She thought it was strangely unfair that only the man was wearing a helmet. Shouldn't they all have helmets? Shouldn't they be in a car? Marybeth wished she had a helmet. She'd pee in it.

When the taxi finally pulled into the driveway of the Oriental Hotel, Marybeth handed the driver a scrunchy wad of funny-looking Thai money and took off running. She ran in a kind of hunched-over scuffle, one hand holding her crotch, applying pressure to keep the urine trapped in her bladder until she reached a toilet.

The bellman understood right away and led her down a hallway past some expensive boutiques to a bathroom. Had anyone been using the toilet when she entered, Marybeth would've killed them. Or she would've stood on the counter and peed in the sink. As it happened, the stalls were unoccupied and Marybeth was able to squat and let loose what can only be described as a torrent of urine worthy of a drunk elephant. She shivered with relief.

After she'd checked in, gone to her room, taken a quick shower, and put on new clothes—a flouncy hippie skirt, no underwear, and her Metal Assassin T-shirt—she went to look for Turk. Her first stop was the bar, where she was surprised not to find him. Then she tried the restaurants and the Authors' Lounge—looking slightly surreal with its white wicker furniture, like Alice had gone to a tea party and ended up in Bangkok. She even looked in the spa. She called his room and left a message. She asked the bellman and the concierge if Turk had left the hotel.

She finally found him eating lunch outside on the veranda.

"You're a hard man to track down."

Turk looked up at her and smiled.

"Marybeth."

He stood up, wiped the spicy Thai noodles off his lips with a napkin, and planted a kiss on her cheek.

"Have a seat. Please."

Marybeth joined him as a waitress appeared and handed her a menu.

"Don't you want to eat inside? It's fucking hot out here, dude."

Turk mopped some sweat off his face and took a long drink of cold Singha.

"Once you eat the food, you forget about the weather."

Marybeth looked at him and smiled. "You look good."

"Considering."

"No. You just plain old look good."

She turned on her smile. Turk nodded. "Thanks. You look nice yourself."

Turk used his spoon to scoop up some food and pop it into his mouth.

"Don't they have chopsticks?"

Turk swallowed. "They don't use 'em here. Everybody eats with a spoon. That's the proper way to do it."

"Who told you that?"

"A waitress at the resort set me straight."

The waitress came over and Marybeth ordered eggs Benedict and a large orange juice. Turk smiled at her.

"You come all the way to the other side of the world and order eggs Benedict?"

"I bet they're good here."

Turk shook his head. "Yeah, you're probably right."

Turk realized that he was sounding a lot like Sheila. Chastising someone for ordering eggs Benedict in Bangkok was something she'd do.

"Is Jon meeting us out here?"

"He couldn't make it."

Turk's face fell.

"Don't worry. He sent me. That's why I'm here."

"To tell me he can't come?"

"No. No. No. I'm here to help you. I'll do anything you want. Whatever you need. I'm here for you."

She smiled again, and Turk caught the meaning behind the smile.

"I want to get Sheila back."

Marybeth kept smiling.

"Right. Exactly. Dude, that's why I'm here. But that doesn't mean I can't help you with your needs. When you pull up to my pump, it ain't self-serve. I'm a full-service personal assistant."

The eggs Benedict arrived, two soft round poached eggs slathered in a bright yellow hollandaise and jiggling on a couple of toasted muffins.

. . .

Jon Heidegger was a good manager, and what a good manager does is anticipate his clients' needs. That way when they ask for something, it's already done. Heidegger had made a few phone calls and tracked down a security consultant in Bangkok. He'd already called and spoken with this man and learned that he was an expert in ransom and retrieval, often spending a good deal of time negotiating the "escape" of American students from Thai prisons, personally escorting them over the border to Cambodia or down to Singapore, where they would be reunited with their wealthy and worried (and, admittedly, disappointed by their children's lack of judgment) parents. He'd also handled the ransom and release of a famous Hong Kong director who had been snatched from a Patpong brothel by a gang of unemployed Thai actors. A former Australian special forces commando, he was well qualified for the job, and Heidegger had already made the appointment for Turk and Marybeth.

...

It hadn't occurred to Turk that someone from the government might be following them—he assumed he'd given them the slip with his coded message—so he hadn't taken any particular precautions, like using cash to pay for his food or wearing a disguise (not that he would have known what to do if someone was following him) as he and Marybeth got in a cab and gave the driver the address of an office building a mile or so down Silom Road.

...

Ben sat in his cab and watched as Turk and Marybeth entered the office building. Having come to the decision that he was going to keep the million dollars, he'd also come to the decision that he had to keep Turk from ransoming his wife. If Turk was successful, he would inevitably get in touch with the Bureau of Immigration and Customs Enforcement and ask for his money back. This would cause complications for Ben, because he had no intention of giving the money back.

In Ben's perfect world, the kidnappers would become bored with holding Sheila hostage and release her. That would be ideal. He could then spin a web of reasonable untruths, telling Turk that it had been a "backdoor negotiation." Of course, he'd exaggerate the story, detailing how he'd violated U.S. law and paid the ransom. Turk would commend Ben for his bravery, for putting compassion and humanity above the law. Ben, in turn, would make Turk swear an oath to never tell a soul; they'd be two men bonded by a secret. Maybe he'd even put Ben + 1 on the guest list at all of his shows. Or better yet, give him an all-access pass.

The next best thing would be for the kidnappers to get bored with holding Sheila and do what frustrated kidnappers do: kill her. Then he could say he gave them the money—again risking his job by putting humanity ahead of U.S. law—but they'd double-crossed him. Ben would make Turk swear an oath to never tell a soul and they'd become two men bonded by tragedy.

The third option, and least palatable, was that Turk would persist with his Don Quixote rescue mission and Ben would have to kill him. It wasn't unheard of. A lot of people had been killed for less than a million dollars.

Ben didn't follow Turk and Marybeth into the building. He didn't have to. He knew who they'd be seeing.

. . .

Lampard International Consulting was one of the largest and most experienced security firms in the world. Headquartered in London, it had more than sixty international branch offices. It handled everything from bodyguard services, personal protection, and risk and threat assessments to the planning, design, and implementation of security systems for your home, office, or corporation. LIC experts handled crisis management, corporate espionage investigations, and hazardous materials situations. They could do just about anything you might want someone to do for you.

The company's specialty was crisis intervention. Say your head of marketing is stuck in some godforsaken country due to a natural disaster or political upheaval; an LIC "quick response team" could be mobilized within the hour to plan and execute a precise extraction of your valued executive from the hostile environment.

LIC had an entire division dedicated to kidnap-for-ransom cases. Due to the frequency of abductions in Latin America, this had become a booming business. Executives and their companies frequently bought kidnap insurance, and LIC worked with the insurers to "protect against financial and accidental loss." Many times this meant tracking kidnappers in Mexico City or Caracas and abruptly putting an end to the *secuestro express*—basically an extended shopping spree, with the victim using his or her credit card to treat the kidnappers to electronic goods, clothes, and luxury items at gunpoint—by planting a well-placed bullet in the kidnapper's cranium.

It was an effective strategy, and LIC had a very high success rate.

. . .

Turk stood in the air-conditioned lobby of the Southeast Asia bureau of Lampard International Consulting studying the framed photographs of cities around the world. There was Rio de Janeiro, Mexico City, Tokyo, Cairo, Johannesburg, and Sydney. Turk smiled when he saw them. They were all places Metal Assassin had played on its world tours, and despite his age and the sheer volume of conquests, Turk could still recall the myriad sexual encounters with fans, groupies, and all kinds of innocent bystanders in porno-film detail. *Funny how a picture of the Sydney Opera House can give you an erection.* Otherwise the office was austere, like a clinic. To the point of being drab.

A nice-looking Thai woman in a red silk dress came out of the back room, greeted them with a *wai,* and escorted them into a conference room. Turk tried to imitate the *wai,* and Marybeth laughed at him. Turk looked at her with some annoyance. He didn't know why, but for some reason the longer he stayed in Thailand the more he wanted to be polite. He liked the way Thais were unfailingly polite to each other; maybe it was contagious.

The conference room proved to be much more impressive than the foyer. Decked out with a state-of-the-art video conferencing system, computers, global tracking monitors, satellite communicators, and some nifty designer furniture from Italy, the conference room was like a high-tech command center. Just standing there you felt better, at ease, like everything was under control.

Before Turk or Marybeth had a chance to sit down, a tall and ruggedly handsome man with short blond hair and a sunburned nose strode into the room. He spoke with a cocky, self-assured Australian accent and gave Turk a warm, confident handshake.

"Mr. Henry? I'm Clive Muggleton, your case officer."

"Thanks for seeing us."

Marybeth shook his hand, the extremely fit Aussie holding hers for longer than he needed to.

"I'm Marybeth. We spoke on the phone."

"Nice to put a face to that voice."

Clive actually winked at Marybeth, then turned to Turk.

"You're here because you want your wife back. Safe and sound."

Turk nodded. "Absolutely."

Marybeth pulled a Metal Assassin CD out of her purse. "I brought you this. So you'd be familiar with the band."

Clive took the CD and studied it. It was easy to pick Turk out on the back cover. He was on the far left, outfitted in black leather pants and some kind of straitjacket made from chain mail, glowering and baring his teeth like a rabid dog.

"Do you know the band?"

Clive cleared his throat. "I've heard of them, of course. Who hasn't? But I can't say I listen to a lot of this kind of music; not really my cup of tea."

Turk tried to steer the conversation back to rescuing Sheila. "What about Sheila? Can you rescue her?"

Marybeth looked at Clive. "Like what bands do you like?"

Turk looked at her, annoyed. "Marybeth, for fuck's sake."

The Australian, not a man above a random nooner with a hot chick like Marybeth, spoke diplomatically.

"Oh, INXS, Midnight Oil, that kind of thing. I'm pretty old-fashioned."

Clive turned back to Turk.

"Mr. Henry. I spoke with your manager this morning, and I want to reassure you that we're prepared to do whatever it takes to see your wife safely repatriated."

Turk sighed. Finally, experts were taking over. Someone was doing something.

"First thing I need to do is run what we call a risk assessment. Find out who might be behind this, what kind of threat they might be, what kind of resources I might utilize to extricate your wife from this situation."

"I just need someone to give these guys the money."

"That's exactly right. But I think it's important we understand who we're dealing with. Don't you?"

Turk didn't answer.

"I'm a former member of the Australian First Commando Regiment. And I know how to plan and execute a tactical rescue. We are experts in this kind of thing. Let me do my job. Trust me, you're in good hands."

Clive smiled, flashing a set of perfectly straight, gleaming white Australian teeth. They were the teeth of the New World, confident and irresistible. Turk nodded. For some reason he felt reassured.

It was true: Clive Muggleton was a former commando, and he did know his stuff. But in the last ten years, stuck behind a desk, he'd let himself go, hardly working out, and spending much of his free time in a Soi Cowboy bar consuming vast quantities of vodka spiked with balls of opium from Chiang Mai. When business was slow he'd scuffle off to a brothel and spend the afternoon drinking beer and fucking fresh young Thai girls just off the farm. It wasn't much of a hobby, but it beat sitting at his desk reading corporate e-mails.

Even though he was only forty-one, Clive realized he was getting older, that his commando days were behind him; he wasn't going to be crawling through the mud with an assault rifle anytime soon. So living in Bangkok had become one extended midlife crisis for him. But if he no longer had the strength or the balls to fast-rope out of a Black Hawk helicopter, he could still party like the young commando he'd once been, could still get wasted and screw women half his age. Although he had to admit to himself that the hangovers had become more and more ferocious as the years passed and his liver disintegrated.

But what Clive lacked in fitness, he more than made up for by being a good salesman, a closer. It wasn't a difficult job. Turk wanted his wife back, but didn't know what to do. He was emotional, confused, and frankly didn't have the skill set to locate a car in a parking garage. Turk would do the sensible thing. He would let the experts take over. It would cost him hundreds of thousands of dollars, but he could go back to doing whatever it was rock stars do.

Turk had one last concern.

"What if something goes wrong?"

Clive leaned in, put on his most serious warrior-like expression, and closed the deal.

"Then I promise you one thing. We will find the people behind this and bring you their heads in a bag."

Turk nodded. Sold. Although it did sound like something he remembered from an old movie.

"How long is it going to take?"

Clive smiled.

"I just need you to sign some papers—our contract and a release form—and then I'll get right on it. I should know something in a few hours. We can meet later tonight, somewhere discreet, and I'll brief you."

...

Turk and Marybeth walked out of the air-conditioned high-rise into the sweltering Bangkok heat. Sweat erupted from Turk's forehead the moment he stepped outside. Marybeth's makeup began breaking down in the thick, humid air, making her look ragged, as if she'd been up partying for days.

They looked for a cab in the fast-moving free-for-all that constituted traffic patterns on Silom Road. It was anarchy in action. There were no stop signs, signal lights, or pedestrian crossings that Turk could see, yet pedestrians crossed the free-flowing bumper car craziness without getting crushed, killed, or pancaked by what looked like a zillion cars, *tuk tuks,* motorcycles, and scooters careening around each other.

"This is some crazy shit."

"Traffic's fucking unbelievable here."

A motorcycle with a food cart strapped to its side stopped in front of them. Turk pointed it out to Marybeth.

"Look at this guy. Instead of driving to the restaurant, he's driving the restaurant. That's so cool." Turk flashed the devil horn salute to the motorcycle driver.

"Rock 'n' fuckin' roll, dude."

Marybeth smiled. She didn't think a guy with a grill strapped to his scooter was all that rock and roll, but then she wasn't a rock star like Turk, so she just kept smiling.

"Yeah."

The motorcyclist nodded, then moved off as traffic de-congested somewhere and the flow resumed. Turk watched as a couple of *tuk tuks* drove along the side of the street, weaving between the cars and the vendors.

"Maybe we should take one of those."

Marybeth wrinkled her nose. "If you want to get high on car exhaust."

"It's better than standing here."

"All that pollution is really bad for your skin."

Marybeth spotted a cab on the other side of the street and pointed. "There's one. Over there."

Turk saw the cab, parked half on the sidewalk, across six lanes of death-on-wheels.

"Great. How do we get there?"

Marybeth grabbed his arm. "C'mon."

She stepped out into the street. Turk pulled her back. "Are you crazy? We'll get killed."

Marybeth pointed out all the locals crossing the road. "We just gotta go like they do. Show me a little faith."

"Show Me a Little Faith" had been a massive hit for Metal Assassin. Turk tried to remember the lyrics, but could only recall the chorus. That's where Steve hit the big high note and a gigantic dove with an olive branch stuck in its beak would suddenly fly from the back of the stadium to the front of the stage. It might not have been as totally metal as their other stunts and pyrotechnics, but the dove had been designed by the same guy who did all the Rose Parade floats and it looked really cool. And chicks dug it. Turk briefly flashed on a memory of crawling in the dove with some crazy groupie and getting it on.

"C'mon."

Marybeth took his hand and led him out into the river of steel. It was almost magical, like Moses parting the Red Sea. Somehow the traffic adjusted for them, swerving around them, braking and accelerating, leaving them enough room to cross. Turk couldn't believe it. He grinned at Marybeth. "That fucking rocked."

...

Turk sat in the back of the cab marveling at the city. He looked out at the shops along the road. Gem dealers, silk traders, custom tailors, currency exchanges, office buildings—it had all the hustle and bustle of New York, the familiar scenes of any metropolis, and yet Bangkok was completely different from any city he'd ever been in. Turk couldn't quite figure out what it was. Sure, some of the architecture was crazy; not like the Guggenheim in New York or Museo Bilbao in Spain or the Disneyland in California—Thai architecture had its own insane style. The temples, the palace, the traditional Thai architecture was like nothing he'd ever seen before. The colors were amazing: shockingly bright reds; vibrant blues, oranges, and greens; blindingly clean white. The shapes were out of control—ornate peaked roofs, intricate and bizarre patterns and details cut into the structures, strange flourishes perched on the corners of the roofs, reaching up to the sky like alien epaulets. Turk laughed to himself. You could use some of these buildings as a set for an extraterrestrial invasion video and people would believe they really came from outer space.

Marybeth broke the silence.

"You look like you need to unwind. Want to go out tonight?"

"For dinner?"

"Yeah. Dinner and then let's go clubbing."

"I don't know."

"Dude, we're in Bangkok. It's like got the most famous nightlife of any city in the world. We gotta go."

Turk felt a shiver go through his body. For him, Bangkok was legendary; it was the world's biggest living breathing *catalytic environment*. It was exactly the kind of place his therapist would not want him to be.

"I don't think so, Marybeth."

Marybeth knew why Turk was being hesitant.

"Turk, dude, you gotta face your fears. And besides, I'll be with you the whole time, holding your hand."

"I was going to get a massage."

"Get a massage and then we'll go out. You need to chill, dude. The rescue guy's working on it; let him do his thing."

Turk didn't answer so Marybeth smiled her sweetest, sexiest smile at him.

"Please."

"I guess you're right. Sheila would want me to see the city."

Ben watched Turk and Marybeth cross the street. In the back of his mind he was hoping for a little luck; an auto accident would be perfect. But that didn't happen. As he watched Marybeth, checking out her cute ass, he made a note to himself. He'd order a background workup on her. That might be fun.

Ben didn't follow them; he figured they'd return to the hotel. He drove off, heading back to his office in the U.S.

Embassy on Wireless Road. Once there he'd send a message to Washington and have the State Department call Lampard International headquarters in London and put the kibosh on this whole thing. When it came to interdicting the aid and support of terrorist organizations, the United States government didn't fuck around.

...

Turk lay on the bed in his hotel room. The masseuse, a squat young Thai woman from the provinces, had made him put on some strange cotton pajamas and was now giving him a traditional Thai massage. It wasn't like any rubdown he'd ever had. She twisted his legs and torqued his body into a series of odd angles and strange poses that were supposed to stretch and relax him. The fact that it was working—he felt great— was a surprise. Turk realized that nothing here was really what it seemed. Or maybe it was exactly what it seemed, only he'd never thought about it that way.

The massage went on and on, lasting almost two hours. When she was done, the masseuse looked at him.

"You want happy finish?"

Turk, who was in a kind of endorphin release trance, blinked.

"I'm sorry."

"You want happy finish? Special massage."

Turk thought about it. Hadn't he just had a special massage? What more could she be offering? He grasped her intent at the exact same moment that she grasped his cock.

"Uh."

"It's okay, mister. Happy finish good."

Turk thought about Sheila, about his marriage vows, about his promise to try and be monogamous for the rest of his life. Is a happy finish the same as sex? Or is it part of the massage, just on a different part of the body? Is getting a massage the same as being unfaithful? Or is getting a massage okay? Turk supposed that if you called it a hand job then it could be considered infidelity. But this was a massage. Happy finish good.

Turk wanted to hold off. To wait and give it further consideration. He wanted to discuss it with his therapist. But by the time he'd come to this decision, he'd ejaculated all over the strange cotton pajamas.

...

The guilt he felt after the masseuse left was overwhelming. All the therapy, all the soul-searching, all the restraint that he was so proud of, everything that he had worked so hard for was tossed out the window in one quick happy finish.

Turk stood up and looked at himself in the mirror. *What have you done?* He couldn't face himself; he turned away from his reflection and sat on the edge of the bed.

He held his face in his hands and began to cry.

Like a lot of heavy metal bass players, Turk wasn't particularly emotional. He didn't cry at movies or weddings. He didn't cry at funerals. He didn't cry when Metal Assassin got their first double platinum album. He didn't cry when they won their Grammy award. He didn't cry when they called it quits.

But now he was blubbering like a prom-jilted teenage girl. Hot tears were freely flowing down his cheeks, strings of mucus were hanging off his nose, his chest heaved with mournful sobs, and he couldn't stop it. He cried because he was disappointed in himself. He wanted to be cured, free of his addiction. He wanted to be stronger. He wanted to be faithful to his poor kidnapped wife.

Turk needed to call his therapist but realized that the time was wrong. It'd be too early or too late or something in L.A. Everything was upside down here. He wanted a pill, some kind of Xanax or antidepressant, a pharmaceutical monkey wrench to shut off the flow of tears, something to numb him out; but he didn't have anything like that. Unable to stop sobbing, he grabbed a Singha out of the minibar and headed into the bathroom to take a shower.

...

By the time Turk got out of the shower he'd stopped crying. He hit the minibar for another brew and, wearing only a towel, went to the window to watch the boats on the Chao Phraya. He didn't know why, but there was something about the view that calmed him. Maybe it was the sense that he was safe in his room while chaos swirled around him. Maybe it was just watching the water taxis flying across the river, cutting in front of barges and tour boats, just like taxis in the streets. Maybe it was the Thai architecture; *Wat Arun*—the guidebook in the hotel called it the "Temple of the Dawn"— was visible across the river, made entirely of ceramic plates and jutting up into the sky. It reminded Turk of the space-ships in the *Star Wars* movies. He liked that he could see an ancient temple from his modern hotel window.

...

In the shower Turk had thought about the happy finish. He started to come up with the usual excuses: he was under enormous stress from dealing with Sheila's abduction; he didn't mean to do it, it just sorta happened; he thought it was part of the massage and didn't want to offend his foreign masseuse by declining. He could keep the justifications coming for hours if he had to. But then he had an epiphany: he decided that he wasn't going to rationalize anymore. He wasn't going to blame someone or something else. He was going to take responsibility for the fact that he had allowed it to happen. His therapist would say that it was part of the cycle of addiction. But Turk didn't know what to think. He was confused. Wasn't blaming the addiction for his behavior just another excuse?

I'm an addict. It's not my fault. It's a disease.

Wasn't that just a cop-out?

...

Marybeth wanted a real Bangkok experience. She wanted to go to a seedy brothel and hire a sexy Thai prostitute—she wasn't a prude when it came to sex and sometimes enjoyed hooking up with a hot lesbian; besides, maybe she could entice Turk into a three-way and kill two birds, so to speak—and she wanted to see what all the fuss was about, why busloads of horny tourists from England, Sweden, and the U.S. came every year just to frolic in the sex clubs of Patpong. Most of all she wanted to see the girl do that trick with the Ping-Pong balls.

Marybeth, dressed somewhat provocatively in a light slip dress covered by a torn denim jacket, met Turk in the hotel lobby. He smiled when he saw her.

"Hungry?"

Marybeth nodded. "I got this."

She handed Turk a business card. It was Clive's. Turk flipped it over and saw the words "The Winchester, 10pm" and an address on Soi Cowboy. Turk was impressed.

"That was fast. This guy doesn't mess around."

Marybeth hooked her arm around Turk's.

"Let's eat. We can celebrate."

...

At Turk's insistence, they took a *tuk tuk* to dinner. He was beginning to appreciate them. The overtaxed air conditioners of the cabs had a close, musty smell and Turk preferred to be out in the wind. Marybeth was annoyed at first; she had spent a good hour and a half removing and reapplying her makeup, and the last thing she wanted was for a layer of Bangkok grit and humidity to destroy those efforts, but Turk seemed to be in better spirits, less worried about Sheila and more his old rock star self, so Marybeth indulged him.

It was her job, of course, to indulge the boyish antics of her company's clients, and she did it very well. In fact she enjoyed it. There was just something kinda cool about watching a bunch of forty-year-old musicians trash a hotel room—break the lamps, turn the furniture into splinters, scrawl obscenities on the wall, and chuck the TV set into the pool. It was all the stuff you wanted to do in high school. Only now their celebrity and bank accounts allowed them to do stupid shit with impunity.

Turk didn't say much, just smiled into the breeze and seemed to enjoy the *tuk tuk* ride like it was a special treat at Disneyland. But for Marybeth it was a little more traumatic as they jounced and swayed past the street life: the open-air restaurants, the markets, the mangy-looking dogs sniffing through piles of garbage, cars, motorcycles, apartments, shops, and everywhere thousands of people out and about, doing their thing. Marybeth saw children playing, old people shopping for food, young couples holding hands: people living their lives out on the street. She found herself feeling shocked, overwhelmed by it all. Bangkok was a whole other kind of animal than what she was used to.

But for Turk it was a completely different experience. He grooved on the humanity of the place. The city pulsed with life. It had the street energy of New York City, only multiplied to the hundredth power. Yet it wasn't frenetic. There was no mania, no anger or rage. Bangkok spun out in a kind of relaxed and vibrant swirl. It was beautiful.

Turk realized that normally he would've just sat in the hotel, ordered room service, and watched a video. That's how he'd seen the world on tour with Metal Assassin. He regretted that now. The cocoon of the tour bus, the luxury and isolation of the hotels, the handlers, managers, and assistants had all kept him from experiencing the world, from engaging with life. He'd never realized until this moment in the *tuk tuk* that he'd missed so much.

Marybeth watched Turk. She was worried about him. He seemed distant, kind of out of it; yet he was smiling. She wondered if he'd smoked a joint earlier.

"Hey! Let's try that."

Marybeth turned to look where Turk was pointing. It was an outdoor restaurant—really just a table and a fire pit on the sidewalk—surrounded by dozens of people eating mysterious food off paper plates.

"You're joking."

"C'mon. It must be good. Look at all the people."

Marybeth shook her head.

"No fucking way. I've got an expense account."

...

Marybeth had seen to the dinner arrangements. The concierge had recommended a funky but chic little place. It was very modern—simple and clean, almost minimalist—and at the same time very Thai. The effect was inviting and relaxing. She could see Turk take a deep breath and exhale as they entered.

"Smells great in here."

It did smell great in the restaurant. A giant display of fresh orchids and gingers exploded out of the hostess station, perfuming the restaurant. After the gut-churning drive through streets fragrant with exhaust, rotting garbage, and the piquant tang of an antiquated sewage system, the restaurant was like an aromatherapy spa.

The hostess seated them and gave them English menus.

"This is the wine list." She handed Turk a thick binder.

Marybeth wasted no time. "I'd like a double Stoli and tonic, please."

Turk looked at her. "You don't want wine?"

"I do. I just want to start with a cocktail."

Turk nodded and looked at the hostess. "Make it two."

The hostess gave Turk a deep *wai* and went off to procure the cocktails. Marybeth turned and smiled at Turk.

"I'm gonna get fucking polluted tonight."

Turk raised an eyebrow at that, but Marybeth wasn't about to be denied her fun.

"C'mon Turkey, we're in Bangkok. Let's get out of our skulls."

Turk smiled at her. "I don't want to get *too* out of my skull. We're meeting the guy, remember?"

Marybeth nodded. "Yeah. But after the briefing, I'm getting wasted. Why not? You know what I mean? Why the fuck not? That's my motto."

Turk looked at the menu.

"That's a good motto."

. . .

Ben watched from the back of a *tuk tuk* as Turk and Marybeth entered the restaurant. He paid the driver and got out, going across the street to a little store for a bottle of water. Ben assumed that Turk and Marybeth were just going out to dinner, but he wanted to make sure. He wouldn't want to see them meeting someone, anyone, who might assist them.

Ben squirted some antibacterial hand cleaning gel onto his palm and rubbed his hands. Then he waited. He figured he'd give them half an hour and if they were still alone, he'd call it a night. He had to be in the office early and check with Washington to make sure they squashed Turk's rescue mission before it started.

. . .

Two hours later, wobbling from the cocktails, the bottle of wine, the intensely spicy food, and the subsequent beers, Turk and Marybeth climbed out of a *tuk tuk* in front of a nightclub called The Winchester. A garish neon sign the size of a school bus flashed above a run-down two-story building in the middle of an alley that seemed to be lined with bars, brothels, and go-go clubs, crammed up against each other like sardines. Above the door a bright Winchester rifle cocked and shot over and over again in neon flipbook animation. Turk looked at Marybeth.

"Are you sure this is right?"

Marybeth nodded. Turk hesitated.

"I don't want to go in. Can you tell him I'm outside?"

Marybeth grabbed Turk's arm. "Don't worry. I'll protect you."

Turk shook his head. "That's what I'm afraid of."

...

If you could get pregnant from breathing, the air in the club would knock you up in no time; it was dense with cigarette smoke, human sweat, the yeasty aroma of beer, and the unmistakable salty perfume of spent semen and wet pussy. Turk had followed Marybeth and the hostess, an older *mamasan* type, past the bar to a booth near the rear of the club. Topless go-go dancers moved to the music—'80s rock classics from The Clash, Blondie, and The Smiths intermixed with new techno tracks from Brazil and Holland—as multicolored lights beamed down on them and a crowd of appreciative Caucasian men stood around white-knuckling their beers and grinning like boob-addled retards.

Marybeth was the only non-Thai woman in the club, and a number of the men exchanged nervous glances when she entered. Turk ordered the drinks and looked around. He didn't see Clive. But he saw lots of men who looked like Clive cuddled up in various booths with Thai women dressed in what can only be called "pay to fuck me" clothes. Turk noticed that a couple of these men were getting special crotch massages while they drank their beers and watched the go-go dancers. Turk was slightly disconcerted by the fact that all of the men were his age or older. Apparently he was the target demographic for a Bangkok brothel.

A pair of British men, sporting shaggy layered haircuts and bushy mustaches, flashed Turk the devil horn salute. One was wearing a Manchester United jersey, the name "Rooney" and a giant number 8 printed on the back. Turk smiled at them and flashed back, which they took for an invitation to come over.

"I fuckin' love Metal Assassin!"

Turk smiled. "Thanks, man."

"What're you doin' here, man? Gettin' a little R&R?"

Turk nodded. "Taking a break from it, you know."

"You came to the right place, man. You can go all night, nonstop. They don't care, man. They just replace the girls."

Turk smiled and nodded his head. "Cool."

Although in all honesty he didn't think it sounded cool. It sounded kind of sweaty and gross to him. Manchester United leaned in, a coconspirator. "I've got some Cialis and some coke if you're interested."

Before Turk could answer, the other guy playfully smacked Manchester United on the head.

"Don't be a prat. This is Turk-fuckin'-Henry. He don't need any help." The friend held his hands about two feet apart to indicate the legendary size of Turk's penis.

Manchester United grinned.

"Be careful you don't hurt any of the girls."

The two Brits burst out laughing. Turk smiled; Marybeth glared.

"Yeah, Tommy Lee came in here and left a trail of dead bodies."

More laughter as beer arrived for Turk, another vodka tonic for Marybeth. The Manchester United fan wobbled unsteadily and handed the waitress a clammy wad of baht. "I got this round."

"You don't have to."

"How many times do I get to buy a rock star a drink? Eh?"

His friend clapped him on the back. "Fuckin' right."

Turk lifted his beer in a toast. "Cheers. Thanks."

Another song started and new dancers hopped up on the bar.

"Showtime."

The men turned their backs on Turk and moved toward the bar, the sex-on-display suddenly more interesting than an old rock star.

Marybeth smiled at Turk. "What do you think?"

Turk watched a young Thai woman lead an inebriated old man up a flight of stairs toward a series of private rooms. He saw men groping and fondling women half their age in the booths as they laughed, their faces flushed with excitement, their eyes wild with drink and testosterone. He looked at the bar, where three young women undulated their smooth brown bodies to the music, their mouths open in seductive pouts, their eyes working the men in the room, promising sensual delight, a return to youth, release.

Turk hadn't really given the situation a whole lot of fore-thought. His penis had checked in, become tumescent the moment they walked into the bar. For a recovering sex addict, this was the worst place to be in the world. Perhaps, he mused, only a Roman orgy would be a more *catalytic environment*.

"I think we should leave."

Marybeth looked at him, surprised, even disappointed. "Leave? We just got here."

Before Turk could insist, Clive slipped into the booth. He smiled at them and put a warm hand on Marybeth's thigh. "Enjoying yourselves?"

Marybeth nodded and moved away from Clive. "This place is wild."

"Sorry I'm late, but I wanted to make sure you weren't followed."

Marybeth looked at Turk. "Has someone been follow-ing you?"

Turk shrugged. "The ICE man knew everything I was doing. I think he tapped my phone or something."

Clive agreed. "That's what they usually do. But it doesn't matter. No one followed you here."

Clive signaled the waitress. "Boodles and tonic."

Then he turned to Turk. "I don't think we're dealing with terrorists."

"How do you know?"

"I put a cell net over the whole western end of Phuket and didn't pick up anyone speaking Arabic, Bahasa Indone-sian, or Tamil."

If the dancers in see-through bikini tops and cowboy hats wiggling their asses on the bar didn't distract Turk enough, the alcohol in his brain wouldn't allow the information to process. It was like trying to understand algebra after drinking a bottle of Stoli. Turk looked at Clive.

"I don't follow."

"We tapped all the cell phones in Phuket and we haven't picked up anything out of the ordinary."

"Maybe they didn't make a call."

"Maybe. But it's unlikely that an organization in the middle of an operation would be silent."

Turk nodded and looked at his beer. Marybeth turned to Clive.

"So who is it?"

Clive shrugged.

"Probably a local gang. Or someone with a grudge against the resort. It's usually something like that."

Clive's cocktail arrived. He took the lime off the rim of the glass and squeezed the juice in, stirring with his finger.

"Once we get some daylight, I'll have our satellites scour the area around the resorts for anything unusual."

He took a long slurp of his cocktail. "Don't worry. We'll find them."

Turk looked over at Marybeth. She was no longer part of the conversation, the gyrations of the go-go dancers having captivated her.

"So what should I do?"

Clive smiled. "You're in Bangkok. Have some fun. We'll have you and your wife reunited in no time. I'll be in touch."

With that Clive stood, patted Turk on the shoulder, and carried his cocktail off in the direction of a young bar girl leaning against the wall.

Turk turned to Marybeth. She was still staring at the dancers. "See something you like?"

Marybeth blushed and gave him a playful shove. "Shut up."

Turk laughed. "I wasn't the one staring at the girls."

Marybeth smiled and picked up her drink. "They are kind of cute."

Turk was about to suggest they call it a night and go back to the hotel when a lithe Thai woman in a diaphanous silk dress slipped into the booth next to him. She casually stroked his crotch as she sat down, her touch as light and fleeting as a puff of smoke. It electrified him. Turk turned to tell her not to do that again, but the words stuck in his throat. She was a stunner. Her skin was a dark creamy brown, like a perfect café latte, she had big brown eyes and small but sensual lips, and her hair was cut short in an asymmetric bob. Her neck was long and slender, and there were a pair of chic Alain Mikli eyeglasses perched on her nose.

"Hi. I'm Wendy."

Marybeth smiled. "Wendy? Is that your real name?"

Wendy lit a cigarette. "Do you mind?"

Turk shook his head. "No."

Wendy exhaled a perfectly shaped plume of smoke. "My real name is Watchara Kunakornpaiboonsiri. But that is too difficult for Westerners. So, I'm Wendy."

"Wendy's a nice name."

Marybeth gave off all the obvious signs and signals of sexual attraction as she flirted with the beautiful Thai prostitute; she leaned toward Wendy, locking eyes, and then unconsciously toyed with her hair, licked her lips, touched her breasts, and stuck a finger in her mouth as they chatted. Turk didn't notice; he was looking at Wendy's body. He could see her slender torso and small, perfectly shaped breasts with dark brown nipples through her blouse. Her legs were long, and her hips and ass were rounded, almost athletic. Turk shuddered. Wendy was perfect. It was as if some evil spirit had drawn up everything that Turk found attractive in a woman and put it in one neat and affordable package. Turk realized he would need all his strength and willpower to survive this evening.

Marybeth reached over and took Wendy's hand. "Wendy? Can I buy you a drink?"

"I would like a glass of tequila."

Turk was surprised by that. "Tequila?"

"I love tequila."

Marybeth grinned. "So do I."

Oh my God! She really is perfect!

Marybeth flagged down the waitress and ordered a bottle of their best tequila and three glasses brought to the table. Wendy leaned forward.

"If you would prefer, we can go back to my room. I have some rambutan there. It's not a lime, but I like it even better."

Marybeth nodded. "Great."

Turk looked at her. "What the fuck're you talking about?"

Marybeth gave Turk a friendly shove. "C'mon, Turkey. Let's go somewhere quiet and have a drink with Wendy. What's the problem with that?"

Turk leaned in and whispered to Marybeth. "The problem is that I don't want to fuck a prostitute."

Marybeth smiled. "Then you can watch me."

. . .

Turk had never seen a hairy fruit before. The fuzz of a peach and the fur of a kiwi hadn't prepared him for the spiky dreadlocks of a rambutan. Turk perched himself on a low wooden stool in a corner of the little room—Wendy and Marybeth sat on the simple wooden bed—and looked at the strange fruit. For all he knew it could be some kind of rodent scrotum.

"What the fuck is this?"

Wendy smiled. "Rambutan. You have to peel it."

She demonstrated, cracking the shaggy shell and then peeling it off to reveal a soft, translucent fruit inside.

"Watch out for the seed. It is rather large."

She poured three shots of tequila and handed Marybeth and Turk glasses. Marybeth raised hers in a toast. "Here's to Bangkok."

Wendy smiled as they clinked glasses. Turk knocked the tequila back in one gulp and then bit into the peeled rambutan. His teeth found the hard, smooth seed right away, but the fruit itself exploded onto his tongue in a tangy sweet-sour blast. The taste was alien; it made his mouth feel like it had just been cleaned with an astringent, but it was also delicious. Wendy was right—rambutan mixed well with the tequila. Turk looked up to ask for a refill and noticed that Wendy was undressing Marybeth.

Had he been thinking clearly he would've recognized the danger signals, the extremely *catalytic environment,* and taken this opportunity to slip discreetly out of the room and wait in the bar until Marybeth was finished. But Turk wasn't thinking clearly. He wanted more tequila. He wanted another rambutan.

Turk stood up—somewhat clumsily, as he had a very strong erection, like a sockful of reinforced concrete, in his pants. He reached over and grabbed the tequila and the bowl of rambutan. Wendy noticed this and held out a glass with one hand; her other hand was busy, her fingers gently teasing Marybeth's nipples. Turk carefully filled her glass—feeling oddly like a nurse assisting a doctor—and then sat back on the stool. He watched as Wendy took a sip of tequila, then dipped her fingers in it, and let Marybeth gently suck the liquor off her fingers. Wendy then fed Marybeth a rambutan, gently placing the pale fruit between Marybeth's lips.

Turk peeled a rambutan and popped it in his mouth. He carefully chewed on the fruit, slowly detaching it from the seed with his teeth. He watched Wendy pull her dress off over her head. She hadn't been wearing anything underneath, and now the two women were both naked. Turk took another shot of tequila and peeled another rambutan.

It suddenly occurred to Turk that he was enjoying himself. If he let the guilt and shame he felt in disappointing his therapist just kind of slide away for a little while, he could relax. He knew he wasn't going to join in; that was a line he wasn't prepared to cross. But why not watch his friend have sex? What was the harm in that? He knew that Marybeth was getting off on being watched. What was the harm in letting her put on a little show?

Turk realized that while his marriage to Sheila had many positive aspects, it had also made him a prude, a suburban soccer mom baking cookies for the church social. That wasn't who he was. He wasn't afraid of the dark side. He wasn't scared by sex. He liked sex. He wasn't Suzy-fucking-Homemaker; he was Turk-fuckin'-Henry from Metal Assassin. He was a rock star. This was his kind of scene.

Marybeth was moaning.

Wendy was gently running her hands over Marybeth's body, starting at her lips and gently brushing down her neck, around her breasts, over the nipples, across the belly, and down to her clitoris. Wendy leaned over and circled her tongue around Marybeth's nipples. Turk could see them stiffen, contracting at the touch of Wendy's wet lips.

Turk realized that he had never seen Marybeth naked. He had always thought of her as kind of chunky and unattractive, not the long and slender model type that he normally went out with. But he had to admit that seeing her like this—with her small and perky breasts, her wisp of black pubic hair, her round ass, and skin that looked soft and comforting—he realized that she was actually very sexy, voluptuous and sensual, not long and bony and hard like some women, like Sheila.

He couldn't help staring. It wasn't just the sex on display, either. Turk found himself fascinated by the contrast between Marybeth's soft white American body and Wendy's lithe brown Thai body. Where Marybeth seemed plush, Rubenesque, and luxuriant, Wendy's body was lean and supple. Marybeth's skin was pale, protected by late nights and sunscreen; Wendy's skin was rich and earthy, her nipples a dark mahogany, like Swiss chocolates. It occurred to Turk that their bodies accurately represented the countries and cultures they were from. Marybeth's was soft, privileged, fed on booze and fancy dinners in restaurants, and slathered in emollients to keep young and firm, the product of an easy American life. Wendy's was flexible, strong, resilient, browned by the tropical sun; it had all the qualities needed for survival.

Turk refilled his tequila and sipped it. He didn't want to get wasted; he just needed to do a little buzz maintenance.

He watched as Wendy began sucking on Marybeth's nipples in earnest. Marybeth arched her back in pleasure and flexed her feet reflexively as Wendy began to follow her tongue down Marybeth's torso, slowly licking her way between her legs.

Turk bit into another rambutan and was struck by the fact that neither woman had fake, phony, inflated, or enhanced breasts. They were both natural, the size of their tits in proportion to their bodies. As Turk watched Wendy eat Marybeth's pussy he realized that so many of the groupies he'd enjoyed over the years, those blond bimbos with their silicone-packed jugs, buns of steel, and teased hair, were actually kind of repulsive. They weren't women—not natural women, not like these two on the bed; they were some kind of freak show by-product of a sick society. A symptom of the American culture's deranged relationship to sex, to fantasy, and to desire. Why were all these women getting their boobs stuffed with plastic goo, their lips pumped full of collagen? Why did they all want to look the same? It was a perversion of the feminine form. Wendy and Marybeth couldn't have looked more different, and yet they were both extremely attractive. Sexy, vibrant, and alive.

It occurred to Turk that maybe he was part of the problem. Maybe it was the fact that those Barbie doll bimbos, the Playboy bunnies with the Godzilla-sized knockers, were exactly the kind of women he was always seen cavorting with. Maybe that sent the wrong message. Maybe he, Turk Henry, was part of the sick society that perpetuated the perversion.

Turk was jolted out of his reverie by Marybeth.

"Turk. Come fuck me."

Her voice was raspy, her breathing ragged.

"I need your cock in me. Now."

Wendy stopped slurping and looked at Turk.

"You know I can't do that, Marybeth."

"Please."

Turk laughed, embarrassed. "I would if I could. Believe me."

"I need your cock. Please."

Turk shook his head and looked to Wendy for help. Wendy smiled. "I have just the thing."

Turk watched as she reached under the bed and pulled out a box of sex toys. Wendy deftly took out a strap-on harness—a large black dildo jutting from the end of it—and buckled it on. She kneeled over Marybeth and rolled a condom down the dildo.

"I think you'll like this."

Marybeth looked and gasped. "Oh yeah."

Turk's pulse was pounding; sweat was sprouting off his forehead. He knocked back the shot of tequila he'd been nursing and poured himself another. Wendy squirted a handful of lubricant onto the dildo and then spread Marybeth's legs. Turk watched as Wendy expertly mounted and entered Marybeth. Marybeth groaned with pleasure, her back arching as she pressed her shoulders into the bed, and squealed. Turk thought he might have to stand up and jack off right then and there.

Wendy began fucking Marybeth in long smooth strokes, pushing the dildo deep into her. Marybeth looked at him.

"Turkey. Let me suck your cock."

Turk blinked. Although right here, right now, in this room in a brothel in Bangkok, Turk would've liked nothing better in the whole wide world than for Marybeth to suck his cock, he had to decline.

"Marybeth. I can't."

Marybeth wailed in frustration. "Please. Please. I won't tell."

Turk's head swam. Why did he put himself into this situation? *This was fucking torture.* His mouth went dry and his body trembled with desire.

"I wish I could."

"Let me suck your thumb."

Turk watched as Wendy began increasing the tempo. Marybeth's legs were up in the air, locked around Wendy's slim body.

"Please. Oh God, please."

Turk stood up and walked over. He took his thumb, parted Marybeth's moist lips, and tenderly slid the digit into her mouth. She immediately began sucking on it full force, like a turbo-charged hoover, as she bucked and groaned underneath Wendy.

The sexual energy being emitted by the two women was too much for Turk. As Marybeth began to have what could only be called a hurricane-force orgasm, Turk unzipped his pants, letting them drop around his ankles, pulled out his throbbing cock, and began stroking it. Marybeth groaned and gasped, but continued to suck on his thumb.

Turk closed his eyes. He was transported by the energy in the room. He could smell the two women—the perfume of their sweat, the juice of their vaginas. He could feel the heat coming off their coupling bodies, humid and animal and real. He could taste the tequila and rambutan in his mouth, delicious and exotic. And he could feel his hard cock in his hand, burning to trigger, stretching to shoot. He opened his eyes and looked over at Wendy and Marybeth. Both women were looking at him. Watching him as he stroked faster and faster, as if he were giving them applause, props for their fucking, a standing ovation for their performance. As Turk tensed and jerked, Marybeth reached over and delicately inserted a finger up his butt.

Turk shot a gob of come as his entire body spasmed. The semen hit the wall and stuck, slowly dripping down, a salty stalactite. Turk stood, holding his cock, looking at the wall, his body heaving, his mind vacant and clear. That's when it happened. A bolt of inspiration, a gift from the Muses.

For the first time since the band had broken up, Turk had an idea for a song.

...

He didn't remember how he got back to the Oriental Hotel. He remembered leaving the room alone—Marybeth wanting to spend another hour with Wendy—and going down to the bar. He remembered drinking beers with the two football hooligans. He remembered a young woman squatting under the table giving the Manchester United fan a blow job while they all sat around and sang Metal Assassin songs like nothing was happening. He remembered the dancers spinning on the bar, flicking their hips, flashing their breasts, smiling at him.

Turk lay in his bed like a shit-battered, deep-fried lump of jetsam. Booze sweat dripped off him, his head feeling like a churning cesspool of pain, guilt, fear, and frustration. He was backsliding, he realized that. It had started with the happy finish and it had picked up steam in that moist little room with Wendy and Marybeth. The excuses came to him, popping into his brain rapid-fire, one after another—the stress of Sheila's abduction, the strange sense of disconnectedness that had overwhelmed him since the band broke up, his *cycles of addiction,* the *catalytic environment*—but Turk didn't want to blame anyone or anything, didn't want to make excuses.

Maybe this is just who I am.

The hangover was more or less what he expected. It felt like an ice pick had been driven through his left eye to the exact center of his brain. It was nothing he couldn't deal with.

Turk sat up, feeling his blood pressure readjust, and hoisted himself into the bathroom. He patted his gut, and was surprised to feel it somewhat smaller than before. It was baffling.

With all the booze I've guzzled? How is that possible?

Maybe it had something to do with the food in Thailand. He'd eaten more rice and vegetables in the last week than he had in his entire life.

Turk took three Advil and drank an entire bottle of Evian before staggering back into bed. He was drifting off again when he remembered something from last night. Something wonderful had come out of all that debauchery. It was the song: raw and magnificent, with a bass line like a volcanic blues riff. The song was heavy. Like the songs of his youth, the music that got him excited about playing. Songs like Black Sabbath's "Ironman," Deep Purple's "Smoke on the Water," and Led Zeppelin's "Kashmir." Classic riffs that every teenage boy was desperate to master. Riffs that revealed the roots of rock, the core, the backbone. This was one of those.

An hour later the phone rang. It was Clive Muggleton of Lampard International Consulting. He needed to talk to Turk.

...

Ben sat in the lobby and watched as Turk ambled out of the elevator. *How could such a lumpy lard-ass be an international sex symbol?* Turk was greeted by Clive like they were old friends, lifelong conspirators. Ben watched as they walked out onto the terrace. He didn't need to follow them. He didn't have to get that close. He knew what Muggleton would say.

...

Dense, humid air rose off the Chao Phraya. Turk followed Clive outside and immediately began to breathe easier. It struck him as unusual. Normally he wouldn't venture outside on a hot day; he'd stay in his studio, with its cooled and filtered air. But there was something about the air in Bangkok. It surprised him, like the air was filled with soulful nutrients. It was as polluted as any air in the world, but there was something else to it, a life and vitality to the stench that was missing in the smoggy air of Los Angeles.

Clive turned to Turk. He smiled and began to act like they were having the most banal conversation in the world.

"Where's your lovely assistant?"

"What?"

Clive spoke in a ragged whisper. "Just play along."

Turk nodded and spoke louder than he normally would have, like he was doing a commercial for something. "We had a late night."

Clive nodded. "Occupational hazard in your line of work."

Turk ordered a coffee from the waitress. "Anything for you?"

Clive shook his head. Then spoke quietly. "I'm afraid I don't have good news."

Turk looked at him, alarmed. "Sheila?"

"No. I don't know anything about her. It's your government. They won't let me take your case."

"It's none of their business."

"They've made it their business."

"But you're Australian."

Clive nodded. He was Australian, and proud of it.

"My company does a lot of business with the U.S. military. Security and whatnot. They'll pull our contracts if we don't play by their rules."

Turk put his face in his hands and sighed. This was not making his hangover any better.

"What the fuck am I supposed to do? Leave my wife to rot in some godforsaken swamp?"

The coffee arrived. Clive looked around, professionally scanning the room. "Look, Mr. Henry. I think I can help."

"But you just said . . ."

"Ssshhh."

Clive lowered his voice. "Privately. Between you and me."

Turk suddenly felt better. "I see."

"Off the books."

"I thought you needed a tactical assault squad or something."

"This isn't about a rescue. You just need to pay the ransom."

"They won't let me."

Clive lowered his head. "We'll just have to work around that."

"What are you talking about?"

"You deliver the money and free your wife and I'll watch your back."

Turk thought about it. "I don't know if I can do it."

"Of course you can. Have a little confidence."

Clive flashed his white teeth and smiled; confidence practically oozed out of him. Turk stared at him. It occurred to him that he felt like throwing up. But it wasn't the coffee or the hangover; it was nerves. Deep down in his heart of hearts, Turk didn't think he was up to it.

"Isn't there someone we can call?"

"Sure, we can call other people. But your government will jump on them just as fast. Meanwhile your wife is out there."

Clive waved his hand to indicate the vast unknown world surrounding them. Turk sighed. A man can have fame, fortune, and a fashion model for a wife, and still life's not perfect.

"Shit."

Clive smiled, reached over, and patted Turk on the shoulder. "I'll be right behind you every step of the way."

Turk took a sip of coffee. He felt it burn its way down into his septic tank of a stomach.

"It's not like I have a fucking choice."

Fourteen

A forensic entomologist can tell how long a body's been rotting in a swamp by collecting the bugs—the insect eggs and larvae—living on the corpse, taking them back to the lab, and watching them hatch and develop. Insect lives are set on precise time lines, and trained scientists will recognize the difference between a teenage maggot and the newly hatched, thus enabling them to calculate a precise date of death.

The Thai policeman standing waist-deep in the muck of the mangrove swamp didn't bother to collect any bug larvae, he didn't worry about disturbing the evidence, he didn't wait for the crime scene investigators to come crawling around the swamp looking for forensic evidence the size of a mosquito penis. The body had been gnawed, nipped, sucked, and munched beyond recognition. It had turned into a bobbing luncheonette for all varieties of fish, crabs, and scavenging seagulls. It was host to a convention of bone-white maggots, skin-eating beetles, leeches, carnivorous wasps, and whatever else happened to be passing by looking for some kind of rotting carrion to do its thing on.

In fact the Thai policeman and his partner had considered just leaving the body to float where it was—who wanted to bag that thing?—until they found a U.S. passport in the floater's clothing. Now they'd have to do everything by the book; they'd be spending their afternoon doing paperwork, filing forms, and waiting for someone from the U.S. consulate to arrive.

Ben took the call on his cell phone. Roy, his assistant, had spoken to the Thai authorities in Phuket. Responding to an anonymous phone call, they'd found the body of the woman from Seattle floating in a mangrove swamp a few meters from a fancy resort. According to police on the scene, the body had been in the water for at least twenty-four hours. Ben thanked Roy and told him to book him a seat on the next available flight to Phuket. Then he hung up the phone and ground his teeth.

Too bad it wasn't Sheila.

He wished he'd been down there to manage the scene, control the flow of information, maybe fix things in his favor. He was encouraged by the fact that the kidnappers had killed the American woman. That meant they'd probably kill Sheila sooner or later. Too bad they didn't decapitate her, then it'd really look like terrorists were behind it.

Those extremists love to lop off the heads.

He thought about what to do next. Ben realized he needed to separate Turk from the Lampard security consultant as soon as possible. The last thing he wanted was for Turk to get a clue, gain competence, or take any useful advice. A blundering, clueless Turk was dangerous enough, but with a little coaching Turk might actually throw a wrench in Ben's plan.

Ben looked around the lobby of the Oriental Hotel. It was considered one of the best hotels in the world, first-class all the way. He'd never stayed in a hotel like this. It was a luxury that he couldn't afford on his salary. But a million dollars could fix that. With a million dollars in the bank he could stay anywhere he wanted. He could live in the Oriental Hotel. Move in and set himself up like a grand poobah.

Ben couldn't help himself—he smiled as he punched Turk's number into his cell phone.

. . .

Turk pounded on Marybeth's door. Why wasn't she answering? She was supposed to call him when she woke up, and it was almost noon. Turk pounded again—this time harder, with a little more urgency, suddenly feeling a sick sensation in his stomach as he flashed to the time Klaus Van Persie, his friend and the drummer in The Mountebank Conspiracy— they dressed up as seventeenth-century aristocracy and played a kind of orchestral arena rock with a flamboyant harpsichord- ist as their leader—hadn't answered his hotel room door. Hotel security was called, and Klaus was found dead, over- dosed in the bathtub. Turk could still see Klaus's body, pale and pruney, withered by drugs, wrinkled by the water; it was not something he wanted to remember.

Turk sighed with relief when he heard muffled footsteps in the room. He hit the door again.

"C'mon. It's me. Turk."

The door opened, and Wendy stuck her head out and smiled.

"*Sawadee krab.*"

Turk was momentarily thrown.

"Where's Marybeth?"

"In the shower."

"I need to talk to her. Now."

Wendy opened the door and Turk entered the room.

The room was murky—the curtains were still drawn—and Turk nearly fell on his face when he stumbled on an empty champagne bottle. Half-eaten plates of food, empty glasses, scattered clothing, an upturned chair . . . the room reminded Turk of the good old days, when Metal Assassin used to sweep through a hotel like a cross between the James gang and a plague of locusts. He turned to Wendy.

"You girls have a party?"

Wendy smiled. "A late breakfast."

Turk opened the bathroom door and saw Marybeth in the shower. She peeked out and blinked with surprise when she saw Turk.

"Turkey. Jump in and scrub my back."

Turk couldn't help himself—he blushed. Not that he wanted to get in the shower with Marybeth, but he felt embarrassed about last night's escapade in the brothel. Even though he hadn't had sex with either woman, his witnessing their sex, allowing her to suck his thumb, masturbating in front of them, it had been a kind of intimacy—a strange kind of intimacy—and now it was something they shared.

Turk looked at Marybeth. He didn't want to snap at her. He needed her support for the coming campaign.

"We've got to go. They found a body in Phuket."

. . .

Sheila slammed her shoulder against her ear. The buzzing stopped. *I'm getting good at this,* she realized. *How many people can kill mosquitoes while handcuffed?*

She leaned back against the wall, adjusted her legs to try and bring some circulation to her numb ass, and sighed. Sheila had missed her book group. Although she wasn't sure what day it was, or even what time it was halfway around the world in Los Angeles, she felt that tonight was probably her book group night and that right now they were all sitting around a table at Panzanella, drinking wine and eating ravioli while they discussed the latest book and shared their anxieties about their children's upcoming bar mitzvahs or SAT tests.

Sheila was surprised at how intensely she missed them. It's not like she socialized with them; they weren't part of the fashion business, they were just a group of women who met once a month to talk about books. They were all attractive and successful—publicists, lawyers, and agents; they were intelligent and self-assured women whom Sheila admired and looked up to. Fashion models aren't known for their brains, yet Sheila never felt intimidated or stupid around them. They accepted her. Even when she argued against reading another novel by Tolstoy, Balzac, or—God forbid—Amy Tan, even when she pleaded with them not to choose some massive nonfiction doorstop-of-a-book (really, did anybody care about Alexander Hamilton?), they didn't mind. Sheila would try to bring in some contemporary fiction, or new age stuff by Deepak Chopra, even a little chick lit. Why not? Shouldn't they have some fun? What's wrong with a little fluff?

Sheila wished she had a book to read now. Sitting, sweating, and swatting mosquitoes with her shoulders got old fast.

Where the hell was the Captain? And what had happened to Turk?

...

Something was wrong; Somporn could feel it. He sat in a bar nursing an orange soda—Green Spot—and watching BBC as the British couple described their harrowing experience in the jungle.

Somporn wondered how releasing the couple next to a girl bar on a tourist-filled street near Patong Beach in Phuket could suddenly become an inspirational story of survival and a triumph of the human spirit. Why didn't they say they were kidnapped? Why lie?

Obviously, someone in a position of authority wanted to keep the kidnapping quiet. But why? Had his kidnapping scheme been hijacked for some kind of political agenda? Was the Thai government worried news of kidnappings would scare away the tourists? Or was the U.S. somehow behind this? It wouldn't surprise him; Uncle Sam was always sticking his nose in places where it didn't belong. As far as Somporn was concerned, the whole war on terror was just an excuse for America to take over the world. He could see them using the tourist kidnapping as some kind of excuse for military or political intervention. Somporn felt insulted. He had no sympathy for terrorism of any kind; he was a criminal, and had no agenda beyond earning some quick cash. There was no profit in terror. He wouldn't waste his time building bombs, not when there was Pai Gow to be played, whiskey to be sipped, and pure alabaster skin to be stroked.

Somporn finished his soda and softly cursed. It suddenly occurred to him that maybe that was why he hadn't heard back from Sheila's husband. Maybe the U.S. government had gotten its hands on the rock star and fed him a bunch of bullshit. Maybe it was intercepting Somporn's messages to him. The Captain realized he'd have to be more discreet, more clever. He'd have to get a message to Turk Henry directly.

. . .

Clive Muggleton put his hand on Turk's shoulder. "You ready for this?"

Turk felt his knees shaking, his hands trembling. It was worse than any stage fright he'd ever had.

"We gotta do it. Right?"

Clive nodded. Marybeth gave Turk a smile. "It's not Sheila. I can tell."

"How can you tell?"

Marybeth shrugged. "It's a vibe I get."

A door opened at the end of the corridor and Ben stepped out with a thin Thai man wearing a white doctor's jacket with a name tag written in indecipherable Thai script. Ben and the doctor came toward them, their shoes clacking and echoing on the shiny linoleum. Clive leaned in to Turk and whispered in his ear, "That the ICE guy?"

Turk nodded. Ben approached Turk and extended his hand. "Mr. Henry. I'm so glad you could come on such short notice."

Turk couldn't help himself; his nerves caused him to blurt, "Is it Sheila?"

Ben shrugged, appearing as sympathetic as he possibly could.

"We were hoping you could tell us."

Turk's voice cracked. "Okay."

Ben looked at the doctor. "This is Dr. Phatharathaananunth."

Ben pronounced the Doctor's unpronounceable name; the doctor smiled, took off his glasses, and wiped them on the tail of his shirt before extending his hand to Turk. He smiled sympathetically to Turk and nodded as they shook hands.

"Thank you, Doctor."

Ben turned his attention to Clive, glaring at him. "Does your boss in London know you're here?"

Clive was not intimidated. He turned on his Aussie charm, his tan seeming to glow a deeper, richer brown as he flashed his gleaming white teeth. "I'm not here professionally. Turk an' me are old mates."

Ben decided not to pursue it. He turned to Marybeth.

"You might want to wait outside. This isn't going to be pretty."

Marybeth shook her head vigorously. There was no way Marybeth was going to miss out on seeing a real dead body. She loved horror movies. Halloween was her favorite holiday. She'd even gone to Oaxaca to see *Dia de los Muertos* celebrations. She had been into the whole Goth thing for a while, too, dressing up as one of the undead before going out to drop some ecstasy and dance all night in a club.

"I knew Sheila, too. I can help with the ID."

Marybeth liked the way she said that. It sounded professional. Ben just shrugged and turned to the Thai doctor.

"Let's proceed."

Turk, Marybeth, and Clive followed Ben and the doctor down the shiny hallway, through a door, and into the Phuket International Hospital morgue.

...

The morgue was cold and gray, lit by dim fluorescent lights. It looked just like a morgue on TV. Silver metal trays full of silver metal scalpels and saws, clamps, and forceps were placed on silver metal rolling carts. There were some pots and large spoons that looked like they had been stolen from a cafeteria. A digital scale sat nearby. There were several large drains cut into the tile floor. Turk was surprised to see a set of screwdrivers and a hammer.

They followed the doctor over to a wall fitted with a dozen small doors. The doctor opened one and, with some effort, slid a sheet-draped body out. Ben looked at Turk. He hoped that the sight of the corpse would scare the crap out of Turk and get him off the case.

"You ready for this?"

"Ready as I'll ever be."

Ben nodded to the doctor, and the doctor pulled back the sheet to reveal the bloated, rotting, insect-gobbled corpse of the woman from Seattle. Turk gasped.

"Fucking hell."

It was the single most disgusting thing he'd ever seen in his entire life. The skin had blackened gangrenous and foul in some places and yet was pale white in others. Festering holes pocked much of the body and the woman's face had been chewed off by something, bits of skull and jawbone poking through where the skin was gone. It was much worse than a dead drummer in a bathtub.

Just when Turk's brain had adjusted to seeing a shredded body, the smell hit him: a potent mix of deep jungle rot and antiseptics—nauseating and at the same time reassuringly medicinal, like roadkill sprayed with Bactine. It made him want to vomit. His body convulsed a little as he fought to keep from puking. Ben noticed this and smiled blandly.

"Take your time."

Turk swallowed and tried not to breathe. A bile-flavored burp rose in his throat. "What happened to her face?"

The doctor pointed to several gaps in the flesh. "Turtle. Maybe eel."

Marybeth, who'd been watching goggle-eyed, finally emitted a sound. "Ewww. A turtle?"

The doctor nodded again. "Maybe eel."

Marybeth thought about all the times she'd eaten eel at sushi bars; in fact, the broiled anago was one of her favorites. She suddenly felt very queasy. Turk looked at Ben.

"It's not Sheila."

Ben knew it wasn't Sheila, but the longer he kept Turk looking at the disgusting corpse, the bigger the psychological effect.

"Can you be certain?"

"Sheila wasn't fat."

"The body's been in the water for a long time. Bloating can give the appearance of weight."

"Maybe. But Sheila had a Brazilian wax. She would never let her pubic hair grow all over the place like that."

Turk turned to go.

"Are you absolutely positive?"

Turk turned and looked Ben right in the eye.

"I'm positive. This isn't Sheila."

Ben gave the doctor a nod, and the doctor covered up the body with the sheet. As Turk turned to leave he realized that he'd been holding hands with Marybeth the entire time.

. . .

Ben caught up with Turk in the hallway of the hospital. "Can we talk? Privately?"

Turk shook his head. He was growing to really dislike Ben. "We can talk right here."

Ben looked at Clive and Marybeth. "Okay. But you might not like what I'm going to say."

Turk interrupted him. "Have you heard anything from the kidnappers?"

"You know we don't negotiate with terrorists."

"That's not what I asked. Have you heard from them?"

Ben shook his head and grimaced. As if Turk was forcing him to reveal bad news in front of everyone.

"And I don't expect to, Mr. Henry. I hate to say this, but your wife's body is probably floating out in some swamp right now. We were lucky to have recovered this one."

Clive finally spoke. "How did you recover this one?"

Ben turned his attention to Clive. "Thai police got a tip."

"An anonymous tip?"

"You'd have to ask them."

"You didn't?"

Ben sighed. "Look, Mr. Muggleton, my job is to protect American interests and American citizens. The first thing

I wanted was to get Mr. Henry down here to help identify the body. I'm going to go interview the police next."

"Mind if we come with you?"

Ben scowled. "Yes. I do. This is government business."

Ben turned to Turk; he attempted a sympathetic expression.

"I know this is hard. But the longer she stays missing the less chance there is of getting her back. It's been almost a week. I think you've got to accept the fact that you may never see your wife again."

Turk glared at Ben.

"That doesn't mean she's dead."

...

Ben watched them walk out of the hospital. What a motley crew. The pudgy rock star waddling away in his black linen pants and oversized sunglasses; the strangely attractive woman who dressed like she was going to a punk rock show in a short skirt with leather Doc Martens, a motorcycle belt, and a ripped-up T-shirt that revealed her hot pink bra straps; and the overtanned Australian commando who smelled vaguely of gin. Ben was disappointed but not discouraged. He'd been hoping for something a little more dramatic. Like Turk's eyes rolling up in his head as he fainted and cracked his skull on the morgue floor. Or maybe Marybeth screaming and crying, hysterical at the sight of the moldy old carcass. They should've reacted—it was disgusting. It made Ben want to faint and puke and look away, and he was ex-military.

But he'd been pleased to see that Turk had gagged. Maybe that's all you could get out of a rock star. Who knew?

The important thing was that Turk had seen what the terrorists were capable of. The seed was planted. It wouldn't be long before Turk began to imagine his wife and her Brazilian wax floating in a swamp, being slowly devoured by turtles and bugs and seagulls and whatever else felt like grabbing a free slice of dead meat floating in the bay. Turk would imagine this, it would haunt him, and then he'd give up. He'd quit the chase, pack his bags, and go home. And Ben would be rich.

. . .

Carole Duchamp was not happy to see Turk and his entourage, but she was the general manager of the resort and had a responsibility to her guests, so she turned on her Gallic charm, managing to be gracious, and greeted Turk at the front desk with an exaggerated smile and promises to help him in any way she could. The resort had managed to rebound from the tsunami, but that was Mother Nature, just one of those things. Kidnappers and terrorists were different. The mere mention of the words struck fear into the hearts of Westerners, especially Americans.

Although the British couple's story got only minor play in the media, Carole rightly assumed that it was just a matter of time before some journalist figured out that something was amiss with the famous rock star and his wife. Adding celebrity to terrorism fears was like throwing fresh meat into a pool of piranhas, guaranteed to create a feeding frenzy of snapping paparazzi and sound-biting reporters, who would descend on the resort and strip it down to the bones in a day. It was not good for business. Carole hoped Turk would only stay for a day or two; then this whole unpleasant incident would blow over.

She handed Turk his room keys. "I hope you are able to resolve your situation as quickly as possible."

Turk thanked her and turned to Clive and Marybeth. "I need a drink. I'll be down by the beach."

Turk walked off, leaving Clive and Marybeth to finish checking in. Clive was immediately struck by the hotel managers' hazel eyes and flashed her his trademark smile.

...

Marybeth found Turk sitting on the end of a chaise longue digging his bare feet into the sand. He held a Singha in his hand and was sipping it distractedly as he stared out at the ocean. Marybeth had picked up a Singapore Sling at the poolside bar before heading out to find Turk. She sat down on the sand.

"It's pretty here."

Turk nodded.

"Quiet, too. I can see why you'd want to come."

Turk belched silently. "It wasn't my idea. I never wanted to come to Thailand."

"Why not?"

Turk shrugged. "I don't know. I guess I thought it was too tropical."

Marybeth laughed. "Too tropical?"

Turk smiled back. "What did I know?"

Marybeth looked out at the ocean and sipped her drink. It was sweet and sour, the gin providing the engine that cranked the cocktail to life, the cherry brandy and Cointreau combining with the lime and pineapple to create a kind of fantasy flavor. Like a tropical Popsicle.

Marybeth noticed all the topless women lounging around. "Is this a nude beach?"

"Nobody wears clothes here."

Marybeth peeled off her T-shirt and unhooked her bra. Her breasts tumbled into the air. Turk looked over at her; he couldn't help himself. He followed a bead of sweat as it rolled down her sternum between her breasts. Turk had to admit that they were lovely. Not too large, but perfectly shaped, with small pink nipples pierced by little silver studs with balls on each end. Funny, he hadn't noticed the piercings in the brothel.

"If it bothers you I'll put my shirt on."

"It doesn't bother me."

"It feels good to be naked. It's hot here."

Turk realized that he'd forgotten how hot it was. He'd grown accustomed to the heat and humidity, the constant trickle of sweat under his arms, the damp collar of his shirts. In fact, he realized, there was something calming about the heat. The spicy food, the muggy air, the scorching sun; it all kind of worked together somehow. Maybe that's what it meant to be tropical.

Marybeth looked at him. "What if you don't get her back?"

"I'll get her back."

"Yeah, but, I'm just saying, what if you don't?"

Turk looked at Marybeth. "I'll get her back."

Marybeth saw that Turk was not going to discuss any other possibility, so she picked up her cocktail and took a long sip. She noticed a young Thai boy walking toward them, waving to Turk. She wondered if she should cover herself.

"Beer, mister?"

Turk smiled at him. The boy's presence was reassuring. He pointed to Turk's almost empty beer.

"You want beer? Cold beer?"

Turk nodded and handed the boy a wad of baht.

"The coldest you've got. Hurry."

The boy smiled at Turk, then turned and sprinted off down the beach. Marybeth was impressed.

"He brings you beer?"

"He doesn't mess around."

Marybeth smiled as she watched the boy run to the end of the beach and hand his parents the money.

"You should take him on tour."

Turk looked at her. "If I ever go on the road again, maybe I will."

Marybeth sipped her drink. "You'll be back on the road in no time. Jon's got plans for you. Don't you worry."

It suddenly occurred to Turk that, even with the new song in his head, he wasn't sure he ever wanted to go on tour or be in a band again. Maybe it would be okay to just sit here on the beach drinking beer for the rest of his life. Why not? Maybe that was enough. No more happy finishes, no more strangely intimate scenes in Bangkok brothels, no more worrying about the band, the fans, his wife, the business. No more stress. No more guilt. Just a beach and beer.

As if to confirm Turk's newfound belief that he was sitting in the best of all possible worlds, the boy arrived with Turk's beer, ice cold.

...

Captain Somporn came back to camp and went directly to the little hut where Sheila was kept. He felt bad leaving her handcuffed and alone for so long, but it served a psychological purpose: it gave her a reality check and reminded her that she was not the one in control of the situation. He wanted her to appreciate the special attention she received.

Somporn entered the hut. Sheila glared at him.

"Where the fuck have you been?"

Somporn didn't react to her anger. It was, after all, entirely natural given the circumstances.

"I apologize. I had some business in town."

"Collecting ransoms?"

"I have been trying to contact your husband."

"What's the problem? Call the hotel."

"It's not that simple. I believe the authorities may be monitoring his phone."

Sheila hung her head in frustration. "Maybe he's checked out."

Somporn shrugged. "It would be easier if he had a mobile phone."

"He doesn't like them."

"My men will locate him. It is only a matter of time."

Sheila looked at Somporn, a bitter expression on her lips. "He's not hard to find. Just look for a fat ass with long hair and a beer in his hand."

Somporn looked at Sheila. She really was beautiful. Even with her hair matted by sweat and her skin dirty and damp, even with her bad mood, she was lovely.

"Would you like to take a shower and have something to eat?"

Sheila nodded. "I'd love to."

Captain Somporn knelt down and tenderly unlocked her handcuffs.

...

Turk sat back in the chaise longue and looked up at the sky. Coconut palms caught the ocean breeze and wiggled overhead in slow motion. Turk wondered what it would be like if Sheila was dead. He'd hardly even had time to get used to being married, and now he was potentially a widower.

He hadn't known that many people who'd died. Sure, he was a friend of Bon Scott's, the AC/DC singer who drowned in his own vomit in a parked car—the one time seat belts didn't save lives—and of course there were Klaus Van Persie and a few others who'd died of drug overdoses. But he'd never lost a girlfriend or a sibling or a parent.

If Sheila was dead, what did that mean? Did he have to have a funeral? A wake? Should he call a florist?

Turk wondered if Sheila's death would change him. Would he be different? Older and wiser? Would her death be meaningless? Would he just go on partying and carrying on, using the tragedy to propel more willing young women into his water bed? Or would it be cathartic and give him insight into the deeper meaning of life? He didn't know the answer. He figured that, if she was dead, he'd find out. But he didn't think it would change him that much. He already wore black.

...

As Sheila undressed, Captain Somporn handed her a bottle of hair conditioner. "I got this for you."

Sheila smiled and pulled her shirt off. By way of thanking him, she unhooked her bra with a flourish. She turned and silently teased him, like a stripper, before taking the conditioner from him, tugging her panties to the floor—despite repeated wearings, the lace was holding up surprisingly well—and with her left foot, flicking them across the room.

Somporn smiled and walked over to the bed. He sat cross-legged on the floor and carefully poured himself a glass of whiskey before lighting a cigarette. He looked up at her expectantly, waiting for the show to begin.

Sheila was suddenly hit by a pang of guilt. Why was she enjoying herself? Here she was, a prisoner, forced to strip and shower in front of some kind of perverted Thai pirate, and yet she found it exhilarating. She liked it. She was getting aroused by her own performance. Maybe it was having such an appreciative audience. He was so focused and sincere in his admiration of her body. He was sweet and caring and respectful, and that made her feel good about herself. And feeling good about herself turned her on. She discovered she liked having an audience; she needed to be adored. Maybe that's why she'd become a model in the first place.

That's the great thing about traveling. You can learn a lot about yourself.

. . .

Somporn sat back and let the whiskey work its magic on his tired muscles. He felt his shoulders relax more and more with each sip. He watched as Sheila unhooked the clamp on the hose and water began to fall gently on her body. He watched her breasts, so white that he could easily see the bluish veins under her skin, the nipples a vibrant pink—like the snapper he used to catch. He waited for her to turn, to see the translucent white skin of her ass. As Sheila turned in the shower—taking her time, teasing—a shock went through his body; he felt a primal energy rise inside him. It was pure, unadulterated desire.

...

Sheila took her time. She soaped up her body, letting the bubbles build into a thick lather, rubbing herself all over. She was hamming it up. Not that the soap and water didn't feel good, but she was touching herself, exaggerating, putting on a show for the Captain. It almost made her laugh out loud; here she was like some actress in a soft-porn movie. *Emmanuelle 15: Thai Prisoner.* It was kind of campy, but it was fun, and she knew the Captain would appreciate it. She looked over at him to see what his reaction was and saw the unmistakable outline of a raging hard-on in his shorts.

Sheila smiled and looked at Somporn. She turned to face him, in all her full frontal nudity.

"Enjoying yourself?"

She pointed at his crotch and smiled. Somporn instantly knew what she meant. He looked down and saw how aroused he was. He'd been so caught up in watching her that he hadn't even noticed his erection. Now that it was the center of attention it was difficult to ignore.

Somporn stood up, with some difficulty, and handed her a towel.

"Dry yourself, please."

He turned and left the hut as quickly as he could.

Once outside he slipped on his flip-flops and moved toward the jungle with quick, agitated steps. It had gotten dark, night falling with a velvet thud, and the moonless sky was bright with stars. Somporn walked about ten feet into the dense foliage, the trees a deep black against the already black sky, and stopped. He listened for a moment, to insects buzzing and chattering, frogs croaking, birds screeching, bats swooping through the air with sonar peeps, the cacophony punctuated by an occasional howl from monkeys mating. Sure that he was alone, swallowed by the black forest, he pulled down his shorts and quickly jerked off into the night.

...

Turk didn't remember how many beers he'd had. Ten? Twenty? A hundred? No, if he'd had a hundred he'd be really drunk. As it was he just felt kinda smashed. Not shitfaced, not three-sheets-to-the-wind, but definitely polluted. He strolled along the beach, chasing the little crabs back into the surf in a kind of stumbly-stagger, occasionally roaring and belching at the scurrying crustaceans, like a drunken tiger with a tranquilizer dart in his ass.

Turk had left Marybeth and Clive at the seaside buffet, Clive working his way through a third bottle of white wine and desperately trying to get Marybeth to go to bed with him. To her credit, she'd shown no interest. Yet Clive was undeterred, letting the Chardonnay wage a war of attrition on her morals and aesthetics until, he hoped, she'd be ready to hump a giant sea cucumber.

Turk laughed out loud. Poor Clive, working his ass off for a piece of tail. That was the best part about being a rock star. You never had to work too hard to get laid.

Turk reached his beachside cabana and stood on the porch looking at the water. He gripped the railing for balance as he swayed in the soft breeze coming off the bay. The cabana was new, a replacement for one that had been yanked off its foundation and dragged out to sea by the tsunami. A couple on their honeymoon had been asleep at the time. Turk shook his head and muttered to himself, "Poor fuckers."

He was almost ready to feel something like a kind of beer-goggle empathy when he realized that it might not be such a bad way to go after all. Everyone wants to die in their sleep with their loved ones near.

He opened the door to the cabana and stopped. Hadn't he locked it when he left? With his beer-impaired memory Turk couldn't be sure, but any fear he might've had was shoved aside by an urgent need to piss. He pushed the door open and flicked on the light before making a beeline to the toilet. He decided he should say something to scare off any potential intruders, and opted for a cheery greeting in the kind of mock singsong voice popular with actors in situation comedies.

"Honey, I'm home."

He walked quickly into the bathroom and stood swaying over the toilet, fumbling with the string on his pants.

"Sorry I'm late. There was a meeting at the lodge."

Turk pulled out his penis and recycled the beer into the basin.

"I may go bowling with Fred tomorrow."

He chuckled at his joke, tears of relief swelling in his eyes, as he squeezed out the last couple of squirts and shook the lingering drops from his dick.

"Maybe you can have bridge night with your girlfriends."

Turk flushed the toilet and walked into the room.

He noticed it right away: a white envelope with his name written on it. Turk opened it and read the short note.

This is a last opportunity to save your wife. We want one million American dollars. You have one day to get the money and then we will contact you. Do not contact the authorities. We are watching.

He read it several times, the bad penmanship of the author and the beers he'd consumed conspiring to make certain parts of it blur and blend like an optical illusion. But Turk knew what it meant: Sheila was alive. He reached for the phone and then stopped. Clive had told him not to use the phone, that it was probably bugged. Everything had to be done discreetly.

Turk burst out of his cabana and jogged down the beach toward the restaurant. He had to show the note to Clive and Marybeth.

...

When Somporn, visibly relieved, came back to the hut, Sheila was wrapped in a towel, sitting on the bed and drinking a glass of whiskey. Somporn couldn't be sure, but it looked like she'd been crying.

She looked up at him. "Did I do something wrong?"

Somporn shook his head. How could he explain his reaction to her? He strongly desired her, it was true, and knew he would love to have sex with her. But he was a disciplined professional criminal and a Buddhist. As a criminal he knew that Thai laws looked at kidnapping one way—carrying a brief prison term—while rape was considered a capital crime and carried the death penalty. The sex between them might be consensual here in the jungle, but once free—and with DNA evidence still on her body—she might have an entirely different story.

As a Buddhist, despite violating all Five Precepts in this lifetime, Somporn realized that the desire he felt rising in him was an emotional response that he could control. He could sever his desire for Sheila with mental discipline—while still realizing the truth behind it—and keep himself from acting impulsively.

"No. You are fine."

"But why did you leave? Don't you like me?"

There was something sad about the way she said it, as if she had been lonely her entire life. It broke Somporn's heart to hear her sound that way. He sat down on the bed next to her and lit a cigarette.

"I like you. Very much."

He exhaled a plume of smoke and reached for the whiskey bottle. He unscrewed the cap and poured a little of the amber liquor into her glass before filling his halfway. He took a sip of the whiskey, as usual loving the way the flavor of the alcohol mixed with the smoke of the cigarettes; it tasted earthy and strong.

"Hand me the oil. You must keep your skin moist."

Without saying a word, Sheila removed the towel and lay naked on the bed as Captain Somporn began to slowly and tenderly rub sweet oil on her body.

...

Marybeth sat back in her chair and watched as Clive goggled his head around and leaned in toward her, flashing his irritatingly white teeth that looked like a theater marquee.

"Listen. What's a bloke got to do to get you to go to bed with him?"

The teeth flashed again; a blinding semaphore smile. Marybeth considered the question. If she thought about her history and answered honestly, she would say, *"Be famous."* But now things had changed; if she were really going to tell the truth, she would say, *"Be Wendy."* She chose to be coy instead of honest.

"I take it on a case-by-case basis."

Clive grinned even wider.

"Allow me to present some evidence to prove my claim."

Marybeth hoped he wasn't going to unzip his pants, but before he could do a thing Turk came racing over to them, sweating profusely and gasping for breath. Marybeth jumped up and moved toward him.

"Oh my God! Turk, are you okay?"

Turk gulped air and nodded.

"Sheila."

He waved the piece of paper in the air. Clive instinctively took command of the situation. "Mr. Henry. Sit."

Clive signaled the waiter. "We need some water over here."

Turk nodded, catching his breath. "And a beer."

While Marybeth used her napkin to mop the sweat from Turk's face, Clive took the piece of paper from Turk's hand and held it up to a candle to read it. Marybeth watched him.

"What is it?"

Clive smiled.

"They've made contact."

...

Ben, neatly disguised with a Yankees baseball cap and a fake mustache, sat on the far side of the beach restaurant. He was about to dig into a second blue crab with chili sauce when he saw Turk running up. Obviously—when had anyone ever seen Turk run?—the kidnappers had made contact. Ben considered taking the million dollars and leaving. Just go on the lam. But he'd need a fake passport, a new name, all the stuff you need when you go underground, and he didn't have the criminal connections for that kind of thing. Besides, he liked being Ben Harding. He didn't want to adopt a new identity and live in Amsterdam. He wanted to go to his twentieth high school reunion and see all his friends, he wanted to visit his parents over the holidays, he wanted to collect on his veteran's benefits. He didn't want a new life. He just wanted to be Ben Harding, millionaire.

But it looked like Turk Henry had other ideas. He just wouldn't give up. You'd think threats of rendition and getting up close and personal with a rotting carcass would be enough to put someone off. But Turk didn't seem fazed by it. He was stubborn. Ben adjusted his baseball cap and watched as Turk talked animatedly with Clive and Marybeth. Perhaps he'd underestimated him.

Ben realized he'd need a plan. The simplest one is usually the best. That's what Ben had learned repairing helicopters, that's what they taught him at the Land Rover customer service seminar, and that's what ICE had preached as well. The simplest plan was to get Turk Henry dead.

As Ben watched Clive shifting into his rescue and recovery expert mode, he realized something. If the terrorists were in touch with Turk, they'd still expect a ransom, and Turk wouldn't be able to get his money back from Ben without exposing himself to arrest. That meant Turk would have to go to the bank and get another million dollars. Ben rubbed his hands together. If he could somehow get Turk parted from that, he'd have two million dollars. And as everyone knows, two million dollars is twice as good as one million dollars.

. . .

Jon Heidegger sipped his glass of wine and looked across the table at his lunch companion, a young A&R guy from Planetary Records. The kid was hip, decked out in baggy pants and a pink Ramones T-shirt under a retro-plaid shirt from Penguin that he left unbuttoned and hanging open. It was the look: sloppy but cool, the features of his face hidden by manicured muttonchops and thick black eyeglass frames peeking out from under a swoop of brown bangs. The kid went by the name Jethro—no last name—and was a real rising star in the business.

The waiter, a handsome and gregarious Italian named Gino, came over and asked Jethro if he'd like a glass of wine.

"Uh. Arnold Palmer? Do you have that here?"

Gino nodded. Heidegger shook his head sadly. That was it, wasn't it? The end of civilization personified by a half-iced tea, half-lemonade monstrosity that everyone in Los Angeles drank for lunch. Heidegger remembered—and he wasn't even that old—when lunches began with a cocktail—a cold martini, a gimlet, a tangy margarita—before giving way to a bottle of wine. If you felt a little drowsy after lunch you'd just open your desk drawer, pull out your little mirror and razor blade, and hoover up a couple lines before your next meeting. Nowadays if you had a glass of wine—a single glass—people looked at you like you had a drinking problem.

That was the trouble with the music business. The film business, too. It wasn't about the lifestyle anymore, it was about sales. Creativity didn't matter; mediocrity was what sold, and mediocrity was easy to market, so mediocrity was what they pumped out. The world was no longer controlled by content providers—the musicians and songwriters—but by marketing teams and focus groups. If you asked a dozen random people plucked out of a shopping mall in Tarzana what kind of music they liked, well, you'd get Britney Spears, 'N Sync, Menudo, or some other lip-synching variation wearing Daisy Dukes and a see-through halter top.

Heidegger hoped it was just a cycle—like a moon wobble —just a phase the world was going through. At the end of the day, shit is shit no matter how pretty the packaging.

You can't polish a turd.

Heidegger knew this to be true, and he was banking on it. He and his team had been snapping up as many of the most outrageous, idiosyncratic, and just plain weird acts as they could find. Heidegger was banking on rebellion, stockpiling bands for the backlash against corporate sludge and vacuous sex doll pop. He remembered the Sex Pistols. It was only a matter of time before people fought back, dumped vodka in their Arnold Palmers and started breaking furniture, if for no other reason than they were bored stiff.

Jethro dipped some bread into a little saucer of olive oil. "So what's this about Metal Assassin? They getting back together?"

"They're still exploring their solo projects. That's what I wanted to talk to you about."

"Who?"

"Turk."

Jethro rolled his eyes. "Sweet Jesus. The bass player? Are you kidding me?"

"He's got a lot of songs."

Jethro shook his head. "A solo album from a bass player. That's such a loser move, man."

Heidegger sipped his wine and looked at Jethro. "Sting is a bass player, as I recall."

Jethro looked skeptical. "I don't know, man."

Heidegger pressed him. "You got the bass player from the biggest heavy metal group in history. Right? That's going to guarantee you go gold."

"Yeah. Some metal heads might buy it. But what about John Q. Public? Do people even know who he is?"

A plate of figs stuffed with Gorgonzola arrived. Heidegger leaned forward.

"When people hear about his wife's kidnapping and his desperate attempt to rescue her from the hands of terrorists in Thailand, everyone will know who he is."

Jethro's expression changed. "You're fucking kidding me."

Heidegger shook his head. "It's happening right now."

. . .

Roy guided his scooter through the morning rush hour and arrived at the U.S. Embassy on Wireless Road only fifteen minutes late for work. He didn't think it would matter; his boss hadn't been in the office for days, and no one else would notice. What was it with these Americans and their mania for punctuality? Roy was running late because he'd been out drinking with some friends the night before and had stopped on his way to work at a little Chinese restaurant for some pork congee to cure his hangover. The soupy rice porridge with shreds of roast pig and dollops of red-hot chili sauce had, temporarily, done the trick. While he didn't exactly have a spring in his step, he was upright, and the pounding headache and queasy churning in his stomach had subsided.

Roy clipped his ID badge onto his shirt and walked up to the security checkpoint. He emptied his keys, his belt, his wristwatch, and a gold ring into a little dish and then crossed through the metal detectors. He went to the staff room and swiped his ID badge through a digital reader. An LED readout announced the time. *Computerized time cards—very un-Thai.*

He entered his office and flicked on the lights. The air-conditioning was already cranking at maximum; he felt like he worked in a giant refrigerator. Roy checked his messages and was alarmed to discover there were already three from his boss.

He immediately picked up the phone and dialed Ben's cell phone number.

"Where have you been?"

"I had an errand to perform."

Ben paused. Maybe Roy had been running an errand for someone on staff. Better not to make a big deal of it.

"Well, I've got another one for you. Ready?"

"Ready."

"This is all black, understand? Don't tell anyone anything. Just do it."

"Okay."

"I need a tactical kit, a light one, sent down here ASAP."

"Shall I liaise with the *Thahan Prahan?*"

Ben shook his head in dismay. *Thahan Prahan* translated roughly as "Hunter Soldiers," and the last thing he wanted was a squad of Thailand's elite trigger-happy special ops commandos running amok in Phuket.

"No. Don't liaise anything through anybody. Just send it to me."

"That's against the protocols."

"I know it is. That's why it's black."

There was a pause on the line.

"Should I check with the Defense Attaché Office?"

"Roy. This isn't a Defense Department operation. Black means black, and this is totally black, understand?"

There was another pause on the line, then Roy spoke.

"Is now a good time to talk to you about getting a higher grade of pay?"

Ben sighed. "Would you like a vacation to go with it?"

"I have always wanted to go to San Francisco."

Sarcasm never worked on the Thais. They just didn't get it. Ben took a breath, tried to control his temper.

"Okay. I'll get you a raise. Now send me the fucking pack."

...

The plan, so far, was pretty simple. Clive had brought a secure satellite phone with him and Marybeth used it to call

Heidegger in Los Angeles. Heidegger was expecting something like this and had the million bucks ready to go. He agreed to wire it to the bank in Phuket, but not before telling her to tell Turk that a deal had been struck with Planetary Records for a solo album and that Turk needed to call him as soon as he could to work out the particulars.

The record deal took Turk by surprise. On the one hand it was good, because he had a new song, but on the other hand he was right in the middle of a hostage negotiation. Couldn't it wait?

With the cash on the way, Marybeth needed to go into town and buy a wheelie suitcase large enough to hold the money. Clive decided he would accompany her as some kind of security guard just in case something happened; it was a lot of money to be dragging around unprotected. Clive tried to reassure Turk and Marybeth by showing them the .9mm handgun that he had stuck in a belt holster underneath his garish Hawaiian shirt, but the reality of the gun just made Turk nauseous.

All of this was discussed as they strolled on the beach, Turk and Clive walking their hangovers off. Clive told them that from now on they would operate on what he called "radio silence": no phones, not even cell phones; no conversations in any of the rooms. In fact, the less they talked about it the better. They should assume someone—either the kidnappers or ICE—was watching them at all times.

Turk was happy to see that Clive was taking charge, organizing and strategizing, and that Marybeth was taking it seriously, and not fucking around.

...

Marybeth walked down the main street of Hat Patong, the tourist-packed beach town a short drive from the pricier resort where they were staying. Clive hurried to keep up, trying to match her determined stride. They were looking for a luggage store, or at least a shop that sold luggage. But Marybeth couldn't help herself, she was distracted by the scene. There were hundreds of tourists, mostly middle-aged Caucasian men wearing cargo shorts and polo shirts, sporting sunburned noses and clutching beers, milling around the street. Marybeth saw that most of the storefronts were bordellos masquerading as beer halls, with dozens of bar girls hanging around—some dancing languidly to disco music in the afternoon heat, others sitting with customers in booths. Only the occasional T-shirt shop, and a surf store selling condoms from Japan, interrupted the wall-to-wall emporiums of beer and sex.

Marybeth saw Clive's eyes lingering on a young bar girl in a white bikini top. The girl shifted on her bar stool, crossing one leg over another, and stared back at Clive with a frank, mercantile gaze. Marybeth tugged on Clive's arm. "You can come back later."

Clive grinned at her. "Believe me, I will."

Seeing the bar girls, Marybeth realized that she missed Wendy. She'd taken Wendy's cell phone number but hadn't called her. She wanted to, but she had been afraid. *What was there to be afraid of?* Marybeth didn't know why she was hesitant. What was so scary? Wendy was a whore. Big deal. Did that make her a bad person? Not at all. In fact, Marybeth had never met a nicer, sweeter, more generous person in her life. And she was easily the best lover Marybeth had ever had. When she compared her slow, sensual tumble between the sheets with Wendy to her experiences with all those long-haired rocker dudes whose leather pants she'd yanked down and whose cocks she'd sucked; when she thought about all the times she'd taken it doggie style on a tour bus; when she recalled all those sweat-drenched quickies backstage before an encore . . . well, there wasn't really a comparison. Marybeth realized she'd had sex with at least two hundred men and that never once had it been about her pleasure. She was always working to get the men off—it was a one-way street, a sexual cul-de-sac. But with Wendy it was different; it was a two-way street. Or, more accurately, it was like one of those round-abouts they have in Europe, where traffic enters from dozens of directions and mixes and blends as it circles.

Marybeth hadn't experienced many epiphanies in her life, but now, out of the blue, she realized what she was afraid of. She was afraid she was falling in love with Wendy. If she was in love with Wendy, didn't that mean she was gay? How could she explain this to her friends? Was she really a lesbian? Or was it just Wendy? Or was it the fact that Wendy was a prostitute? Was that the appeal? A kind of rock and roll bad boy danger thing? What was she afraid of? Didn't they make movies about guys who fall in love with whores? Wasn't that like a standard Hollywood thing?

They stopped in front of a sundries store, the kind that had clothes and hats, sunscreen and sandals, backpacks and a few suitcases.

"Here we are. You go ahead and pick it out. I'll be right back."

Marybeth watched as Clive turned and headed back toward the girl in the white bikini top. She shook her head. "Thanks for watching my back, asshole."

Neither of them noticed Ben, dressed as a tourist, window-shopping in the street behind them.

...

The bar girl in the white bikini knew what she was doing. She'd seen Clive ogling her as he walked by and had made eye contact with him. Although she was only sixteen, she'd been a bar girl for three years and was well practiced—like an expert fisherman—in the art of baiting a hook. She knew he'd taken the bait, but she didn't make a move, just sat there patiently. The worst thing was to appear overeager. She didn't want to spook her prey; she'd wait for Clive to take enough line, to look back at her as he walked down the street, then she'd set the hook and he'd reel himself in. The bar girl in the white bikini understood that men, like fish, were not particularly complicated animals.

For Clive it was a different experience altogether. It was like she saw into his soul and found his weakness, his craving. Somehow she'd managed to touch something inside him, to flick a switch that kicked his desire into action. Clive couldn't resist her—he had to have her or be had by her; it was an unstoppable urge.

Clive entered the bar and smiled at the girl in the white bikini. He asked if she'd like to join him for a drink. Although the outcome of their encounter—quick and sweaty sex on a rickety cot in a tiny back room—was guaranteed, there was still an etiquette to follow, the protocols of sex for sale.

Clive and the bar girl settled into a booth in the back. He ordered a double Belvedere vodka and Pepsi for himself, a glass of champagne—that he was sure was ginger ale—for her. Then he slipped his hand under her white bikini top and began to caress her breast.

...

People always say that you can't put a price on a human life; that a human being is something sacred, mysterious, and more precious than anything else in the world. But Ben could put a price on it: one million dollars a head. That seemed fair and reasonable to him. Not too cheap—nothing insulting—but not out of reach for a man who'd suddenly found himself a near beneficiary of two million bucks. Ben realized that he needed to get Turk alone, mano a mano, if he had a chance of snatching the second million. But that would have to wait. First things first, and first he needed to kill Turk's adviser.

Ben sipped a beer at the bar and watched out of the corner of his eye as Clive fondled the bar girl. Several other bar girls approached Ben. Although they were slender and attractive, Ben wasn't interested. He chatted with them, non-committal, a shopper, until they got bored and went off after easier customers.

Ben watched as Clive gave the telltale signal that he was going upstairs: he drained his glass and stood. Even from across the room, Ben could see that he was aroused. The bar girl in the white bikini took Clive by the hand and led him through a door in the back. Ben watched them go; he'd wait until they were in the middle of it, then he'd make his move.

Not that he knew what move to make. He wasn't a trained killer. He remembered some basic hand-to-hand combat techniques from boot camp, but it wasn't like he'd ever had to use them. He'd never even been in a fistfight. Ben wished his tactical kit had arrived; then he could just shoot the fucker. That would be easy, decisive. But it wasn't here yet, so Ben would have to improvise; he'd have to be careful, because Clive was ex-military, and wouldn't go down easy if he could help it. Ben knew he'd have to take Clive at his most vulnerable, when he least expected it. That would be his edge, his only chance.

Ben finished his beer and asked the bartender where the bathroom was. The bartender pointed toward the back door, the same one Clive and the bar girl had used. Ben sauntered back, walking slowly. Unless Clive was a premature ejaculator, he had time. When he crossed through the back door he saw a short hallway, with a bathroom on the right and a flight of steps leading upstairs on the left. Ben walked up the stairs as quietly and casually as he could.

At the top of the stairs, he stopped and listened. There were six rooms, three on each side, running down a narrow hallway. Ben could hear a German man grunting and muttering at the first door, his guttural "ya, ya" growing ever-louder and more emphatic. Ben peeked through the crack in the doorframe and saw a massive pink-skinned man being straddled by a tiny brown Thai woman. The girl looked like a tattoo on the big man's body.

Ben heard someone speaking English across the hall and crept over to see a young American man, probably seventeen, banging away on an equally young girl. He moved toward the end of the hall. He suddenly heard Clive's Australian accent coming from behind a door. He heard him say, "Ride the baloney pony, baby." That's when he stopped feeling bad about killing Clive.

...

Clive was beginning to feel slightly gypped. Sure, the bar girl in the white bikini was alluring and beautiful; her expansive smile and the naughty twinkle in her dark eyes were almost as arousing as her tight body and beautiful young ass. But once money had changed hands and the white bikini had come off, her dazzling smile, the flirtatious twinkle, the salacious licking of her lips all vanished. She'd sucked his cock with all the interest and enthusiasm of someone peeling a pile of potatoes. Now she was on top of him, bouncing up and down with a minimum of effort and a distant, distracted look in her eye like she wished there was something good on TV. Every now and then she would say something encouraging like "You're so big! I hope it doesn't hurt my tight Asian pussy." Or, "You make me feel so good!" But she didn't say it with any passion; there was no gusto or verve in her performance at all. She sounded like the recorded voice outside of airports warning about parking in restricted zones.

...

Ben waited outside the door. He wasn't sure exactly what he was waiting for, but he hoped he'd know it when he saw it. He watched as Clive flipped her over and mounted her, holding himself over her with his arms extended, thrusting toward climax.

Ben moved quickly. Clive was moaning. The bar girl's eyes were closed; she'd seen the faces of too many orgasming *farangs* to bother watching another. As Clive's body shuddered, Ben entered the room and crept up behind him. He wrapped his right arm around Clive's head and then twisted as hard as he could. Clive grunted and flailed, instinctively reaching for Ben's arm. Ben wrenched harder and was surprised to hear a distinct, sickening snap. His neck broken, Clive went limp and dropped forward onto the bar girl, pinning her to the bed. For her part, she just thought the *farang* was a freak with a violent spasm, and didn't bother opening her eyes.

Ben walked out of the room, down the steps, and through the back door of the bar.

...

Sheila stood in the shower and shivered. A storm was building out at sea, thunderheads looming, turning the sky into a boiling black. The breeze blowing in off the ocean was cool and she felt goose bumps erupt across her arms and legs, felt her nipples contract into hard little nubs. Somporn came up to her and handed her a towel.

"It's too cold."

Somporn stood close to her, his eyes studying her body. "You should dry yourself."

Sheila could smell the fresh cigarette on his breath. Somporn turned his gaze from her pallid breasts to her face. Their eyes met and held until Sheila felt herself blush. She looked down at the floor.

She took the towel from him and began to dry off. "Thank you."

Somporn walked back and sat on the bed. They had slept there last night, but nothing had happened. The Captain had wrapped himself around her—she had felt his erection pulsing gently against her thigh—and held her as he fell asleep. Sheila had lain awake feeling very confused. When was the last time a man with an erection had lain next to her and done nothing? Had it ever happened? Even once? Sheila wondered—and not for the first time, plagued as she was by a fashion model's insecurities—if something was wrong with her.

She didn't bother wrapping the towel around her. She dried her hair and looked at Somporn.

"Do you want to have sex with me?"

The cigarette dropped out of Somporn's mouth.

"What?"

"Do you want to have sex with me? You can. If you want to."

Somporn retrieved his cigarette and shook his head. "I don't think that's a good idea."

Sheila walked over and sat next to him on the bed. "You want to. Don't you?"

"I will not lie. You are a beautiful woman. But you are also my hostage."

Sheila looked him in the eye, her tongue automatically flicking out and moistening her lips.

"That's right. I'm your prisoner—you can do whatever you want with me."

Somporn hesitated for a second, then stood up from the bed, his pants tenting up in the crotch, and moved away from her.

"Please understand that this is a business. I am not a dishonest criminal."

Sheila shifted on the bed so that her legs were slightly spread, just enough to give Somporn a view of her pussy.

"I won't tell."

Somporn focused his mind; he saw desire—grasping, at its most primal level—arising inside him. He recognized the emotion for what it was, respected its power while maintaining his discipline, his mental strength. Sometimes it paid to be a Buddhist.

"Your husband is paying a lot for your safe return. I'm sure he'd like you unused."

Sheila blinked. She realized she hadn't thought of Turk in what seemed like weeks.

"He fucks other people all the time. He won't care. And I won't tell him."

Somporn dropped his cigarette on the floor and ground it out with a bare foot.

"It won't be long now."

He turned and walked out of the hut.

. . .

Ben was in the shower. Scalding water turned his skin red as he scrubbed his body with antiseptic soap, trying to disinfect himself, desperate to wash off the taint of seedy brothels, broken necks, and infected whores. He was interrupted by an insistent knocking at the door. For a brief, horrible second, he thought it might be the police, and he was visibly relieved when he opened the door to reveal a courier with his special package. Ben signed for it and closed the door without a word. He probably should've tipped the courier, but he didn't; he wasn't in the mood for generosity or magnanimity or even common courtesy.

He put the box down on the bed and ripped it open. Inside was a small tactical kit; a lightweight nylon shoulder harness with a Smith & Wesson M&P .9mm handgun and four extra clips, a tactical ballistic vest, camouflage pants and jacket, waterproof boots, a pair of small binoculars, night vision goggles, a belt stuffed with a GPS positioning device, handcuffs and pepper spray, and an M67 fragmentation-type hand grenade.

Ben found a note from Roy. It read:

Boss,

Ops wouldn't let me take a rifle or shotgun. Use hand grenade in emergency only. I promised to return it.

P.S. Don't forget about my raise!

Ben sat on the bed and loaded the handgun. He suddenly wished he'd put in some extra hours at the range. He hadn't planned on having to get close to Turk to kill him.

...

It was almost one o'clock in the morning Los Angeles time when the call came through. The weird thing, the part that Heidegger still couldn't wrap his mind around, was that it was early afternoon of the same day in Thailand. Just how did the international date line work? It was easier to understand wormholes and time matrix nebulae on a *Star Trek* episode.

He was glad to get the call. He'd been waiting for it, sitting up in bed nursing a tumbler of aged reposado tequila—the honey-colored liquor tasting of prickly pear, caramel, and smoke—and listening to Lou Reed's early '70s classic *Transformer*. It was a vinyl album, a large thin black plastic disc that was pulled from a cardboard jacket and played on something called a turntable. Heidegger had over three thousand vinyl albums, his collection alphabetized and displayed in several classic Eames shelving units—and not reproductions; originals —along one wall of his bedroom. He preferred the sound of vinyl. Some people said it had a warmth that CDs and MP3s didn't, and Heidegger agreed. To his ears the music just sounded better. He liked the hiss and pops as the needle rolled along the grooves. For some strange reason he found it comforting. It gave the sterile, digital world a human patina.

Like the way the original antique furniture was better than the new knockoffs. It was something that had been lived in. The nicks, scratches, and scuff marks, the sun-faded fabrics made him feel like he wasn't alone in the world. They were signs of life, evidence of existence. Someone sat on this fifty years ago, I'm sitting on it now, and in another fifty years someone else will be sitting on it. It was evidence of the continuity of life, and he liked that. He was old-school that way.

Heidegger spoke to the bank manager in Phuket, who politely informed him that the money had been collected and asked if there was anything else he could do to help. Heidegger thanked the manager and hung up, then dialed Takako Mitsuzake in Tokyo.

Takako had been the Japanese publicist for Metal Assassin for years, and Jon knew her well. He'd already spoken to her about how to handle the news of Sheila's kidnapping. Takako had suggested they wait until the last minute, avoiding the media frenzy the news would generate, and then she would dispatch a journalist and photographer to Phuket, giving them the scoop of a lifetime. Heidegger gave her a quick update, telling her that the money was on the move; Turk would probably be making the drop very soon.

The last minute had arrived.

...

The storm had passed, blowing across the island in less than an hour. Marybeth avoided the rain while counting money in the bank. She took an air-conditioned cab back to the hotel, watching wisps of steam rise off the boiling pavement, the air somehow even hotter after the cool rain.

When she entered the hotel, Marybeth felt like she was in a scene from a Doris Day/Rock Hudson movie. She was Doris Day, of course, pulling her suitcase across the floor of the hotel lobby, a swing in her step, a song in her heart, and a smile on her face.

The reason she felt like Doris Day had more to do with the suitcase she'd bought than the million dollars inside it. With Clive disappearing for a quick fuck with the bar girl, Marybeth had been left to choose between several suitcases. There were the black ones—too conspicuously serious, she thought, almost broadcasting the money inside. There were a couple covered in bright Hawaiian hibiscus patterns that announced themselves with a gaudy fluorescence. They were a bit much; not quite rock star enough for the mission at hand.

Eventually she discovered the perfect suitcase buried under a pile of sham Hello Kitty gear and a stack of counterfeit Louis Vuitton Murakami purses.

Covered in a psychedelic pattern of happy-face cartoon daisies, it was perfectly incognito—who would carry a million dollars in something so ridiculous?—and yet still kind of groovy. Best of all, it made her feel like she was a perky '60s movie star when she pulled it through the hotel lobby.

She found Turk sitting out by the beach, a cold beer in front of him, his legs kicked up on a chaise longue, snoring under a palm frond *palapa*. The afternoon showers hadn't seemed to disturb him.

"Turk. Turkey. C'mon."

Marybeth gently shook him awake. Turk pulled off his sunglasses and looked at her.

"Hey. You get everything?"

Marybeth patted the suitcase. "No problem."

Turk saw the suitcase and sat up. "What the fuck is that?"

"You don't like it?"

Turk had to think about it. "It's not that I don't like it. I do. But, is it appropriate?"

Marybeth nodded. "Totally."

Turk looked around. "Where's Clive?"

"He'll be back soon. He had to stop and drop a load in a bar girl."

Turk shook his head. "That's all anyone does around here. The whole country's just about fucking and getting massages. And the massages are a lot like fucking."

Turk sat back on the chaise. "Paradise. Really."

She laughed. "So the bag's okay?"

"Peachy."

She reached over and took a swig of his beer. "You're in a good mood."

"I'm just trying to be cheerful instead of freaking out."

"You won't freak out."

Turk shrugged. "We'll find out soon enough."

Marybeth sat down and put her arm around him. She gave him a reassuring kiss on the cheek. They sat there like that for a moment.

"What're you going to do after?"

"After what?"

"After you get Sheila back."

Turk turned and looked at Marybeth. "She's my wife."

Marybeth pulled her arm away from Turk, but she kept looking at him. "I know that."

"Honestly, Marybeth, I don't know what I'm going to do about anything. I really don't. I'm just a bass player."

There was no bitterness in Turk's voice. He was happy to be a bass player. Marybeth smiled at him and said, "You're a great bass player."

The boy came running up to Turk and Marybeth, sand flying. He pulled an envelope out of his shorts and handed it to Turk. "This for you, mister."

Turk took the envelope, his hand shaking. "Who gave it to you?"

The boy shrugged. "You want beer, mister?"

Turk stared at the envelope. He didn't want to open it. He looked at the boy. "Bring two."

Turk reached into his pocket and handed the boy a hundred baht. The boy turned and took off running. Marybeth looked at Turk.

"Is it from them?"

"Has to be."

Turk still didn't open it. He sat there, trembling.

"They might be watching. You should probably open it."

Turk heaved a sigh. "I need a beer."

He stared out at the horizon, watching soft waves whisper in off the Andaman Sea.

"Hard to believe that they had a tsunami here."

Marybeth was impatient. "You want me to open it?"

...

Captain Somporn realized he wasn't dealing with the brightest bulb on the planet, so he had made his instructions to Turk as simple as possible. An inflatable boat with a motor and a GPS positioning device was going to be waiting for Turk on the beach near the hotel at four o'clock. He was supposed to use the GPS and drive the boat about twelve miles north to a secluded cove surrounded by mangroves. There he would find a date palm with a red bandanna tied on the trunk. He would leave the suitcase with the money next to the tree and return to the hotel. Once the money was counted, Sheila would be released in town.

The only tricky part, Somporn knew, was navigating through the overgrown mangroves without getting lost. The GPS should lead him to the spot without any problems. But if he took too long it would get dark. This complicated the drop—and Turk's safe return to the resort—but it gave Somporn and his men some protection. If Turk had gone to the Thai police, any sea or air support they might muster would be useless at night.

Somporn hoped Turk would follow the plan and not try anything clever. He'd hate to have to kill Sheila.

...

Ben sat in a chair on the beach, watching Turk and Marybeth read the message from the terrorists. He had a beach bag next to him, his waterproof boots, fatigues, gear, gun, and grenade all tucked inside and covered by a towel and a tube of sunscreen.

A topless woman—judging from her straight blond hair and perfect teeth she was probably Norwegian—came strolling by. Ben's eyes followed her briefly, before he reminded himself of his mission. He turned back toward Turk and Marybeth. He could hang out with topless Norwegians when he was a millionaire.

...

Turk looked at Marybeth. "I'm hungry. Feel like lunch?"

Marybeth shook her head. "I'm going to take a shower. I'm stinky."

Turk stood up. "That's just part of your charm. I'll meet you back here at three-thirty. If you see Clive, tell him what the deal is."

Marybeth gave him a reassuring smile. "Okey dokey."

Turk turned and walked up the stairs, toward the restaurant on the terrace overlooking the pool. Uncharacteristically, he didn't bother looking at the dozen or so topless women arrayed around the pool like a Nordic smorgasbord.

He *waied* to the Thai hostess and she dutifully led him to a table. It was a nice table, with a view of the pool and the ocean beyond it, the hard cobalt of the sky and the shifting azure of the ocean contrasting and blending, all framed by coconut palms and dotted by fluffy white clouds and topless Scandinavians. Turk had barely had time to look at the menu when Ben Harding walked up to him.

"Mr. Henry. May I join you?"

Turk nodded. "Any news? Or do you want to show me another dead body?"

Ben tried not to snap. "I'm sorry if I upset you, Mr. Henry. But nobody ever said fighting terrorism was pleasant."

"You keep saying they're terrorists."

"I think the statements the other hostages made were conclusive."

"What do you mean? They said they were lost in the woods."

"That, as you might have guessed, was what we wanted the world to hear. Trust me, their debriefing was conclusive about the fact that, whether you like it or not, we're dealing with an international terrorist organization."

Turk didn't respond.

"But we haven't stopped working. We're exhausting all the possibilities. My team in Bangkok has been on it twenty-four-seven."

He looked Turk right in the eye, using a technique they'd taught him in interrogation class. Ben was hoping Turk would confide in him, tell him what the plan was, give him some kind of inkling about when things were going to go down. It was difficult to do a round-the-clock surveillance without a team of operatives covering from a variety of angles. Any little hint—a time, a place, a tiny tidbit of information—would make it that much easier for Ben to follow Turk and kill him.

"How about you? Any word? Have the terrorists tried to contact you?"

Turk felt the message from the kidnappers burning a hole in his pants pocket. He wondered why Ben was so curious about the terrorists all of a sudden. He hadn't bothered to ask before. Did it mean that he knew what was going on?

The last thing Turk wanted was more interference from the U.S. government.

"Nope. Not a peep."

Ben could tell by the way Turk's pupils dilated when he answered the question that he was lying. Not that he needed any more confirmation than what he'd already witnessed. A waitress came over and Turk ordered a papaya stuffed with blue crab salad and green mango.

"Hungry?"

Ben shook his head. "I've got a lot of work to do. Trying to get your wife back."

"You told me she was probably floating in the bay."

Ben looked a little sheepish, like a kid caught lying. "I— honestly, Mr. Henry, I don't know. We don't know. Anything is possible at this point."

"You made me go to a morgue."

"I needed you to ID a body. I'm sorry—I know it wasn't pleasant, but it was necessary. Just like it would be necessary for you to tell me if the terrorists contact you, as I'm positive they will, if they haven't already."

Turk felt a surge of conflicting emotions jolt through his body. He wanted to laugh at Ben and at the same time he wanted to pile-drive his fist into Ben's soft pink face. He looked down and saw that his right hand was clenched in a tight fist, the knuckles white. He shook it off. It wouldn't do any good to punch the guy. Probably end up in Siberia or Romania, or worse, with a lawsuit to settle and an unflattering mention in *People* magazine. Turk took a breath. He thought about his therapist. Keep cool. Breathe. Try and detach from the urge. Don't let your emotions push you to do something you'd regret later, like strangling the ICE asshole sitting across the table from you. Turk finally spoke, measuring his words carefully.

"I appreciate your concern. If any terrorist tries to contact me, you'll be the first to know."

"This isn't easy for anyone, Mr. Henry."

Turk nodded. It wasn't easy. It wasn't easy to keep from telling this guy to go fuck himself, despite the consequences of whatever the Patriot Act might bring.

"What about my money?"

Ben felt a shudder run through his body. He'd grown so used to thinking of the money as his that he felt a sudden shock of jealousy. Ben had been hoping that Turk would forget about the money. Wouldn't that be easiest? Couldn't Turk just give him the money?

"Your money?"

"Yeah, remember? The million bucks you impounded?"

"Oh." Ben nodded. "Don't worry. It's safe."

"You've got it?"

"ICE has it."

"Well, how could I pay the terrorists if you've got the money?"

Ben sighed. "Mr. Henry. We're not stupid. We know that you've got resources. Don't mess with the United States government."

Turk couldn't help himself—he laughed in his face. "Go fuck yourself."

Ben bristled. "What?"

"Fuck off."

That wasn't how you talk to the authorities. Maybe you could tell a Land Rover customer service rep to fuck off, maybe you could even tell a helicopter repairman that. But that's not what you say to America's first line of defense. No one tells them to fuck off. It isn't patriotic.

"I understand that you're under considerable stress, but I don't think that's the way to talk to someone who is trying to resolve your case."

Turk considered that. "You're right. It's probably not the way to talk to someone like you. But I can't help it. So, fuck off."

Ben looked at Turk. The conversation was, apparently, over. Ben stood up. "You'll regret that."

Turk didn't blink. "I doubt it."

...

Marybeth didn't shower right away. She sat on the bed in her little bungalow, picked up her cell phone, and called Wendy in Bangkok. Marybeth wasn't sure what she'd say to Wendy. What *was* there to say? Did Wendy feel the same way about her? Or was Wendy just a really superb hooker who fulfilled her client's fantasies? But Marybeth had felt a connection. It wasn't just sexual, it was bigger than that—big, fresh, unfamiliar, and unsettling. Marybeth didn't know what it was exactly that she was feeling, but whatever it was, it was there. Living and breathing and growing inside her.

Wendy answered, and when her voice came on the line, Marybeth hesitated. For a split second she considered hanging up the phone and never calling again.

Just hit "delete."

Falling in love is a scary thing, especially when it packs a surprise, suggests something you'd never imagined about yourself, like maybe you could be in love with a prostitute from Bangkok. But the sound of Wendy's voice made Marybeth's heart leap.

"Hey. It's me."

"Marybeth. I was hoping you'd call."

That did it. Marybeth was overwhelmed by the wave of genuine affection and excitement she felt coming through the phone.

"I said I would."

"I'm glad you did."

"Can you come down here? Please? It's not that far and I'll pay for your ticket."

"Are you all right?"

"I just wish you were here."

Marybeth couldn't believe what she was saying, but she couldn't stop herself, it just came out of her in a big sloppy blurt.

"I think I'm in love with you."

There was a pause on the line. Marybeth cringed. She couldn't believe she'd just said that; maybe she'd blown it. But it was exactly what Wendy was hoping to hear.

"I'll see you tomorrow."

. . .

Wendy hung up her phone and smiled. She had just received the phone call that every prostitute dreams about. A rich American was in love with her. Of course, normally it was some middle-aged man, lonely and desperate for some companionship, who would take the lucky girl back to Michigan or some other exotic place and marry her. Wendy didn't mind that a woman was in love with her. She took it as a compliment. Besides, sex was sex, it didn't really matter who it was with as long as it put food on the table. Wendy was practical that way. Although she had to admit that she enjoyed having sex with Marybeth. Usually she had no feeling about it one way or the other.

She went to the window in her tiny apartment and looked out at the jumbled-up architecture of the city. Power lines were strung along the alleyway next to her building like spaghetti, and several small stores spilled out below them. There was constant noise from the traffic and the small motorcycle repair shop, smells of charcoal and grilling meat from the *satay* stand, and the almost nonstop blare of Thai pop music from the little kiosk on the corner. For someone who worked nights and tried to sleep during the day, it was far from ideal. She realized, with a wry smile, that she wouldn't miss this view.

Wendy opened the door of her armoire and looked at her clothes. She didn't have a lot. She'd come to the city with just a change of clothes and, except for the see-through dresses she wore when she worked at the club, she had added only a few blouses and slacks. Hanging in the back of the armoire Wendy saw the yellow and orange silk dress she'd worn for her first performance at the Ram Thai Academy.

She'd come from the provinces; her parents raised ducks by a small lake surrounded by rice fields. They lived near the ruins of Sukhothai, a massive city that had risen amidst the rolling hills in the thirteenth century. The ruins were a popular tourist destination, and Wendy had been plucked from school at a young age to learn the intricacies of *khon,* the traditional Thai dance. Wendy was graceful and athletic and she enjoyed learning the postures, steps, and hand gestures. By the time she was eleven she was one of the lead dancers performing at the *Loy Krathong,* the festival to mark the end of the rainy season and the beginning of the rice harvest.

A teacher at the academy in Bangkok had seen her perform at the *Loy Krathong* and offered her a scholarship.

But life in Bangkok was hard and there were not a lot of jobs available, even for a graduate of the academy and a gifted *khon* dancer, and it was only a few years before she began working as a go-go dancer in nightclubs and bars along Soi Cowboy. One thing led to another, as it almost always does, and Wendy soon found herself employed as a very successful, highly paid prostitute.

She was ready for a change.

...

Fuck ICE. Fuck Homeland Security. That's right.

Turk found himself shaking with anger as he tried to finish his lunch. All this time he'd played it cool, tried to be a reasonable, helpful guy, and then the ICE man cometh, getting up in his face, trying to sweat him. *Fuck him.*

Turk flagged down the waitress and ordered a beer. He needed something to calm his pounding heart. Something to distract his brain from all the fucking bullshit he'd been putting up with since Sheila disappeared.

The beer arrived and Turk downed it in a couple greedy guzzles. He nodded for another. Did the ICE agent know that the kidnappers had contacted him? Or was he just fishing?

Turk replayed the scene in his head. He couldn't help but smile when he got to the part where he told the guy to fuck off. *That felt good.* He wished he'd told Steve to fuck off when Steve was pissing and moaning about how the band wasn't fulfilling his "artistic vision." He wished he'd told Bruno to fuck off when he said that Turk had to play the bass a certain way. Maybe the band would still be together if he hadn't let them walk all over him. Maybe they'd still be together if he'd just told them to fuck off every now and then. At least they would've treated him with a little more respect.

In fact, the more he thought about it the more Turk realized that he should've been telling people to fuck off for years. Maybe even his whole life. Like the high school football coach who told him he couldn't be on the team unless he cut his hair. That guy deserved it. But instead of telling the coach to fuck off, Turk cut his hair and watched pathetically as Carrie Parsley—the girl with the best tits in the eleventh grade—dumped him for a guy with long hair and a motorcycle. Turk had never really had a steady girlfriend since then. If he'd told the coach to fuck off, maybe he'd still be with Carrie Parsley. Or maybe he would've told her to fuck off, too. Once you get the ball rolling, well, who knows who you'll tell to fuck off. Turk realized that the power of saying "fuck off" had a dark side, a side that found you beaten to death or locked up in jail. As with all powerful things, the "fuck off" had to be used responsibly.

But if he had employed these magic words a few times in his life he wouldn't have been stepped on, used as a doormat; the guy in the back playing the bass who let everyone else make the big decisions and get all the fame and glory. Not that Turk didn't have some fame and glory, but nothing like Steve and Bruno's.

Turk let out a long, low, crab-scented belch, and the riff came to him. An insistent low rumble tumbling through his head, the bass line for another new song. There were lyrics, too: a story of standing up and empowering yourself. He'd call it: "Fuck the Man in Charge."

Turk realized that the song would never be played on the radio, and that they'd have to sticker the CD with "Parental Advisory" labels, but it made him want to stand up and sing at the top of his lungs.

"Fuck the man in charge! Come on!"

Fifteen

TOKYO

Takako Mitsuzake spoke quickly into her cell phone.

"Gotta go. My flight's boarding."

She snapped the phone shut and handed her boarding pass to the flight attendant. She was lucky to be on the flight—first-class to Phuket, with a brief layover in Bangkok.

She sat by the window, her tiny body almost getting lost in the first-class chair, and went through the list of editors and reporters she'd put together and stored on her Treo. She was excited, energized. It was a juicy story; there'd already been a couple of deaths related to the kidnapping—bodies abandoned by a shopping center, floating in a swamp—and nothing sells like a mix of celebrity, murder, and terrorism. News of this magnitude had to be handled carefully—let's face it, it wasn't every day that the supermodel wife of a rock star was kidnapped, much less rescued by that same rock star. She wanted to maximize the exposure but at the same time control it. It wouldn't be any good to anyone if the news landed on the back page of some random newspaper. She didn't want Reuters or the Associated Press to put the story out over the wire. This had to be placed on the front cover of *US Weekly,*

People, Rolling Stone, and any number of other glossy magazines. That would be the initial wave. Then feature stories in the serious media. Maybe an exclusive interview with *Vanity Fair.* Lastly, when interest had ebbed, she'd leak private photos to select Web sites around the world. She'd already contracted a photographer she knew from Singapore—he did fashion shoots for *Hong Kong Vogue* and slick publications in Tokyo—and he was meeting her in Phuket.

Takako kicked off her Prada shoes and settled in for a long, boring flight. It'd take her eight hours to get to Phuket. She hoped she'd make it in time to be there to art-direct the exclusive photographs.

· · ·

Heidegger stood in line in the Bradley Terminal at LAX. He was waiting in the Royal Orchid first-class queue and was a little annoyed that it wasn't moving more quickly. I mean, what's the point of coughing up the money to be a Royal Orchid if you aren't given every possible shortcut? He could see what the problem was: a young couple going on their honeymoon, holding hands and smooching at the Thai Airlines ticket counter like no one else in the world existed. Young love fresh out of the can and on display for everyone to see. They were a real "you complete me" pair. A perfect union of perfect-for-each-other people untainted by the ill winds of life and commerce and ego and aging. How could you get mad at them for being in love? Heidegger was no psychic, but he was a cynic, and he could see the future for this wonderful couple. The first few years of happiness, then the difficulties, the monogamy fatigue, followed by betrayals, disappointments, the accusations and reprisals all culminating in the inexorable, inevitable divorce. That's why he didn't say anything. He didn't clear his throat or look at his watch or give off any sign of impatience, letting them enjoy the moment. It might be all they got.

Going to Thailand was the last thing Heidegger wanted to do. He was up to his ass in alligators, so to speak, with several deals to close, the planning of Rocketside's big summer tour to promote its new CD, photo shoots to supervise, demos to listen to. Flying halfway around the world was low on his list of priorities. But Takako had told him he needed to be there. He would be the person she'd steer the press to for quotes; neither one of them was willing to trust Turk to actually sound coherent or intelligent on the subject of international terrorism, kidnappings, and the rescue of his beloved wife. So Heidegger had thrown a swimsuit and a casual outfit—khakis and a vintage Hawaiian shirt—along with some underwear and sandals into a small carry-on and here he was at the airport, standing in line for his Royal Orchid seat.

...

The boat was waiting, just like the note said. It was small, just one seat, and made out of some kind of inflatable plastic. It looked, basically, like a life raft with a small motor. The word ZODIAC was painted on the front. A small plastic bag containing instructions and a battery-powered GPS was duct-taped to the seat. There was a plastic paddle, a life jacket, and an outboard motor. Turk and Marybeth stood there, looking at it like it was some kind of alien spacecraft.

"Have you ever driven a boat?"

"When I was fourteen."

"Maybe I should go with you."

"I'm supposed to go alone. Besides, do you know how to drive a boat?"

Marybeth shook her head. "No. But how hard can it be?"

Turk flicked on the GPS and it beeped to life, the coordinates preprogrammed in. "I guess I just drive to that dot."

Turk looked at the tiny device in his hand. Drive a boat to some dot? He was baffled, lost, in over his head. Why couldn't the kidnappers just show up and take the cash? What was their problem? "I wish Clive were here."

Marybeth gave him a pat on the back. "C'mon, Turkey, you've played live at Budokan, you've headlined Madison Square Garden—you can drive a stupid boat."

Turk wasn't so sure if the experiences were comparable, but he nodded in agreement. "The show must go on."

. . .

Ben had thought he was prepared. But as he watched Turk and Marybeth standing next to an inflatable boat he realized that he hadn't planned for an exchange at sea. Ben sauntered over to the resort's lifeguard station, where several hard plastic canoes and kayaks sat on the sand next to a pile of Styrofoam boogie boards and a couple of Sea-Doo Jet Skis. Flashing his badge didn't impress the lifeguard, but five thousand baht did the trick, and Ben quickly put the Jet Ski into the water, started it up, and roared off toward open ocean with a little salty geyser of seawater spewing up behind him.

Driving the Sea-Doo turned out to be a lot of fun. Ben thought it would be cool to buy a pair. He'd get a little trailer to pull them behind the new Cadillac Escalade he was planning to purchase. He'd take them to the beach, maybe meet some cool chick who'd want to go ride around on the waves with him. That was the great thing about Sea-Doos—girls wore bikinis when they rode on them. Maybe he'd even pack a picnic lunch. They could find a deserted beach somewhere, park their Sea-Doos, eat some shrimp cocktails, and drink some champagne. Then, well, who knows what could happen.

Ben was jolted out of his daydream when he hit his first real wave. Outside the protection of the cove, driving became a little trickier. He almost crashed, and worse, his tactical kit disguised as a beach bag almost fell overboard. Ben slowed down and regained control of the Sea-Doo. He couldn't help himself. He smiled.

These things are fun!

When he was far enough out that he didn't think anyone could see him, Ben quickly changed clothes. He put on his tactical camouflage and holstered the handgun. He let the binoculars dangle from his neck and stuffed the other equipment into a small backpack that he strapped on tightly. As a last touch he clipped the grenade to the backpack strap.

He let the Sea-Doo idle as he bobbed in the waves. He focused the binoculars and scanned the shore. Sure enough, he saw Marybeth wheeling the psychedelic daisy suitcase toward Turk. Ben was impressed. The suitcase wasn't small; in fact, it looked a little bigger than the other one. *Maybe the ransom went up. Maybe there's more than a million dollars in it.*

Ben smiled to himself. Now all he had to do was wait and hope that no one noticed a lone gunman wearing jungle camouflage sitting on a bright yellow Sea-Doo in the middle of the ocean.

...

Sheila wasn't used to rejection. Not from men, anyway. But despite her advances, the Captain had rejected her—and really, had anyone ever said no to that move where she bit her lower lip and spread her legs slightly? Now Somporn was off doing something, preparing for the exchange, the ambush, the getaway, whatever task it was that kidnappers did. He was too busy to spend time with her and had lunch delivered by one of his men. Sheila had thought about seducing that guy just to show Somporn what he was missing, but it was the guy who'd stolen her Chanel sunglasses and there was no way she was gonna fuck him.

So she ate her rice with dried shrimp, chilis, and some kind of green leafy vegetable and thought about Turk. She wasn't looking forward to seeing him. For one thing, after paying her ransom he'd have her on the hook; he'd want sexual favors for the rest of her life. Favors she didn't feel like providing anymore. For Sheila, the thrill was gone.

Their marriage had been forged in rehab; they'd bonded in recovery, a two-person support network. But she wasn't addicted anymore, was she? She didn't need grams of coke or to be Mrs. Rock Star. She was over that. Now she wanted to take care of herself. She sure as hell didn't want to take care of Turk. Turk was a baby. A forty-five-year-old baby wrapped in black leather and tattoos, driven by infantile needs and childish desires. When he wanted sex he was like a toddler begging for a piece of candy. He wouldn't stop whining or trying to make her feel guilty until she let him get on her and get it over with. She shuddered, thinking of the gratitude he'd demand for rescuing her. She wasn't grateful. She hadn't been mistreated or abused. If anything, she'd learned more about herself in the last few days then she had in twelve years of therapy.

She considered escaping. Let Somporn send his men out searching frantically through the jungle. That would get his attention. He would lose his hostage and the chance to collect what she assumed was a healthy ransom. Would he be so cavalier then? Would he regret snubbing her? But the more she thought about it, the more she realized that it wasn't going to work. How could she escape? She didn't have a plan. She didn't know where she was or which way to go. And after all the pampering and coconut oil treatments her skin was looking really lovely. Why go slogging through a hot swamp and ruin her complexion? Not to mention all the bug bites she'd get.

Sheila suddenly realized the she wouldn't be escaping for the purpose of getting free; she'd be escaping for the pleasure of being caught. Discovered and chased, tackled and hog-tied. Maybe he'd even spank her for trying to get away. Sheila felt a jolt of adrenaline, a little shiver of erotic delight, run through her body and then—she couldn't help herself—she smiled.

When did I become so kinky?

...

Turk hefted the suitcase into the inflatable boat and bent over to roll up his pants legs. He was wearing flip-flops; they were waterproof, but he wanted to keep his pants dry. He was going to be uncomfortable enough driving the little boat. Satisfied that his pants were secure above his knees—his legs a pale pinkish beige, like raw chicken—Turk pushed the boat out into the water.

"Need a hand?"

"I got it."

Marybeth handed him a paper bag from the hotel.

"Some bottled water and a sandwich."

Turk took the bag and looked at Marybeth. He didn't really know what to say to her, but he was genuinely touched by her thoughtfulness. "Thanks."

It hadn't even occurred to him that he might need some food or water for the trip. He wondered what else he might've forgotten. Marybeth smiled.

"And a beer. You know. For emergencies."

Turk smiled back. "You think of everything."

Marybeth nodded. Turk looked at her. He was nervous, hesitant. "Well . . ."

He turned and looked out at the open ocean, then down to the beeping GPS in his hand. Marybeth couldn't take it. She ran out into the water and gave Turk a hug.

"You be careful, Turkey."

She held on to him for a long time.

...

Ben watched from his Sea-Doo. He saw Turk and Marybeth embracing in the water for what seemed like ten minutes. How long was this going to take? Wasn't this guy supposed to be married? But maybe that was the way rock stars did it: a wife, a mistress, assorted groupies and hookers.

It rankled him, to be honest; having all those women seemed well, unpatriotic. America was built on values, things like family and freedom and justice, things that were important. That's what the country stood for. If Turk Henry was not a family values kind of guy that meant he wasn't a red-blooded American. If he wasn't an American, then perhaps he was an enemy of America. Ben remembered something the president had said.

You're either for freedom and American values or you're on the side of the terrorists.

If Turk was a terrorist then Ben was just doing his duty. Killing terrorists was his job.

Ben was getting antsy; it seemed like he'd been bobbing out here for hours and he was now in some pain. He had brought some food with him but when he tried to eat his sandwich it attracted the attention of a flock of seagulls. They were brazen, swooping down on him and snatching half the sandwich out of his hand before he could even get it up to his mouth. The birds hovered around him, cawing and squawking, trying to land on his head, on the Sea-Doo, swooping down to snag his food. Ben worried that the birds were attracting unwanted attention, so he'd maced one of the little marauders with a blast of pepper spray. The bird had fallen into the water, splashing and flailing wildly for a few minutes until it drowned and sank like a rock. Unfortunately, some of the pepper spray had blown back into Ben's face, his eyes stinging like a motherfucker, and the flailing of the bird had, apparently, attracted some kind of large shark that was now circling the Sea-Doo.

. . .

Turk gave the cord a firm yank—just like starting a lawn mower—and the engine roared to life. He gave a wave to Marybeth—she blew him a kiss—and twisted the throttle. The little Zodiac jerked forward, moving across the bay toward the ocean and a little blinking dot on the GPS screen.

. . .

Ben looked through his binoculars with his one good eye— the one not swollen shut from the pepper spray—and watched as Turk left the cove. He would follow, staying as far behind as possible, until he was sure no one was around. Then he would make his move. Ben wiped the stream of tears from his good eye with the sleeve of his camouflage T-shirt and goosed the throttle. Even though the air stung his tender eyes, it was good to be moving. Ben wanted to get away from the shark.

. . .

Captain Somporn's cell phone rang. Somewhat perversely, he'd downloaded a Metal Assassin ringtone, and a digital approximation of "Drop in the Bucket" began chirping from his pocket. He checked the number and answered. The news he got was good. Turk had left in the boat, alone, and with a suitcase. Somporn ended the phone call and checked the time. He figured it would take Turk two hours to get to the GPS drop.

Somporn entered the hut and found Sheila sulking on the bed, a glass of whiskey in her hand. She glanced over at him and gave him a sneer.

"Well, well, well. Look who's returned to the scene of the crime."

Somporn went over and picked the bottle of whiskey off the floor. He noted that it was more than a quarter gone.

"What are you doing?"

Sheila stuck out her lower lip in a pout she'd made famous in a Moschino campaign in the late '80s. She spoke slowly, punctuating her words with a hurt expression.

"I was bored."

"I am sorry. I had many things to attend to."

"Like making me go back."

Somporn nodded. "You can't be my hostage forever."

Sheila looked at him. "Why not? Why can't you just keep me?"

Somporn sat down on the cot next to her and picked up her hand. He stroked it tenderly and looked into her eyes. "I would love to keep you. But . . . my men, myself—we need money."

"I could give you money."

Sheila's bottom lip had begun to quiver uncontrollably. Somporn shook his head and stood up. "Your husband is on his way."

Somporn walked across the room and picked up a fresh pack of cigarettes. He turned to see Sheila sobbing quietly.

"Don't cry. This is all for the best."

Sheila wiped a string of mucus from her nose. "Can I see you? After?"

"What do you mean?"

"After you let me go. You know? We can meet somewhere. In Bangkok or someplace."

Captain Somporn thought about it, but the thought of trying to rendezvous with a former hostage set off alarm bells in his criminal mind. It would be too easy for her to go to the police and organize a trap. He'd never be able to trust her. He exhaled a plume of smoke into the air, chasing some mosquitoes out of the room.

"Perhaps."

Sheila jumped up and into Somporn's arms. Somporn reeled backward, surprised by her ardor.

"Thank you. Thank you."

She clung to him fiercely, and for the first time Somporn felt the full strength and suppleness of her Pilates- and yoga-enhanced supermodel body. He pulled her hands free and looked her in the eye.

"But right now, you must get ready to leave."

Sheila grinned. "When can we meet? Where?"

"I'll contact you when it's safe."

Sheila couldn't help herself—she kissed him. Full on. For his part, Captain Somporn was not about to deny this once-in-a-lifetime chance to French-kiss a supermodel. He returned her kiss with a passion that took him by surprise. In fact, the feelings that were suddenly and undeniably welling up from deep inside him did even more than take him by surprise. They freaked him out.

Sheila broke from the kiss and held Somporn's face in her hands. She leaned in close, her voice husky and hoarse with desire, and whispered, "Promise?"

Somporn looked in her eyes and nodded.

"Promise me you'll stay out of the sun."

. . .

Salty ocean spray blew up and hit Turk in the face as the Zodiac bounced through the surf. Turk was impressed with the little boat; it handled the waves with ease. All he had to do was keep the front part pointed in the right direction. The tiny flashing dot on the GPS screen moved left or right depending on which way Turk steered, telling him when he was getting off course, keeping him honest. It wasn't nearly as difficult as he had thought it would be.

As he left the protection of the cove and started out into open water, Turk relaxed. Despite his current circumstances, he felt pretty good. The sky was blue, the sun was shining, and, though he'd grown used to the tropical heat, a cool breeze was blowing along the water. It was peaceful. The churning of the small engine had turned into a muffled purr, the boat slapping against the waves in a kind of steady, syncopated rhythm.

As he motored along, the GPS signal having him running north and parallel to the coast, Turk's boat was joined by a small pod of dolphins. They surfed in the wake of the Zodiac, jumping and gliding all around the boat. Turk remembered something Sheila had told him about dolphins when she was working with that Heal the Bay group in Malibu. Apparently they were just as intelligent as humans, with their own language and a kind of organized society, and they were the only species besides humans that had sex for pleasure. Sheila had gone on to describe the mating habits of dolphins—they tended toward wanton group sex with multiple partners—and how the pod becomes like an extended family. They lived, essentially, like a rock band on tour.

Turk looked at the dolphins swimming next to the Zodiac and for a moment he was jealous. They didn't have to

deal with marriage and commitment; they weren't monogamous creatures, and didn't pretend to be. They swam around
all day without a care in the world, without jobs or bills to
pay or cell phones to answer, and spent their lives eating
sashimi and fucking. It occurred to Turk that maybe dolphins
were the more highly evolved species.

The thought that human beings were not naturally
monogamous was not a new one for Turk. In rehab the sexual
addiction counselor had told him that the compulsion to mate
with multiple partners was something biological, part of the
survival-of-the-species instinct encoded in the DNA of every
human. The counselor had told Turk that despite his quite
normal biological urge to get it on with every woman he en-
countered, society had different rules, and it was those rules
he needed to learn to play by. He was urged to become monogamous, if only to preserve his mental health and the public peace.

Turk had been true to Sheila—not counting the happy
finish—but he wondered if it was as good for his state of mind
as the counselor had suggested it would be. He wasn't happy.
He couldn't necessarily lay the blame for his misery on his
marriage; he knew that a lot of it stemmed from the breakup
of the band, the fact that he wasn't playing music, wasn't
doing what he loved to do most. But the fact remained, he
wasn't happy. He was distinctly unhappy, and until recently
he hadn't even been aware of how unhappy he was. He'd been
slowly sliding into a beer-blurred monogamous monotony
that was turning to borderline clinical depression. Sheila's
abduction, and his subsequent time by himself, had forced
him to realize this. This marriage thing just wasn't working
out the way he'd hoped.

Turk watched the dolphins. They seemed pretty happy. He'd never heard of a dolphin dropping dead from stress. What if being promiscuous was just part of the natural world? What if having multiple partners was how things were supposed to be? What if society's demand for marriage was actually unnatural? What if sexual addiction was just some kind of made-up "illness" to keep people from straying?

It slowly dawned on Turk that maybe, just maybe, he wasn't a sex addict at all. Maybe he was just kind of slutty. Like a dolphin.

. . .

Ben followed the slow-moving Zodiac from as far away as he could. He realized he could quickly close the gap between them if he needed to; the Sea-Doo was much more powerful than the poky little engine clamped to the back of the Zodiac. That's what he wanted to do. Overtake the Zodiac and plug a couple of holes into Turk. But he couldn't do it right this second. Not right now. There was a surprising amount of boat traffic out on the water. There were small fishing boats, sightseeing boats, kayaking tourists, and boats filled with scuba divers either on their way to a dive site or returning from one. Ben didn't want to take the chance that someone might see him kill Turk and take the suitcase. He realized he'd have to wait until Turk got closer to shore. Surely the terrorists had planned for the exchange to be in some secluded location. It would be too risky on the open sea.

. . .

Marybeth stood on the beach and looked at the ocean. Turk had been gone for at least an hour, but she couldn't bring herself to move. She didn't know what to do or where to go. She was worried about Turk. She was scared shitless she might never see him again. Her stomach bunched up in a tight, nervous ball and warm, salty tears welled up in her eyes.

Turk is the bravest man I've ever met.

It was inspirational. Really. Turk risking life and limb to rescue his wife. That takes some stones, some *cojones,* some real courage. Marybeth knew that she'd need that same kind of courage. She was about to embark on her own risky journey. She didn't know where her relationship with Wendy would go—what it might lead to or if it would last. She would need some of Turk's guts and audacity to come out to her friends and family. She would have to be brave. What else could she do? She was in love.

"Ms. Monahan?"

Marybeth turned and saw Carole, the hotel manager, standing with a pair of Thai policemen. She gulped.

"Yeah?"

"These officers would like to talk to you."

Marybeth's body went rigid as she mutely nodded. There were so many things to worry about that she wasn't sure which one to choose. Was it Turk? Was it the money? Was it Wendy? Was it news about Sheila?

She followed them up the steps of the hotel, past the pool, into the lobby, and out to the big circular driveway, where a police car was waiting. One of the officers opened the back door of the car and gestured for her to get in. Marybeth turned to Carole.

"What's going on?"

"I'm afraid something has happened to your friend."

Marybeth felt her knees start to go. She was confused. How could anything have happened to Turk? It was too soon. Carole helped her into the back of the car.

"It'll be okay."

She closed the door. Marybeth wasn't sure she'd be okay. She'd lost feeling in her body and her brain refused to generate a single thought. It was like being in suspended animation; like something out of a science fiction story.

The police didn't seem to notice that their passenger was freaking out. They sat in front and listened to some kind of talk radio show. Maybe it was the police radio, but it seemed more like one of those call-in shows like they had in Los Angeles. Dumb-asses spouting their moronic, ill-informed opinions to bigger dumb-asses who phoned in and expanded on the moronic, ill-informed opinions with even bigger, stupider, and more ill-informed—if that was even possible—generalizations and bogus calls to action, except this was in Thai and Marybeth had no idea what they were really saying.

They took her to the same hospital, the same bright corridor, the same double doors, the same pathologist with the incredibly long and unpronounceable name. Marybeth shuffled along, dazed and confused, numbly following the police officers into the morgue.

Because she didn't speak Thai and the officers' English was extremely limited, there was a lot of pointing and nodding going on. The doctor opened one of the steel refrigerators and pulled a body out. He unzipped the white PVC body bag and revealed the deceased.

Marybeth's first reaction was one of relief. She gasped, not at seeing Clive's strangely purple face, but at not seeing Turk in the bag. She'd never been so happy to see a dead man.

The police and the doctor had a rapid exchange in Thai and then the doctor turned to her.

"You know him?"

"Yes. That's Clive. Clive Muggleton."

The police asked a question, the doctor translated. "When was the last time you saw him?"

"On Patpong Beach. He went into a bar and said he'd see me later."

The doctor translated that to the police. There was another question. "Is he your husband? Your boyfriend?"

Marybeth shook her head. "I'm gay."

That was how she came out. With two simple words, telling some uncomprehending strangers and a dead Australian that she preferred to have sex with women.

...

It wasn't until they were almost back at the hotel that the reality of Clive's death sunk in. The doctor had told her that Clive had been murdered, his neck broken by someone. The police had no leads. All they had was the testimony of the bar girl, who said she didn't see anything because her eyes were closed. The police and the doctor were sure of one thing: the bar girl wasn't strong enough to snap Clive's neck. So someone must've entered the room and killed him while he was having sex. They asked her a number of other questions—afterward, Marybeth couldn't really remember what they were—and she answered them as best she could without telling them anything about Turk, the money, or the ransom drop that was in progress. But Marybeth's mind was spinning. Was this related to Sheila's kidnapping? Was it random? Was Turk okay? Marybeth didn't know what to think. Although she was pretty sure that if Clive had to die, he'd probably have wanted to go while boning a bar girl.

...

The setting sun cast a golden glow across the sky, turning the clouds orange and the water deep green. Flocks of birds rose up from the jungle as the little boat motored along.

Turk thought about Sheila. It'd been almost two weeks since she'd been kidnapped. He wondered what he'd say to her when they finally met. But what if they didn't? For the first time it occurred to him that maybe something bad had happened to her. What if she was dead? What if she'd been beaten? What if she'd been raped? Up until this point Turk had been operating on the assumption that the kidnappers were, somehow, honorable businessmen. They wanted money in exchange for Sheila. A tit for a tat. But he had to remember that they were criminals. Why wouldn't they just take the money, kill everyone, and go on their merry way? It was like what they always told you about wild animals: they might look cute, but they'll bite you if you get too close.

Turk's blood pressure went up; he felt a lump of fear harden in his throat. What if the ICE agent was right? What if they took Turk's money and took flying lessons or built a dirty bomb? Turk gripped the throttle of the little outboard motor tightly, his knuckles turning white. He tried to reassure himself. These guys didn't seem like terrorists. They weren't speaking Arabic or releasing wobbly home videos of their hostages reading some kind of prepared statements while the kidnapper-terrorists stood behind them with shopping bags on their heads. That was what Turk didn't get about terrorists. Clearly they weren't using their money for A/V equipment or film school.

Turk realized that the nervousness he felt now was the same nervousness he felt before going on stage. He didn't have stage fright, he just got nervous, but the other members of the band used to tease him about it. Of course Steve, that megalomaniac, didn't get nervous. Steve loved the spotlight, the roar of the crowd. It fed the insatiable appetite of his outsize ego. Bruno never got nervous, but then he was always drunk.

Turk gritted his teeth. He'd just have to suck it up, see this thing through. Even if he now had second thoughts about his marriage, it didn't mean he was going to leave Sheila in the clutches of criminals. That just wasn't the way he was raised.

...

Sheila slipped out of her clothes, carefully folding them on the bed, and stood under the shower hose. Even though Captain Somporn wasn't there, Sheila felt like she was performing. Not for an audience exactly; it was more like she was performing a ritual for herself. Careful not to waste the water, she washed herself—she didn't have time to wash her hair—lathering up with soap and feeling her body becoming slick and clean as she rinsed. She dried herself thoroughly with one of the nice towels Somporn had provided.

Sheila sat on the bed and began to spread coconut oil on her body. She tried to imitate the soft touch of the Captain, meticulously coating every fold and curve with the moisturizing emollient.

Even though Somporn wasn't there to watch her and spread the oil on her skin, Sheila felt herself getting aroused. She slid her oily hand over her breasts and, slowly, down along her belly until she reached between her legs and allowed herself to do something she hadn't done since she was kidnapped: Sheila lay back on the little cot and masturbated.

...

Ben's left eye had turned a bright scarlet and was swollen shut. He tried to open it with his fingers but it was too difficult on the bouncing Sea-Doo, and too painful besides. It wasn't getting better. In fact, it was getting worse. It might, he realized, require a trip to the hospital when he was done murdering Turk and stealing the money. He immediately caught himself. He wasn't necessarily *murdering* Turk. Sure, he was going to kill him, make no doubt about that. But he was killing him to keep him from giving money to a terrorist organization. That he was keeping the money, well, maybe that wasn't the most ethical choice, but it was a whole hell of a lot better than giving it to al-Qaeda. Ben Harding wasn't a murderer. He was a hero. And heroes did whatever needed to be done.

Ben's eye began to throb and ooze some kind of toxic pus. He decided he needed to act now, before it got any worse. He hit the throttle and shortened the distance between himself and Turk. When he got to about a hundred yards—the length of a football field—from Turk's Zodiac he stopped the Sea-Doo, unholstered his gun, and took aim. Out in the open water, Turk was a sitting duck. There was no cover, nothing to get in the way of the bullet, and nowhere for Turk to run.

Ben looked around. A fishing boat was off to the left, maybe a quarter mile away; the shore of the island looked deserted, an uninhabited tangle of mangroves. Ben held the gun in a modified Weber grip—his hands overlapping for stability—took aim, and squeezed off two shots.

...

Turk had played for years standing behind Steve and Bruno, stuck in the back next to Chaps as the muscle-bound drummer had pounded his kit and hammered his cymbals like a beat-happy gorilla on crystal meth. The proximity to Chap's crash cymbal had had the unfortunate side effect of damaging Turk's hearing. The ear specialist he'd visited figured he'd lost a good portion of the high-frequency sensitivity in his left ear; that had been the side that faced the cymbals. So Turk didn't hear the shots. He didn't notice the strange whining whistle that cut through the air as the first bullet flew past his head, missing by an inch or two. He didn't notice the second bullet either. It punctured the side of the Zodiac, flew across at an angle, and blew a second hole on the other side as it exited. But Turk did notice that the nifty little boat was no longer handling so well. In fact, it was melting in on itself like a Salvador Dali clock.

Turk didn't hesitate; he turned the boat toward the shore and hit the gas. Even though he had a pool at his Hollywood Hills home and used to swim laps every day to stay in some kind of shape between tours, he wasn't a great swimmer. He wanted to be as close to shore as possible when the boat finally went down.

As the boat began to fill with water, Turk quickly fastened the life jacket around the psychedelic-daisy suitcase. He then secured the GPS in his pants pocket. He was determined to get the money to the little blinking dot, even if he had to walk through the fucking jungle to do it.

As it continued to deflate, the boat began to lose its shape; it appeared to be dissolving, slowly being sucked under. It looked as if Turk was straddling a giant used condom.

Turk grabbed the suitcase and hit the water. His weight pulled him under for a moment, but then he pulled himself up on the suitcase, the money growing quickly wet and heavy, and began to kick toward the shore.

...

Ben held the binoculars up to his good eye and watched as Turk floundered with the suitcase through the waves. It was another stroke of luck. It was much better if the rock star's body washed up and the cause of death was accidental drowning. With no bullet holes to explain, there wouldn't be an investigation; it'd just be a news item. Turk's fans would lay flowers and candles in front of the Rainbow Room on the Sunset Strip—where Metal Assassin played its first show— and Turk would get a special tribute in the Rock and Roll Hall of Fame in Cleveland.

Ben scanned the shoreline, trying to determine where the suitcase might wash up. He could see a dense thicket of mangroves lining the shore. His swollen eye was beginning to throb with pain. Ben realized that the salt water spraying up when he drove the Sea-Doo wasn't helping.

He squinted through the binoculars—he had trouble scanning the waves with only one eye—trying to monitor Turk's progress. He saw the suitcase—wrapped in a bright orange life vest, it was easy to spot—bobbing in the waves. But no sign of the pudgy rocker.

Ben gripped the throttle; he was about to race over and grab the suitcase when he saw Turk's arm raise up and go down, followed by his other arm. Turk was doing the backstroke. Ben considered running him over with the Sea-Doo, but then decided he'd take the long way around, cut through the mangroves, and be waiting for Turk when he finally washed ashore.

. . .

Captain Somporn lit another cigarette. He'd already smoked half a pack. It wasn't like him—normally he was the coolest of customers—but for some reason he was nervous. He never should have gotten entangled with Sheila. It was obvious. Rule number one for kidnappers and fugitive pirates: don't get emotionally attached to your victims. There were a number of reasons for this, all of them good, but it really boiled down to the simple fact that if you had to pull the trigger, you couldn't hesitate.

Maybe that's why he was so nervous. He knew he couldn't kill her. If everything went haywire and the CIA or the Thai police or, worse, the *Thahan Prahan* showed up, Somporn wouldn't be able to pull the trigger; he would lose face in front of his men and—perhaps a more honorable option—he would be killed himself.

His cell phone rang, "Drop in the Bucket" chirping out in digital glory. He answered it, and grimaced. The news was not good. Even though Turk had left in the Zodiac and headed off in the right direction, for some reason he hadn't made it to the drop point. Somporn cursed. He'd thought about having one of his men shadow Turk's boat, just to make sure nothing went wrong, but had decided that it was too risky out on the water; it would be easy for the police to spot. Besides, Somporn didn't want any of his men to be there when the money was exchanged. He had plans of his own.

...

Heidegger was groggy when he woke up. It took him a couple of minutes to figure out where he was. It was dark, the gloom lit by the glow of distant doorways and the beams of overhead reading lights. The *No Smoking* sign was lit, with its icon of a burning cigarette and the red circle and slash. The dull roar of jet engines also confirmed to him that he was in an airplane.

He turned his head and saw a Japanese couple sitting across the aisle from him watching some kind of pornographic cartoon on their laptop computer while their hands busied themselves underneath a blanket. *Hentai anime*—he knew what that was. A slender Thai woman in a traditional silk dress walked down the aisle and smiled at him as if she knew him. A crazy martial arts movie from Hong Kong was playing on the little TV screen mounted in front of him. He craned his neck, looking behind him. The perfect couple from the ticket counter at LAX slept snuggled together in their seats. She had her head on his shoulder, he leaned his head onto hers. They had a blanket tucked up under their necks. They looked like a Hallmark card for honeymooners.

Heidegger looked at his watch. He'd been asleep for twelve hours. As he started to come to his senses and regain feeling in his body, he realized that his bladder was about to explode.

He stood in the little airplane bathroom and urinated for such a long time that he almost fell back asleep. He pulled a paper towel out of the dispenser and wiped up the area around the toilet where he'd missed, then turned and looked at his reflection in the mirror. There was a long and shiny trail of drool down the left side of his cheek, like a slug had crawled up his face and into his mouth while he was sleeping. Heidegger washed his face and slowly began to wake up.

He remembered he'd wanted to take a sleeping pill and had asked the flight attendant for a glass of water. She'd brought him a tumbler and he'd popped the pill and downed the clear cold liquid in one big gulp. Language is a tricky thing, and when a person says "water" it's understandable that someone else, in this instance a flight attendant, might hear "vodka."

Heidegger had coughed and gagged, surprised and slightly alarmed as the equivalent of six martinis burned its way down his esophagus and into his stomach. The effect had been immediate and powerful.

He should've been angry—the combination of booze and a sleeping pill could have been fatal—but he had to admit that, although he felt a little dehydrated, he'd gotten a really good night's sleep. Now he just needed to see if there was anything to eat. He was ravenous.

. . .

Sheila sat up when Somporn entered the hut. She'd been sleeping, lying out naked on the cot for anyone to see. Somporn stopped and looked at her.

"You should get dressed."

"What's happening?"

Somporn knelt by the cot and pulled a long wooden box out from under where Sheila lay.

Sheila looked at the box. "What's that?"

Somporn quickly spun the padlock that held it latched shut and opened the box. Sheila gasped. "What's going on?"

"Your husband was on his way. Now he is not."

Somporn pulled the wooden stock of an AK-47 out of the box and quickly began to assemble the gun. This was not, of course, one of the original AK-47s designed by Mikhail Kalashnikov in 1949, but it was a high-quality Chinese knock-off that was every bit as good at a fraction of the price.

"Is he okay?"

Somporn didn't look up as he fixed the barrel to the stock, checked that everything was aligned, and slammed a clip home. There was a sureness and precision to his movements that impressed Sheila.

"I don't know."

Somporn stood and headed toward the door. Sheila sat up, her pale breasts swinging from the movement and catching Somporn's eye.

"What do you want me to do?"

Somporn turned and looked at her.

"Get dressed."

...

Captain Somporn slung the AK-47 over his shoulder and walked quickly down the beach to where one of the boats was waiting. He looked up at the sky; it would be dark in another hour. That would make finding Turk and the money nearly impossible.

Saksan and Kittisak intercepted him. Where was he going with a gun? Somporn told them about the disturbing phone call. He was going to the drop site to check and see what was going on. The men offered to go with him, but Somporn told them it was too dangerous. If it was a trap, it was better only one of them got captured. They should stay behind to pack up the gear and get ready; they might have to abandon camp quickly.

Somporn shoved one of the wooden boats out into the water. He jumped in, pulled the cord, and fired up the motor. As he sailed out of the cove and negotiated the tangle of mangroves, he shook his head in dismay. *What the hell am I doing?* He had always prided himself on being a smart, cautious, almost conservative criminal. That was how you stayed alive and out of prison. So what was he doing now? This went against everything he knew, all his instincts and all his years of experience. Normally he would just pack up camp, kill the hostage, and disappear into the jungle. He'd drift around for a few months and then turn up at the little beer hall in Bangkok, where his crew would be waiting. What he was doing now was stupid. He was risking capture and imprisonment, possibly death. But Captain Somporn, scourge of the South China Sea, couldn't help it. It was crazy, but he was in love.

. . .

Turk had seen a TV show about sea turtles. How they are shoved and bullied by the surf as they wallow their way onto the beach to lay their eggs. *That's what I must look like.* Despite the life jacket, the suitcase was getting heavier and heavier, and the choppy surf wasn't helping, finally pushing him into a tangle of trees. The suitcase snagged on the branches, and the roots caught and tugged at his legs like there were little sea monsters trying to pull him under.

But Turk wasn't going to give up. He yanked on the suitcase, breaking branches and jostling the trees, sending birds shrieking into the air. He kicked at the roots of the mangroves, cutting his foot on some sharp underwater branches. Eventually he found some footing and was able to stand. He slogged through what smelled like an open sewer and felt like slimy quicksand, dragging a thousand-pound suitcase filled with a million soggy dollars.

The tangle of mangroves gave way to a shallow canal and he was able to wade to a small spit of sand. He collapsed on the ground, spent and exhausted, flopping on his back and gasping for air. For a scary couple of minutes, as he tried to catch his breath, he felt like he might be having a heart attack. His heart pounded as if it was about to leap out of his chest, his lungs burned, and his legs ached.

Turk rolled over onto his back and looked up at the sky. It had shifted from a pale blue to a deeper violet, and the setting sun was kissing the tops of several coconut palms, their fronds shimmering in the gold light like fireworks. A few birds flew overhead, now reduced to black shapes against the darkening sky. Turk looked up and realized that this view might be the last thing he ever saw; this might be the end of Turk Henry, bass player. And for some reason, he was okay with it. If you've got to go, what better place than right here, right now?

After a few minutes, Turk started to feel better. He sat up and tried to see where he was. Off to his right, a three-foot-long cobra was relaxing on a rock, catching the last rays of the setting sun. The birds had returned to the mangroves—kingfishers sat in the branches while a pair of large herons waded in the shallows, catching crabs with their sharp bills. Dozens of bats started appearing, swirling and diving in the air as they fed on masses of late-afternoon mosquitoes. Turk reached in his pocket and found the GPS. He flicked it on and was pleased to see it blink to life. He looked over at the cobra. It wasn't going anywhere. Turk inched a little closer to the snake to warm himself in a shaft of sunlight filtering through the trees, and opened the beer Marybeth had given him.

He took a sip and raised the can in a toast to the cobra. "Rock 'n' roll."

Turk drank deeply.

...

The Sea-Doo bobbed in a tangle of mangrove trunks. Ben squinted through his binoculars and watched as Turk sat on the beach and drank from a can. What was he doing? Drinking a beer?

Ben wiped the pus weeping from his swollen eye and looked again. He scanned the shoreline for any potential witnesses. The coast was clear. This entire escapade in Phuket had been one wretched fuckup after another, and now it was time to put an end to it.

Ben pulled the sidearm out of his holster and slid off the Sea-Doo into the water. He crept silently through the tangle of branches. He was going to get as close to Turk as possible. He wasn't going to miss this time.

...

Turk finished the beer and crushed the can. He then dug a little hole in the sand and buried it. He smiled at the cobra.

"Leave only footprints."

Turk lay back, letting the beer begin to metabolize, feeling the alcohol climb up his spine to his brain. He wished he'd brought a six-pack. He could use another, and he thought Sheila might want one, too.

Turk let out a long, deeply felt, and slightly hoppy belch. It sounded like some strange Buddhist chant drifting skyward.

...

If you look it up, you'll learn that mangrove forests are made up of taxonomically diverse, salt-tolerant trees and other plant species that thrive in intertidal zones of sheltered tropical shores. If you're actually walking through one, waist-deep in black water, you'll discover that it's a fetid, foul-smelling breeding ground for every biting, stinging, and swarming insect on the planet. It might be good for the earth's ecology, but it's no fun to creep through.

Ben didn't like it, but he let the bugs feed. The last thing he wanted to do was attract Turk's attention. If Turk took off running he'd have a big head start on Ben. The tangle of branches was intense; it was like a spiderweb made out of wood.

Ben ducked and shimmied, turned and wriggled, trying to slip through the mangrove tendrils as discreetly as possible.

It's common knowledge that the M-67 fragmentation-type hand grenade used by the U.S. military comes equipped with a safety pin. The design of the grenade is extremely simple, efficient, and effective. When the safety pin is withdrawn, the safety lever is released from the grenade's body. The release of the lever causes the striker to rotate and spark the primer. The flash from the primer ignites the delay element, which gives you four or five seconds to throw the grenade. Once the delay element burns to the detonator . . . well, in military terms the main charge is ignited. In more human terms, shit blows up.

When Ben had hooked the grenade to his backpack, he didn't imagine he'd be creeping through a mangrove swamp, and he for sure never thought that a teeny tiny little branch from a mangrove tree would snag on the safety pin and pull it out. But that's exactly what happened.

Ben heard the grenade splash in the water and smelled the primer simultaneously. He couldn't run—he was too tangled in the branches—so he bent down, groping frantically in the black water, not worrying about being quiet now, to get the grenade and throw it somewhere, anywhere. The last things he felt were soft mud and mangrove roots.

. . .

Fortunately for Turk, he was lying on his back, belching on the sand, when the grenade exploded. The blast was followed by a geyser of stinky water as krill, baby crabs, and young shrimp took their first flight. Burning-hot pieces of shrapnel rocketed out in all directions, cutting branches and shredding leaves, killing a kingfisher and a couple of bats, but missing the rock star on the beach. Turk sat up.

"What the fuck?"

The backsplash came raining down, Ben's biobits dropping from the sky, followed by leaves and fragments of twigs. Turk looked over and saw that the cobra was gone. It had crawled under a log, not waiting around to see what would happen next.

Turk stood up and looked toward the explosion. The water was still boiling; the trees, blown out of their roots, were smoldering. Behind the hole in the mangroves he saw a bright yellow Sea-Doo drifting toward shore.

Somporn had gotten as close to the drop point as he thought he could before cutting the motor. He'd been drifting there, watching and waiting, for about thirty minutes when he heard an explosion about a half-kilometer away. He didn't know what possessed him, but he started the motor and headed toward the blast, cradling the AK-47 on his lap.

Sixteen

omporn cut the motor and drifted toward the mangroves. He could still see a bit of smoke rising from where the explosion had occurred. He pulled back the firing lever on his gun, racking the first shell into the chamber, and let the boat drift in.

As he rounded the tangle of trees, he saw Turk Henry, bass player for mega-platinum-selling superstar rock band Metal Assassin, waist-deep in muck, trying to drag a Sea-Doo toward the shore. A quick scan revealed that Turk was alone and that a suitcase decorated with psychedelic daisies stood on the beach.

Turk looked up and saw Somporn. Then he saw the gun. He raised his hands in the air. "Don't shoot."

"What are you doing?"

"I need a ride. Can I borrow your boat?"

Somporn looked at the Sea-Doo. "What happened to the Zodiac?"

It dawned on Turk that he was talking to one of the kidnappers.

"Where's Sheila?"

"She's good. Where's the boat?"

"It sank. I had to swim."

Somporn pointed to the Sea-Doo. "What's that doing here?"

Turk shrugged. "Fuck if I know."

Somporn pointed his gun at Turk. "You were supposed to come alone."

"I did. Honest, man. There was an explosion and all of a sudden this thing was here."

Somporn studied Turk for any sign of deception. Turk shrugged, baffled. "Maybe it's a magic trick."

Captain Somporn didn't know what to think. Turk seemed to be telling the truth—the boat was missing; but the Sea-Doo? The explosion? Turk interrupted his thoughts. "Are you a terrorist?"

Somporn looked at him, surprised. "Why do you think I'm a terrorist?"

"They said you were, man. I never thought that."

Somporn looked Turk in the eye. "I'm a pirate."

Turk couldn't believe his ears. "What?"

Somporn enunciated. "A pirate."

Turk nodded. "Like with a peg leg and the skull and crossbones?"

"Exactly."

"I didn't think you were a terrorist. I told them that."

Somporn changed the subject. "Did you bring the money?"

Turk turned and pointed to the suitcase on the beach. "It's all there."

Somporn hopped out of his boat and dragged it ashore. He walked down toward the suitcase. Turk called out after him. "Watch out for the cobra."

Turk followed Somporn to the suitcase. Somporn lay it down and unzipped it. He saw the money and looked up at Turk.

"I'm a big fan of your band."

Turk nodded. "Thanks."

Somporn began pulling the wet stacks of cash out of the suitcase.

"I want to see Sheila."

"Sit down and be quiet."

Turk didn't feel like arguing with the gunman, even if he was a fan. So he sat on the beach and watched as Somporn counted the money in the suitcase, dividing it into two piles. The big pile he wrapped in a plastic trash bag and, using his hands to scoop out the soft sand, buried near a tall tree. The smaller pile he stuck back in the suitcase. Somporn then stood over the buried loot, took a small GPS device out, and locked in the coordinates.

. . .

Turk sat in the front of the boat with his back to the bow. He was facing Somporn, who was holding the gun with one hand and driving the boat with the other. Somporn leaned forward and spoke over the exertions of the outboard.

"Why did you break up?"

"What?"

"Why did Metal Assassin break up?"

Turk thought about it.

"Why did you kidnap my wife?"

"For the money."

Turk spread his hands in a kind of "voila" gesture. "Exactly."

Turk watched as Somporn processed that. He could see that Somporn was an intelligent, thoughtful man. And surprisingly handsome. For some reason Turk had assumed that the kidnappers would either be ragged, toothless orc-like cretins or bearded, turban-wearing fanatics. To discover that the criminal was actually a kind of beach bum Chow Yun-Fat . . . well, it unnerved him.

...

Somporn couldn't risk taking his boat out on the open water. For all he knew a police helicopter or a CIA submarine might be lurking, just waiting for a glimpse of him, a clean shot at his head. He wasn't being paranoid; someone had been on that Sea-Doo, and something had to explain the explosion.

So he took the back way, expertly guiding his little boat through the narrow channels that naturally develop in mangroves. It would take a little longer, but he'd already called his men and told them he had the money. They should break camp. They needed to disappear tonight.

...

Sheila watched as Kittisak ran out of his hut and began barking orders. The men and women dropped what they were doing, a couple of men taking machine guns and running off in different directions to guard the camp, while two women took pots of rice off the fire and dumped the contents into the sea and others began to pack up their belongings as quickly as possible. It wasn't like they were panicked; it was simply that it was time to go.

Saksan approached her with a length of rope. He roughly grabbed her arm and dragged her toward a palm tree. Sheila tried to pull away from him, but that only made him grip her more tightly.

"You're hurting me."

"Sorry. Captain say."

Sheila was suddenly nervous; things were changing too fast. Her lower lip quivered and tears sprung out of her eyes.

"But why? What's going on?"

Saksan shoved her against the trunk of the tree, yanked her arms behind her back, and tied them. He then came around to face her. "Don't worry. It's part of the show."

Sheila swallowed and nodded. "Okay."

Saksan turned and looked around, making sure no one was watching, and then he quickly copped a feel, grabbing her breasts in both his hands.

Sheila recoiled at his rough touch. "What are you doing?"

Saksan smiled, and one of his gold teeth glinted. "American girl."

With that he walked off.

Turk didn't know what to expect. As the boat cut through the mangroves he saw fires illuminating a clump of huts along a tree line and a couple of boats beached on the sand. Silhouettes flickered in and out of the blackness as people moved quickly and purposefully around what looked like a camp. Turk saw Sheila, off to the side, tied to the trunk of a palm tree.

He turned to Somporn. "You're going to let her go now."

It wasn't a question. It was a statement, though Turk needed some reassurance. Somporn nodded. "One of my men will drive you into town. But if you make a noise or attract the police, he has my permission to shoot you. Understood?"

"Understood."

Turk turned and waved to Sheila. It looked like she smiled at him, but he couldn't be sure.

Saksan waded out into the water and helped Somporn land the boat. Kittisak and another man then joined them. Somporn told them to take the money back to Bangkok and divide it there. He didn't know if the police were after them, or the Army, or what, but the last thing they needed was for any of them to be caught in town spending U.S. dollars. He told them about the explosion. Kittisak nodded and, with Saksan's help, began transferring the wet stacks of greenbacks into a ratty-looking canvas sack. They had already arranged for a fishing boat to ferry them to the mainland in an hour. After that a train would take them north to Bangkok, where they would melt into the metropolis.

Somporn looked up and saw that Turk was walking toward Sheila. He decided to give them a minute alone, after which he would have them taken into town.

. . .

Turk couldn't hug her because she was still bound to the tree, so he just stood in front of her for a moment, not really knowing what to say. Finally, he said, "Hi."

Sheila nodded. "I didn't think you'd come."

Turk scratched his head. "Sorry, it got kind of complicated."

"It got kind of complicated here, too."

He moved closer to her.

"You smell like beer."

Turk shrugged. What could he say? Smelling like beer was kind of his chronic condition.

"You want me to untie you?"

. . .

Captain Somporn watched as his men scrambled to get their belongings collected. He was going to leave by boat; hopefully any law enforcement that might be watching would follow him. He promised to meet them back in Bangkok when things cooled off. Somporn told them to make sure the American rock star and his wife made it back to town safely. It was important that the Americans were returned unharmed.

Somporn gave his men a salute, got back in the boat, and motored off into the darkness.

. . .

Sheila looked for the Captain, but he was nowhere to be seen. There would be no tearful good-byes, no promises to call or write or get in touch; there were just a couple of men with machine guns shoving her and Turk into the back of a *tuk tuk* and roaring off into the night.

It was pitch black. There were no lights on the road, no houses or stores; it was just a deserted two-lane illuminated by the single dirty headlight of the *tuk tuk*. As the *tuk tuk* whisked them toward the distant glow of Phuket Town, the warm night air—filled with the sweet scent of tropical flowers mixed with the acrid blast of unleaded exhaust—swirled around them. In any other circumstances it might've been romantic, like a horse-driven carriage ride through Central Park. Sheila reached over and took Turk's hand in hers; she turned to him with a heartbreakingly sincere expression on her face.

"I think I want a divorce."

Turk didn't blink.

"Okay."

Seventeen

PHUKET

Heidegger was at the back of a long line of tourists—they all seemed to be German—going through passport control. He was looking forward to getting to the hotel. He needed a cocktail and a shower, not necessarily in that order, and had arranged for a tailor to meet him in his room and measure him for some tropical-weight clothes. Some trousers and short-sleeved shirts. *Maybe a nice seersucker suit.* That's what you did in Thailand—you had clothes custom-made by expert tailors for next to nothing. The big companies that moved their factories to Southeast Asia knew what they were doing.

Heidegger was expecting Marybeth to meet him at the airport; he was not expecting Marybeth to be accompanied by someone else. Especially not a woman that she was sneaking kisses to.

Heidegger got his passport stamped, picked up his little carry-on, and walked into the main lobby. Marybeth and the woman—Heidegger had to admit she was lovely—were standing side by side, arms intertwined as if they were schoolgirls.

When Marybeth saw him, she let out a squeal and rushed to hug him.

"About fucking time you got here."

She jumped into his arms and gave him a squeeze. Mary-beth's smile was infectious, and Heidegger found himself grinning from ear to ear like a schoolboy with a really good secret.

"Who's your new friend?"

Marybeth blushed a deep red and stammered as she introduced Wendy. "Uh, Wendy. This is my boss, Jon."

Wendy clasped her hands in front of her and bent forward in a *wai*. Heidegger imitated the movement, then extended his hand. His eyes met hers, and he understood right away what was going on. Like the perfect couple on the plane, love was in the air.

"Nice to meet you."

Wendy shook his hand. "Marybeth has told me a lot about you."

Heidegger cocked an eyebrow and shot a look at Marybeth. "She hasn't told me anything about you."

Marybeth stood there getting more and more embarrassed. "I've been busy."

Heidegger grinned; he couldn't help himself. "I bet you have."

...

Turk had wanted to go straight to the police. In fact, when he saw one of the Thai Tourist Policemen—easily identifiable in their jaunty berets—standing outside of a beer hall, he waved to him. But Sheila refused to have anything to do with the police. She wasn't going to tell her story. She wasn't going to press charges or file a complaint. All she wanted was to go back to the hotel, eat a meal, and sleep on a soft bed. Alone.

. ...

There was no celebration when the taxi dropped them off at the hotel. No crowds of reporters, no paparazzi. There were no champagne corks popping, no ticker tape parade; just two tired and dirty people—the fat one smelling faintly swampy— hobbling out of a car and walking into a hotel.

Sheila went to the front desk and asked for a room. There was some clacking of keyboards and signing of papers and then a key was slid across the counter. Turk stood by and watched. He reached over and put his hand gently on Sheila's shoulder.

"You okay?"

Sheila nodded. "I'm really tired. We can talk tomorrow."

He watched her follow the bellhop toward her room.

...

Marybeth and Wendy—discreetly holding hands under the table—sat with Takako and Heidegger in the hotel restaurant. If Heidegger was concerned about Turk's safety, he didn't show it. He ordered a martini and a green papaya salad. Wendy suggested they get an order of *kaeng pladuk chuchi,* which was, apparently, a dip made out of dry curried catfish and chilis. Heidegger, still hungry from his long nap on the plane, also wanted some *pad thai,* and Wendy had told the waiter—in Thai, of course—that they should use fresh shrimp and not the frozen kind so often pawned off on unsuspecting tourists. This would be followed by a spicy crab curry and bowls of steamed rice.

But Marybeth was worried about Turk. He should've been back hours ago. Not that she knew what the plan was after he dropped off the money—maybe the kidnappers had dumped Turk and Sheila on some deserted beach somewhere—but she still didn't think it should take this long. Takako too, was concerned. She had wondered aloud if they shouldn't make a police report, just so the authorities would be on the lookout for a stranded American couple.

All of the anxiety—spoken and unspoken—lifted when Turk ambled into the bar looking for a cold beer.

"Turkey!"

Marybeth jumped out of her chair and gave Turk a hug. "I was so worried about you."

"I'm okay."

She detected something in his voice that made her pull her head back and look at him. "What happened?"

"Nothing."

"Is Sheila okay?"

Turk nodded. "I really need a beer."

Turk broke away from Marybeth and moved toward the table. Heidegger stood and gave him a bear hug.

"You're a fuckin' hero, man."

Turk shrugged. He didn't feel particularly heroic at the moment. "Good to see you, man. Thanks for coming."

He bent forward, giving Wendy a *wai*. "Hey, Wendy. Good to see you."

Heidegger looked from Turk to Wendy to over where Marybeth was getting a beer at the bar. "I obviously missed something."

Turk slumped, exhausted, into a chair. "Yeah, bro, Thailand rocks."

...

Sheila entered the hotel room and locked the door behind her. She sat on the bed and stared at the floor. She was free: no longer a prisoner, no longer subject to the humiliations, degradations, and perversions of the pirate captain. She could do what she wanted, when she wanted, and no one could stop her. She could return to her old life of privilege and haute couture. She could eat the freshest sushi and take Pilates classes; she could spend all day getting treatments at a groovy day spa and then go out and drink the best wines California could produce; she could go first-class all the way back to her big Spanish-style hacienda in Los Angeles and live in air-conditioned splendor swathed in the finest cotton sheets from Italy.

She could go home and be miserable.

Sheila went into the bathroom and turned on the shower. She didn't need to worry about conservation now; the hot water never runs out in a five-star hotel. She carefully took off her clothes and folded them, placing them on a little settee near the bed. When the water was hot, almost scalding, Sheila entered the shower and slowly, deliciously, began soaping her body.

She missed Captain Somporn's watchful eye.

...

Takako Mitsuzake was pissed. She went back to her room, opened up her laptop, and tried to go online. It took her several tries with a variety of adapters to finally get the dataport on the little desk up and running. A half hour later she had the necessary dial-up codes installed—don't these people have DSL?—and was listening to the old-fashioned growling-beeping-swirly sound of her modem connecting. She was pissed, because she knew she'd be up all night dropping e-mails to her various contacts telling them that the juicy scoop she'd promised would need to be delayed. Takako needed to start sowing the seeds of damage control immediately. She couldn't just come out and tell them that it looked like Turk Henry and his supermodel wife were headed for Splitsville. That was the kind of information she wanted to keep out of the papers. Yet without some kind of happy ending to the kidnapping story, well, where was the story? All good stories need a beginning, middle, and end. It was preferable, with stories like this, that it be a happy ending. No one wants to see the hero rescue the girl and then get shit on by her. That's not uplifting or redemptive.

Takako was also pissed because she ate a lot of that spicy food that Heidegger had ordered and now her guts were burning like she'd swallowed a lit hibachi.

As she was typing up her e-mails, Takako had a brainstorm. She didn't care if Turk and Sheila got divorced; she didn't care if Sheila hated his guts. All she needed was for Turk and Sheila to stay together—at least in the short term—for a couple of photos and an interview or two. What's that? A month? Maybe six weeks? Takako realized she'd have to sell the idea to Heidegger, not to mention Turk and Sheila, but she thought it could be done. Why throw away a great story? What was the point of that? Where was the upside? What did Turk and Sheila have to lose by pretending to stay together for a little while? People in Hollywood did it all the time; marriages of convenience, marriages for promotional purposes, marriages to hide the fact that both the husband and wife would prefer to be with members of their same sex. She just needed to convince them to stay together until Turk's CD was recorded. Then Takako would craft and manage the announcement of their separation and divorce and blame it on "post-traumatic stress disorder as a result of her abduction." Oh, yeah. The world's eyes would fill with tears, hearts would pang, and Kleenex stock would jump over that one. Turk's CD would leap ten spots on the *Billboard* chart and Heidegger could negotiate the official, as-told-to, ghostwritten autobiography of Turk Henry for mid-six figures. Heroism and heartbreak went well together. Just not on the same day.

...

If beer goggles really existed, if they were a kind of ocular device that balanced on your nose and warped your perception of the world, then Turk was wearing a pair that was as thick as a Coke bottle.

After Wendy and Marybeth had kissed him good night and gone off for a reunion of their own, Turk sat in the bar and ordered what might as well have been his two hundredth beer.

He had decided to get drunk. *He had his reasons.* He drank to silence the swirl of questions, the jumble of thoughts and dog pile of feelings in his head. He drank to numb his body; he had a variety of aches and pains from wrestling with a wet suitcase and a mangrove swamp. He drank because he was beyond understanding what was happening. Whatever

Sheila thought or felt, whatever made her want a divorce; it didn't matter. A couple is a pair. Both people have to want to be in the partnership or it won't work out. It's not a tulip or a daffodil; you can't force it to grow. You can nurture it. You can urge it forward. But ultimately it has to happen because both people want it to.

Turk drank because he was relieved. The marriage thing, the monogamy, it just wasn't his thing. Sheila asking for the divorce had saved him the trouble of having to ask for one himself. The relief he felt made him feel guilty. Was he finally succumbing to the *catalytic environment?* Was he falling off the sexual sobriety wagon like a big bale of hay?

It was too much, too fast. Too many questions with answers that were difficult or painful or just out of his reach at the moment. Turk realized—with the woozy lucidity of the beer-goggled—that beer itself was a kind of answer to many of life's questions. Unless, of course, the questions were about weight loss.

Heidegger sat with him, drinking a tiny thimble of hot sake. Turk let out a long, low, extended beer belch solo. Heidegger shook his head. "Nice."

Turk grinned. "Remind you of a song?"

"Not one I care to recall."

Turk finished his bottle of beer and wiggled it in the air to get the waitress's attention. When she looked at him he flashed two fingers, not in an effort to buy a round for himself and Heidegger, but to get the waitress to save herself a trip and bring him two at once.

"I've got some new songs."

Heidegger sat up in his chair. "Really? That's excellent news. Did you lay down some tracks?"

Turk pointed to his head. "I've got 'em up here."

Heidegger laughed. "Well, don't wash them out with a beer tsunami."

Turk looked at him, suddenly serious. "Don't joke about the tsunami. Not around here."

Heidegger, who was three sheets to the wind, waved his hand in the air. "My apologies to the people of Phuket. I'm truly sorry. I meant no harm."

Satisfied, Turk put a beer to his lips and nursed like a starving infant. Heidegger leaned forward. "What are you going to do about Sheila?"

Turk goggled his head around. Belched. "Sheila?"

"Yeah, your wife."

Turk thought about it. "I'm gonna do what I always do."

"What's that?"

"Give her what she wants."

. . .

Roy had been enjoying his life of leisure. With Ben away on some kind of cloak-and-dagger mission, he had nothing to do. He'd convinced a colleague to take his backup ID card and swipe it through the time clock for him. That way it looked like he had come in on time.

With the annoyance of punctuality taken care of, Roy would spend his evenings drinking beer and dancing at discos and clubs before rolling into his brothel of choice, where he would stay drinking whiskey and having sex with Chinese prostitutes—for some reason Roy refused to pay a Thai girl for sex—until sunrise. Then he'd grab a fortifying breakfast of thick congee or Vietnamese *pho* before rolling into the embassy around ten o'clock. He'd spend his workday in Ben's office, the door locked, sleeping on the couch.

He knew that this minivacation from work wouldn't last forever, but he was hoping he could stretch it for a few more days. So he was understandably grumpy and annoyed when Bussakorn—everyone called her "Nat"—banged on Ben's door around noon. Roy blinked awake and stumbled forward, taking a moment to blast a shot of breath freshener into his mouth, before opening the door. Nat informed him that the Defense Attaché Office had been looking for Ben and, when the search had proved futile, decided they needed to talk to Ben's assistant. Nat looked at him and asked in Thai, "What are you doing?"

Roy scratched his head and replied in English, "I was sleeping."

It's one thing to be sent to the principal's office for talking during a lecture or making out with a girl in the closet of the biology lab; it's another thing to be called into your boss's office and asked what the hell you were doing sleeping on the job; but it is a unique and rarefied kind of torture to be riding the crest of a crushing hangover, with only two hours of sleep, and find yourself in a conference room with a team of pissed-off military professionals who want to get to the bottom of something you know nothing about. The latter situation was the one in which Roy now found himself.

After three hours of grilling by the Americans—during which Roy was accused more than once of sniffing glue on the job—it was finally decided that he would be sent to Phuket to retrieve his boss. The DAO case officer had traced Ben's credit card to a hotel there. They assumed he had met some girl and gone on a bender. It had happened to others before.

Despite the uncomfortable chair, intense glares, and bad breath of his inquisitors, Roy had somehow managed to not tell them about the tactical kit, the hand grenade, or Ben's strange blathering about "black ops." Roy really didn't know what Ben was up to, but he was sure it had nothing to do with a woman.

. . .

Marybeth woke to find a lithe brown arm wrapped around her. She felt Wendy's warm, firm body pressed against her back. The heat of the two women spooned together under the covers—their pores opened, their sweat mixing—was a moist, reassuring sensation. Marybeth smiled as she remembered making love with Wendy. How they were tender and rough with each other. She remembered licking the sweat off Wendy's neck; it had tasted salty.

Marybeth studied Wendy's arm—the smooth skin, the simple bracelet studded with aquamarines looping over her delicate wrist. Wendy's long and graceful fingers were capped by fingernails cut clean and short, recently manicured and coated with a pale gold polish that made her brown skin look like it was glowing. Wendy had the most beautiful hands she'd ever seen. Marybeth reached over and interlaced their fingers. Wendy let out a low, sweet moan.

Marybeth sighed contentedly. She'd never felt so relaxed, so comfortable in her own skin. She was deeply happy, ecstatic. So grateful for having found someone she could love that the emotions welled up inside her and manifested themselves as a little tear that appeared in the corner of her left eye and rolled down her cheek to be absorbed into the soft pillow.

...

Sheila opened the paper parasol, shading her face, and stepped out of her cabin. She had purchased the parasol at the gift shop and, at the time, hadn't even noticed the brightly colored geometric designs on the stiff paper; she'd just wanted to keep the harmful UV rays off her face. Now that it was open, pulled taut above her head, she saw that the parasol glowed in the sun like an illuminated manuscript. She congratulated herself on being fashionable as she adjusted her long-sleeved cotton shirt, tugging the cuffs as far down as they could go, stretching them to cover her wrists. She set out for a walk along the beach, streaks of SPF 60 sunscreen still visible on her face and neck.

She strolled past the palm frond *palapas* lining the beach, past the early-morning sunbathers stretched out topless and oiled on the chaise longues like appetizers broiling on a grill. The soft sand was sticking to the sunblock she'd smeared on her bare feet, giving the impression she was wearing socks made out of sand.

She walked down to the end of the beach and stared out at the horizon. Somporn was out there somewhere—her pirate, her Captain. She hoped he'd gotten away. That he was safe and en route to Hong Kong or Singapore, wherever he was headed. She had to see him again, that she knew for certain. He was the only man she'd ever met who didn't want her as some kind of accessory. He didn't desire her because she made him look good, important, or virile. It wasn't about his ego; Somporn desired her for who she was. It was plain, simple, and pure. She'd given him her e-mail address, and wondered how long she would have to wait before he contacted her. She hoped it was soon.

Turk sat on a chair on the beach and watched as a group of pelicans hunted for fish, swooping a few feet above the water, rising and falling with the waves. Every now and then one would dive into the water and come rocketing out with a bill full of raw fish.

The thought of sashimi for breakfast sent a fresh jolt of nausea through Turk's beer-battered intestinal tract. A low buzzing pain had taken up residence in his head, and the gentle sloshing of the ocean wasn't helping. It wasn't the worst hangover he'd ever had to deal with, but you don't drink that many beers and not pay for it somehow.

You'd think I'd know better.

Turk sipped some bottled water and waited for the tropical heat to open up his pores and sweat the toxins out of his body. That was the best plan he could think of, and it required no effort on his part.

He adjusted his heavy sunglasses and saw Sheila walking along the beach. She carried a brightly colored parasol, decorated with some kind of vibrant Thai design, and appeared to be dressed for dinner. He saw her look up and see him, so he raised his arm and waved weakly. He didn't want to talk to her. Not that it would be painful or open up deep wounds or send him back to rehab. It wasn't anything like that; it would just be kind of a drag. Better to leave all the details to the lawyers and tax accountants, the appraisers and adjusters, the mediators and judges who would soon be swarming all over their shit like a hundred hungry flies.

Sheila strolled up to him and took a seat in the shade of the *palapa.*

"I suppose I owe you an explanation."

It hadn't occurred to Turk that there was anything to explain. To him, the feelings that he had were just part and parcel of the natural human experience. He assumed that Sheila's feelings would be the same as his. Why wouldn't they be? Marriage was a socializing agreement between two people. It had nothing to do with biology or human nature or the ways of the world. Turk supposed that, at the beginning of civilization, men and women got married to pool their assets, protect against invaders, and produce a line of heirs to either work the fields or inherit the wealth. Monogamy and marriage were for survival. It was a very practical invention.

But he'd come to realize that people weren't necessarily built for that. Not in the modern world, anyway. It wasn't human nature to be trapped with only one mate. In fact, marriage was a kind of denial of human nature; that's what caused all the problems between men and women. Turk was beginning to believe that marriage was a setup, a con, a game of three-card monte with your heart and genitals. Marriage had an inherent design flaw; a built-in poison pill clause. It was made to fail because it didn't take into account our very unmonogamous animal instinct. People expect to be monogamous and then when they're attracted to someone other than their spouse, they overreact. They decide they must be in love with the other person, that the new infatuation is "the one." Betrayals, heartbreak, recrimination, finger-pointing, and divorce follow.

Turk was coming to feel that if people would just be honest, just admit that they're attracted to someone else, that it's a natural thing and has nothing to do with marriage and everything to do with biology and chemistry, maybe they wouldn't get divorced. Maybe they'd say, "Of course I want to fuck her, she's hot," but they wouldn't have to do it. They would understand that it's not "true love," or the fault of their spouse, or a midlife crisis; it's normal. Why else would Internet porn be so popular? So married people could indulge their innate, animal urges, without consequence. *It's life.* We are all sluts; we just don't want to admit it.

Turk had come to understand this, but he didn't know how he could explain it to Sheila, and didn't even know if he wanted to.

"It's cool."

"I should explain. I want to."

Turk nodded. It looked like he couldn't stop her.

"I should never have married you. I'm sorry. This was a mistake."

Turk was sarcastic; he couldn't help himself. "That's your explanation?"

Sheila shook her head. "No. There's more to it. I just don't know if you want to hear it."

"You want to split, I'm not going to make you stay. Anyway, I'm not sure I want you to stay."

Turk felt a bile-filled burp crawl up his throat, a sign that his liver was beginning to fight back. He washed the bitter acid taste down with a gulp of water. Sheila watched him.

"You rescued me."

He had rescued her; it was true.

"Why'd you do that?"

Turk shrugged. "Seemed like the right thing to do."

Sheila couldn't bring herself to look at him. She stared off at the ocean. Turk reached over and touched her hand.

"We had some fun. I can't ask for anything more than that."

Sheila turned and smiled at him. "Yeah. We did have fun."

...

Heidegger stood on a wooden box in the middle of his room. Marybeth sat on the bed, drinking a cup of coffee. Takako Mitsuzake sat on the edge of the sofa, her laptop balanced on her knees. A tailor, an older Thai man, his mouth filled with pins as if he'd just swallowed a porcupine, busied himself around Heidegger, fitting a rough-cut suit pattern around his lanky frame.

Heidegger was holding a book filled with fabric swatches. He flipped through the cottons, silks, and linens, looking for the perfect texture.

"Can you do one in seersucker?"

The tailor nodded. Marybeth snorted out a laugh.

"Seersucker? That'll look great at the Spider Club."

Heidegger cranked his head around and shot her an impatient look. "Don't underestimate the power of a good seersucker suit."

Takako dropped her head into her hands and moaned. "We're screwed."

That got Heidegger's attention. "What's happening?"

"It looks like the *Post* is going to run something about Sheila's abduction."

"How'd they find out?"

Takako shrugged. "They have sources. They're like the CIA."

"I don't see how it hurts us."

"Have you spoken to Turk yet?"

Marybeth saw Takako and Heidegger exchange a look. "What's going on?"

Heidegger looked at her. "We need them to stay together for a little while."

"Why?"

Takako turned to her. "First we need to sell the story of the kidnapping and rescue. Let that sink in."

Heidegger chimed in, "And sell a few million CDs."

"Then we release the sad news that Sheila has post-traumatic stress syndrome related to her abduction and is being treated for it in a private facility somewhere."

"Selling another five hundred thousand, easy."

"Until the sad day when Turk tearfully announces that they have irreconcilable differences caused by her captivity and he wishes her well."

"And we go double platinum."

Marybeth stared at the two of them. "God, you guys are evil."

Heidegger smiled.

"Evil geniuses, I like to think."

The tailor stretched his measuring tape along the inside of Heidegger's leg, measuring the inseam. He looked up at Heidegger. "Dress left or right?"

Heidegger smiled. "Like my politics. Long and to the left."

. . .

Wendy was sitting at a table on the terrace, enjoying the beautiful view, nibbling on a mango, and drinking a cappuccino while she waited for Marybeth. She was dressed like the other guests, wearing flip-flops, khaki Capri pants, and one of Marybeth's rock and roll T-shirts, and she had a room key that she'd showed to the hostess before she was granted a table. Yet she wasn't like the people eating bacon and eggs and oversized waffles at the other tables. The other guests in the dining room were all Caucasian, people from Europe, Canada, Australia, and the United States. Wendy was the only Thai who wasn't working, although most of the employees of the resort assumed she was working in a way.

It was a strange kind of disconnect for Wendy. She had come to Phuket at Marybeth's request, fully expecting to have everything paid for in exchange for sex, secretly hoping she would secure some kind of offer to come to the United States. But now, everything had been turned on its head. Marybeth hadn't mentioned anything about coming to Los Angeles, and Wendy was struck with the dreadful euphoria of infatuation, maybe love. It was the worst thing that could happen to a prostitute. A voice in the back of Wendy's brain, the voice that gave her advice on survival and self-preservation, had told her to leave. To go directly to the airport and back to Bangkok. But Wendy couldn't do it. She had it bad.

A seasoned sex industry professional, Wendy could see the faces of the men as they ate their breakfast. They were glancing her way, calculating her price; the retail cost of quenching their desire. It was the first time in her life that this unspoken appraisal made her feel uncomfortable. She didn't invite the looks; she didn't return them. She was off the market, out of stock indefinitely. She didn't want to be for sale anymore.

It scared her, to be honest. She had never fallen in love before. In fact she had purposefully kept that dreaded, dangerous emotion in check, never once allowing herself to feel anything more than a passing affection toward another person, the kind of fondness you might have for a puppy. She was a Buddhist, so the practice of compassion and kindness were always present, but romantic love was something she avoided like a bad virus. Marybeth had somehow slipped through her defenses in a stealth attack, blindsiding her. Maybe it was because she was a woman, maybe it was just because she was who she was. There was probably some karmic connection binding them together in this life. Whatever it was, she'd never expected to be swept off her feet, to fall head-over-heels. But that's what had happened.

As she sat on the terrace and felt the sun warm her skin, a cold shiver of fear crept into her heart. What happens next? Where do we go from here?

She turned her attention to watch a thin blond woman attack the buffet line like she was a refugee from a famine, stacking her plate high with cold cuts, salami, and chunks of cheese. Wendy shuddered. Could she live in the West? Could she live anywhere people ate whole pigs for breakfast?

She was relieved to see Marybeth enter the dining room and walk out onto the terrace.

The two women couldn't help themselves; they couldn't contain their feelings. They reached for each other, their cool skin touching, zapping each other with sensual static, and embraced. Marybeth gave Wendy a sweet kiss on the lips and then sat down to eat some breakfast. Wendy recommended Marybeth try something traditionally Thai for breakfast. Even though it wasn't on the menu, Wendy convinced the waiter to have the kitchen whip up a couple bowls of *khao tom,* a soup of boiled rice topped with dried chilis and crispy squid.

...

Heidegger and Takako had spent the better part of the morning trying to convince Sheila and Turk that they should "stay together for the kids."

The photographer had come and taken a couple of shots of Turk and Sheila—the parasol caused some lighting problems, as did Sheila's steadfast refusal to stand in the sunlight or have it bounced into her face with one of those shiny reflectors—for the press release that Takako was crafting. The pictures didn't do anyone any favors, Turk looking haggard and hungover, Sheila appearing underlit and distracted. The background didn't help either—the palm trees and ocean making it look more like a vacation travelogue than a story of abduction and rescue—but the colors would reproduce well in the glossy magazines.

Sheila and Turk listened respectfully to Heidegger's take on the situation. There were, according to him, millions of dollars to be made and a musical career to resurrect. Sheila wasn't interested in the money or, for that matter, Turk's musical ambitions. She had things she wanted to do. Things she didn't want to talk about.

Turk was ready to take her side and just forget about it when she said something that pissed him off. She turned to him with an almost accusatory expression and said, "It's your fault I don't love you anymore. If you'd paid the ransom on time, I wouldn't have discovered myself."

Turk held his hands up in the air. "My fault? I paid it as fast as I fucking could."

Sheila turned away from him. "Whatever. It's too late now."

"And what do you mean you 'discovered' yourself?"

"I had a lot of time to think. That's all."

Heidegger intervened. "You don't have to sleep together. Just cohabitate for a little while. Until we get the record finished."

Sheila was silent for a moment, as if she were actually considering it. Then she turned to Heidegger.

"I'm sorry."

"Sheila. Please. You don't have to decide now. Think about it."

Sheila looked off at the ocean; she thought about Somporn.

"I want to do some traveling."

Heidegger nodded. "That's fine. No problem. You can come on tour with the band."

Sheila shook her head. "I want to travel by myself."

Turk could see that she was crying, the tears streaming down her face as she tried not to break down. He couldn't stand to see her like that.

"Fuck it."

Heidegger and Takako turned to look at him.

"What?"

"Fuck it. We're not going to do it. We're not going to pretend anything."

"You need to think this through. As your manager, please listen to me and sleep on it. We don't have to decide anything right now."

Takako didn't like the sound of that. "However, sooner would be better."

Turk pointed to Sheila. "She can't do it, and I'm not going to make her."

Heidegger heaved a sigh. "Think about it, Turk. You're throwing away a great deal. It's everything you told me you wanted. You'd get to play music again, but on your own terms with your own band. Do you really want to give that up?"

They were all staring at him: Sheila, Heidegger, and Takako. They all wanted something from him. Each with their own agenda. But what did Turk want? What was his agenda?

What Turk wanted was a beer. In fact, he needed a beer now more than he could ever remember. He raised his hand to signal the waiter to order one; and yet, when the waiter came over and Turk opened his mouth to ask for a beer, the words "iced tea" came out instead, surprising everyone at the table, Turk more than anyone.

...

Roy stood in the taxi line and watched with growing irritation as the nice, air-conditioned cars took all the Western tourists. Eventually he signaled to a *tuk tuk* driver and climbed in. It was annoying, but he didn't take it personally; he hadn't planned on tipping anyway.

The *tuk tuk* took him to Ben's hotel. Roy had already called the hotel manager and told him to seal off Ben's room. If there was any evidence, say a loose hand grenade under the pillow, Roy wanted to find it before the housekeeper did.

He knew that Ben was dead; he just did. Not that he and Ben were on the same wavelength. Ben had never been the nicest boss—he was demanding, pushy, and always worried about germs. If Ben were alive he'd have been on the phone, yelling at him, telling him to do stuff, admonishing him to wash his hands with sanitizing gel.

Roy arrived at the hotel and showed his identification—and a thousand baht—to the hotel manager. That got him the room key. Roy also made arrangements to keep the room for an extra day. Why not take a little time and see the sights. He'd never been to Phuket.

Roy slipped the electronic card into the slot and the little light turned green. He withdrew the card and turned the handle. He opened the door slowly, half expecting to find a dead Ben moldering in the bathtub. But the room was empty. No body, no tactical kit. Just Ben's clothes hanging in the closet, his toothbrush and electric shaver sitting by the bathroom sink.

Roy didn't know what to do exactly, but he'd seen enough movies to know that he should make a thorough search of the room and Ben's effects. He began by rifling through the pockets of Ben's jacket and pants. He found receipts from various restaurants. He found about two hundred baht worth of loose change in the pants. He found four small bottles of hand sanitizing gel, and he found a slip of paper with a strange list written on it. Roy studied the list, but couldn't make sense of what it might mean. It read: *Maui (golf all year), Nassau (banking), Vermont or Alaska (maybe).*

Roy decided he needed to be systematic. He pulled Ben's small suitcase out of the closet, went through every pouch, and then placed it on the bed and began filling it with clothes once he'd searched them. He'd stick his hands in every pocket, feel the lining and lapels of every shirt and jacket, the cuffs and waistband of every pair of pants that Ben owned. Even the socks got turned inside out. The underwear—those tight white briefs that American men wore—he tossed on the floor.

When he had exhausted all the clothing and gone through every drawer, even looking in the minibar—taking a beer—and behind the television, he sat down on the overstuffed chair. That's when it occurred to him that he needed to search the chair, the mattress, and the little area behind the toilet where people always hid things in the movies.

He rifled the chair, flipping it upside down and poking a hole in the netting underneath. He discovered nothing but kapok. He started to lift the mattress up, then got on his hands and knees and looked under the bed. There, he found a suitcase.

Roy pulled the suitcase out and kneeled in front of it. As he pulled the zipper down, he had the nauseating thought that he might find Ben, sliced and diced and packaged in little plastic bags, in the suitcase. To his relief—in every possible way a person can be relieved—he found a million dollars in cash.

Roy sat back on the chair and helped himself to another beer. He stared at the pile of cash. He didn't know where it had come from or what Ben had been up to down here, but he knew one thing for sure. He wasn't going back to Bangkok.

...

Heidegger sat on a chaise longue, drinking a cocktail and talking on his cell phone. He was in full damage control mode, trying to convince the record company that despite the complications, Turk's record was going to be a megahit. He felt slightly out of place. All around him people were relaxing, unwinding, forgetting their troubles. And here he was, yelling into his cell phone to some sleepy A&R guy in Los Angeles. It made him realize that he needed a vacation. Turk and Sheila had made up their minds and that was that, there wasn't anything he could do but try and salvage something for Turk. He had made his pitch to the record company. But without the media glare and the extensive coverage, they weren't interested in the solo effort of an aging heavy metal bass player. Heidegger hung up, flipping his phone shut with a distinct snap; he had done what he could do. A manager has only so much control.

He leaned back in his chair and heaved a sigh. He looked at the beach, at the clear, perfect water, and at the topless women lying in the sun, and thought, *Maybe I should stay on a few extra days.*

...

Takako was back in her room, listening to the diabolical sounds of a molasses-slow dial-up connection and wondering what she was going to say to people. She was annoyed to the point of rage. What was wrong with these people? Didn't they understand that she wasn't just a publicist? She was a fucking publicist-as-artist. The scenario she had concocted was a masterpiece, probably her greatest work ever. She felt like Michelangelo learning that the Pope had suddenly decided to put in a drop ceiling with acoustical tiles after he'd painted the Sistine Chapel ceiling. *Philistines.* Especially Sheila. What was that woman's problem?

Takako searched through her luggage for one of the vitamin drinks she'd packed. Maybe it was a placebo effect, maybe it was the B vitamins, the ginkgo, or the royal jelly, but the sour-tasting drinks always left her feeling energized and clear-headed. And right now, she needed the boost. She had a long day ahead of her.

. . .

Turk had been lying there for at least an hour. Letting the masseuse massage away his aches and pains, the knots that had gripped his neck and shoulders like a vise, the stress and tension that gave him a migraine. Sheila was safe; he could let go of that. She would move on and live her life the way she wanted. Who was he to tell her anything different? He had nothing to offer her but a prenuptially arranged cash bonus. The kidnappers and government agent were, with any luck, in the past. Without the press coverage of a happy couple reunited, the record deal was off, and Turk didn't care. It wasn't about a media circus, it was about the music, and if the record company didn't think that way, Turk didn't want to be with them anyway. No wife, no band, no record deal. You'd think he'd be depressed, but in fact he was feeling happy, pounds lighter and years younger. He was even letting go of the resentment he felt toward Steve and Bruno for disbanding Metal Assassin.

His schedule was cleared; there was nothing on his plate. He was free to do whatever he wanted with his life. Turk realized he was in an enviable position; not many people could afford to do nothing if they wanted. But he wasn't going to do nothing. He knew, deep in his heart, what he wanted to do. He wanted to rock. That's who he was.

Turk realized that it was time for him to step forward, to live life his way. It's what his shrink had told him in rehab. It's what they try to get you to do in group therapy. They always say, "Be true to yourself." But then they never want you to embrace your inner slut. They never want you to be a headbanger, to crank the volume up to eleven on your Marshall backline and blow out the windows with a heavy-metal hurricane. What they mean is "Be like everyone else." But Turk finally understood who he was, he knew how to honor his true self, and he knew what to say to the shrinks who had convinced him he was a sex addict.

Fuck you.

That's what he'd say.

Turk let out a moan of pleasure. He liked the Thai style of massage, the loose cotton pajamas they made you wear, the fact that they stretched you out like in a yoga class but you didn't have to do any of the work. Even though he was relaxed, deeply relaxed, he could feel his cock stiffening. He was excited. Anticipating the happy finish to come.

. . .

Wendy and Marybeth lay together, naked, on top of the bed in their hotel room. Although it was hot out and they'd just made love, neither one of them drifted off to sleep. Instead there was a kind of quiet anxiety buzzing in the air, like some kind of mosquito who'd suck the infatuation right out of your blood if he bit you.

They lay there, arms and legs and bodies intertwined, just holding each other, breathing, neither one of them willing to speak, to break the spell, to say the wrong thing or the right thing or anything that could fuck everything up.

But finally, someone had to say something.

"There's really good Thai food in Los Angeles. You'd feel right at home."

Wendy looked at Marybeth.

"You want me to come with you?"

Marybeth nodded. That should've been enough, but she couldn't stop herself, she couldn't believe what came out of her mouth. It violated all the rules she'd lived by, all the expectations she'd had for her entire life.

"I love you."

"I love you, too."

"How do you say that in Thai?"

Eighteen

OSLO

Captain Somporn sat at a table in front of the Café Tenerife looking out at a bustling open-air market. Kiosks sold fruits and vegetables, honey, clothes, all kinds of things. Several street musicians, bearded young men in jeans, played acoustic guitars and sang in English as locals passed by, ignoring their protest songs and the guitar cases gaping on the ground, hungry for spare change.

Somporn was glad he was here. Everyone was handsome, tall and blond with pale white skin. He hadn't planned to come to Norway; for some reason Sweden had seemed like the place to go. Perhaps it had been seeing Ursula Andress in those old movies that made him think of Sweden. But he had found a brochure about Norway in a Bangalore travel agency office and decided to come here instead.

This plaza, called the Youngstorget, was perfect for his plans. There was a convergence of streets, a large fountain dominating the center of the square, and a crowd of tourists to disappear into if he had to make a dash.

He was surprised he'd contacted her. He thought he'd never see her again.

When he'd left Turk and Sheila with his men, he had planned to go to Hong Kong and invest the money. But as he returned to the cove, retraced his steps, and began to dig up the buried treasure, he decided that he couldn't go back to the pirate life. It was too dangerous. He just wasn't bloodthirsty anymore. To be a successful pirate—and he had been successful by any standards—you needed to be cutthroat, fearless, and strategically smart. Although he was confident enough in his planning abilities, he didn't feel particularly ruthless. Sheila had changed that. Her presence in the camp had exposed his weakness. She had made him soft, sentimental. One thing he knew for sure: a sentimental pirate wouldn't last long on the South China Sea. Any weakness would be exploited—if not by his men, then by the authorities. He'd end up dead or in jail waiting to die, and he wasn't about to let that happen.

Instead of going to Hong Kong, he'd diverted his trip and taken a cargo ship to Singapore. There he bribed a sympathetic banker and converted his cash into a sizable bank account with a firm headquartered in Geneva. With the money in the bank, he took his time. He laid low. He watched movies to try and improve his English. He quit smoking.

One day he picked up an Australian magazine and saw the photographs of Turk and Sheila in Phuket, along with an announcement that their divorce had been finalized. It had been six months since he'd seen Sheila, but he thought about her every day. Maybe now would be the time to take a risk and contact her. So he flew to Oslo from India—he had moved there because he liked the food—and began scouting for a safe location to meet.

Once he had determined that the Youngstorget was ideal for this kind of thing, he found an Internet café and wrote

Sheila a quick e-mail. It said simply: *Youngstorget, Oslo, Norway. Fourteen hundred hours. Forty-eight hours from today.* He didn't sign it.

Now he waited, eating some fresh grilled shrimp and drinking a very tasty Norwegian lager in front of the Café Tenerife.

Sheila had to scramble to get a ticket. She had managed to get on a flight to Gatwick from LAX with about two minutes to spare and then had a six-hour layover before getting on a connecting flight to Oslo. If her calculations were correct, she had an hour and a half to get from the Oslo airport to some place called Youngstorget.

For months she'd been waiting to hear from the Captain. Compulsively checking her e-mail almost hourly for any word. But as the months passed and the search for a new home—she moved into a nice apartment in Santa Monica—and the divorce negotiations began to take up more and more of her time, she began to check only once a day. Not hearing from him, opening her e-mail in-box and finding nothing each time, became too depressing to bear—each time, it was like a little stab in the heart. She'd begun to believe that something bad had happened to him, that he was shipwrecked somewhere, or being held in a Thai prison.

Then the e-mail arrived and now here she was, in the back of a cab, heading toward downtown Oslo.

...

Somporn saw her first and broke out in a big grin. She was hard to miss with the bright Thai parasol raised above her head. He watched as Sheila sat on a bench by the fountain, checking her watch. He scanned the area around her, looking for signs of a trap, of law enforcement lurking. It might be the biggest risk of his life, but he couldn't help it. He had to see her beautiful skin again.

Somporn finished his beer and paid his check. He didn't want her to be in the sun too long.

Nineteen

LOS ANGELES

Turk stopped and leaned against the wall of the Viper Room. His amp—tiny compared to the size of the gear he used to use—stood on a dolly next to him. Turk lifted his sunglasses and wiped the sweat that was dripping off his forehead, rolling down his neck. Now he understood why Metal Assassin had employed a dozen roadies and guitar techs. Who wants to lug this heavy shit around? Even with the dolly, pulling the equipment up a hill was serious work.

Dani, the drummer, walked past him carrying one of her drum cases.

"You okay?"

Turk nodded. "I need a lighter amp."

Dani smiled at him. "When we get a deal, we'll hire some roadies."

Her belief in the music, the concept of making it as a band, was so pure and optimistic that Turk grinned. "Right on."

Dani laughed. The idea that someone might actually use the expression *"Right on"* struck her as comically old-fashioned.

"You want a hand?"

"Nah. I got it."

Dani nodded and let out a whoop.

"For those about to rock!"

She carried her gear toward the club's door. Turk followed, dragging his amp behind him.

...

Marybeth leaned in close to the mirror, concentrating as she drew a black line along the lower lid of her eye. Recently she'd stopped wearing such dramatic makeup, but tonight she was going to see Turk's new band play at the Viper Room and she wanted to look the part. She was wearing knee-high leather boots, fishnets, a leather miniskirt, and a silver leather bomber jacket over a see-through black bra. She put her hair up in a high ponytail, cinching it with a studded leather bracelet. She looked at herself in the mirror and laughed. It was like playing dress-up. She hoped it wouldn't freak Wendy out.

Marybeth had gotten Wendy a green card through an immigration official she had worked with before—all those British bands needed work permits—and it had only cost her a Stratocaster autographed by Metal Assassin. In turn, Wendy had introduced Marybeth to Thai Buddhism. They now spent every Sunday morning at the *Wat Thai* in North Hollywood, Marybeth learning about Buddhism and the Thai language, Wendy playing a vicious fast game of badminton.

Marybeth had been amazed at how quickly Wendy—and her own new sexual orientation—had been accepted by her friends and family. Her college roommate even told her that she wasn't surprised; she'd always thought she was gay. Even her mother approved, calling Wendy a "real keeper." It felt a little strange. The idea that people might know more about you than you know about yourself.

Wendy burst out laughing when she saw Marybeth; she thought her girlfriend looked adorable. But then she worried that she herself wasn't dressed for the occasion. Somehow the slinky silk dress and simple flat shoes that she wore working as a hostess at a fancy Thai restaurant just weren't appropriate for the mosh pit at the Viper Room. Marybeth thought the same thing, and pulled a black leather jacket—a Metal Assassin logo crudely splattered on the back—and a pair of black boots from the backseat of her car. Wendy laughed, put on the jacket, and then, using some of Marybeth's makeup, added deep purple streaks to her eyelids and a smear of bright red to her lips.

The effect took Marybeth's breath away. She wanted to park the car and fuck Wendy in the backseat right then and there. But she didn't; she could wait. Anticipating it was half the fun.

. . .

The band was blisteringly loud; Heidegger was glad he'd remembered his earplugs. He stood in the back and scanned the room, noting the reaction of the crowd. L.A. audiences are notoriously hard to impress, often giving even the best bands the cold shoulder. But tonight they seemed to be into it.

Heidegger watched Turk patrol the stage, moving up front, racing across, banging into the guitarist, hopping around like the other members of the band—musicians half his age, or younger—like a maniac elder statesman of hard rock. Heidegger had wanted to call the band the Turk Henry Group, but the manager now saw what Turk was after. He wanted to be in a band. A member of something bigger than himself. Although Turk had written most of the songs with the singer, this new band shared songwriting credits equally and made all the important decisions together. Heidegger even liked the name they'd chosen: Bangkok Claptrap. It wasn't as commercial as some of the names he'd put forward, but it had a certain underground charm. Whatever the name, the music was working. It rocked, with driving drums, a crunching powerful bass line as its foundation, and searing guitar interplay over some very interesting lyrics screamed out by a serviceable singer.

It would never go mega-anything, but Heidegger didn't care. He was just happy to see Turk playing music again.

...

If drums are the heart of rock music—the earthbound source of the beat—and the soaring screams of the guitar are the heavens, then the foundation that holds the earth and sky together is the bass line.

And Turk loved playing the bass guitar. It vibrated something in his soul; it filled him with a kind of electric charge, a life force coming straight out of the wall socket, connecting to his fingers and the strings of his guitar, fed back through an amplifier, then blasting into the universe. Turk was like Atlas, condemned by Zeus to hold the earth on his shoulders, to keep heaven and earth from colliding or, worse, tearing away from each other. It was an unglamorous job. The heavy lifting of heavy metal.

Turk walked to the edge of the stage, something he hadn't been allowed to do in his old band, and looked out at the audience. It was a crush of hair and leather, head-banging boys with their devil horn salutes flailing in the air, young women in skintight shirts flipping their hair as they danced.

Turk looked out on this pulsating mass of humanity and smiled; he couldn't help himself. The crowd moved him: the individuals who came to dance and thrash and mosh, putting aside the grind of daily existence to celebrate their animal natures in a timeless pagan debauch. It was rock and roll as spiritual communion. The music of the gods at crush volume.

They loved the music, and Turk, in turn, loved them back. Especially one woman, a dazzling redhead in a tight green tank top that displayed her wonderful, natural cleavage as she spun and danced with untamed abandon.

Turk made eye contact with her, and she smiled. He'd see her after the show.

Acknowledgments

It takes a lot of people to turn a manuscript into a book, and this book wouldn't exist without the intelligence, enthusiasm, and energy of Morgan Entrekin, Eric Price, Deb Seager, Jamison Stoltz, and all the great people at Grove/Atlantic.

Agents and editors around the world deserve some props! Thanks to Chandler Crawford, Michelle Lapautre, Devin McIntyre, Halfdan Freihow, Knut Ola Ulvestad, Elisabetta Sgarbi, François Guérif, Toby Mundy, Christopher Donnelly, Bill Weinstein, Tom Strickler, and Scott Seidel.

Big thanks to: Diana Faust, David Liss, William J. Overton, and Seth Greenland for early reads and advice, and to Jon King, Andy Gill, Hugo Burnham, and Dave Allen of the Gang of Four for all the backstage passes over the years.

And to Olivia and Jules for taking me to Thailand in the first place.

One

"T HIS IS SO fuckin' cool, man." Morris burst through the doors of the lab carrying what looked like a log wrapped in black plastic. His white cotton smock, bearing the name United Pathology, flapped around his bony frame as he rushed forward. Morris was excited, breathless. He had something really good. His sneakers squeaked on the tile floor as he skidded to a stop in front of a young man with tall black hair.

"Bob. Dude. Check this out."

Bob didn't look up from the computer. He slouched his skateboarder-lanky body in a stylish black chair designed to improve his posture, draping one of his legs across the desk so that one scuffy black shoe touched the side of the monitor while his other foot twitched to some unheard autonomic beat on the floor. He kept his eyes on the screen, thoughtfully stroking his trim goatee, as he scrolled through a digital gallery of young Canadian virgins on the Internet. He eyed the young blondes intently, staring at their pert breasts, ice-cream-scoop butts, and spread patches of pink surrounded by wisps of blond curls. They could have been Swedish or maybe Norwegian, but they were definitely from some frosty part of the world. Cold and clean and young. Their bodies promising sex fresh as mountain air, clear as spring water, and as pure as new-fallen snow. Like a beer ad. Bob twisted in his seat, his pants suddenly too small.

Morris cleared his throat.

"Dude, it's totally grisly."

"Can't you see I'm busy?"

Undaunted by Bob's lack of enthusiasm, Morris put the package down on the desk in front of him and began to unwrap it.

"It smells a little."

"Then don't open it."

"I thought you liked tattoos."

Bob heaved a sigh and moused his way out of the porn site.

"Put it in a tray, all right?"

Morris nodded and crossed the lab to the sink. He pulled out a large stainless steel examining tray and carried it back.

"Good idea, Bob. These things are always seepin' a little."

Morris gently plopped the package in the tray and pulled the plastic away, unveiling his prize. Bob recoiled at the sight, instinctively covering his mouth and nose. Morris looked at him, surprised.

"You gonna puke?"

Bob shook his head.

"Check out the tattoos, dude. Check 'em out."

Morris picked up the severed arm and rolled it over. Congealing blood oozed out and smeared the surgical tray. It was a tough-looking arm. Muscular and hairy. Tattoos were scattered up and down, inside and out. The letters *H-O-L-A* etched into the knuckles. Morris rotated the arm again and Bob saw an exceptionally beautiful tattoo of a woman laying naked on her back with her legs in the air. A man lay with her, his head buried between her thighs.

"What'dya think, man?"

Bob covered his nostrils and leaned in close. The tattoo was skillfully drawn, with real flair. The woman's body seemed to quiver, as if she were coming.

"Good, isn't it?"

Bob looked up at Morris.

"It's amazing."

Bob opened the bottom drawer of his desk and pulled out a Polaroid camera.

"Rotate the arm a couple of inches up."

"Like this?"

"Up."

Morris complied. Bob got close to the arm and then pushed the button. Flash, whir, ding. The camera spit out a photo. Bob stuck the picture in his pocket and put the camera back in the drawer. He looked at Morris.

"I'm thinking about making a coffee run. You want some?"

"Let me go. I've spent too much time with the arm. I need a break."

Bob looked at the arm.

"What are we supposed to do with it anyway?"

Morris wrapped the appendage in the plastic.

"I gotta take it to the lab at Parker Center tomorrow morning after they drain it or whatever."

Bob shot Morris a look of disbelief.

"This is evidence?"

Morris shifted his weight from foot to foot, something he did when he was nervous or really had to pee. He took his sunglasses out of his pocket and stuck them on his nose so he wouldn't have to look Bob in the eye.

"Bob. Dude. I don't know that it's evidence for sure."

"Is it from a crime scene?"

Morris finished wrapping the arm.

"Double latte, right?"

Bob shook his head.

"Whatever, man."

Morris spun on his heel and left. Bob sighed, picked up the arm, and walked it over to a large freezer. He swung the big silver door open and slid the arm onto a shelf filled with hundreds of other lumps, bumps, cysts, clippings, cuttings, kibbles, and bits. Bob sat back down in front of the computer, but the blondes had lost their allure.

He pulled the Polaroid out of his pocket and watched it slowly finish developing. It was a clear picture of the tattoo. The artist was obviously very talented. Bob looked closer, studying the woman. Intricately drawn, her breasts hung voluptuously, spreading across her chest and swinging down just a little toward her armpits. She had a full head of long black hair that flowed away from her body. Her legs, arms, and ass were perfectly proportioned, not thin or skinny; there was nothing girly about her, she had a womanly weight. A sensual mass. Her mouth was a half smile, half grimace, as her body bucked and kicked in the throws of orgasm. Her eyes wide open as if surprised by the sensation.

Bob looked at her and felt a strange sensation of his own. It was as if he knew her. Or maybe, closer to the truth, as if she were the woman he wanted to know. His idea of what a sexy woman looked like. Bob felt a pang of jealousy when he looked at the man's body. Although Bob was considered by many people to be a good-looking dude in relatively robust shape, he couldn't compete with the taught and articulated muscles, the pure sexual power of the man in the tattoo. All that energy focused between a woman's legs.

Bob ran his finger over the Polaroid, following the line that detailed her thigh to her belly to her breasts to her lips. He surprised himself when a little moan came out of his mouth.

Bob absently traced a line with his finger slowly down his chest, across his belly, to his crotch. He felt a swelling.

It was a very good tattoo.